# NOCTURNE, OPUS 1: SEA FOAM

# NOCTURNE, OPUS 1:
# SEA FOAM

Norene Moskalski

Divinity Press
Delaware

An Original Publication of DIVINITY PRESS, Delaware, USA
www.DivinityPress.com

First Edition, October 2012



Library of Congress Control Number: 2012950579

ISBN 978-0-988-38116-2 Hardback
ISBN 978-0-988-38117-9 Trade paperback
ISBN 978-0-988-38118-6 Electronic book

Typesetting and formatting services by STEVE PASSIOURAS

Printed in the United States of America
10 9 8 7 6 5 4 3 2 1

*For Mike, Susanne, Lisa, Doug, Parker*

**To My Readers,**

The idea of building the framework for a novel upon the structure of a musical composition has always fascinated me. It would be like watching a movie with perfectly matched music. But in a novel, would anyone other than the author sense the musical movements? I thought I'd like to try using a Chopin nocturne as the underlying structure on which to build a timeline of scenes for *Nocturne, Opus 1: Sea Foam*, and if it worked, continue using various musical structures to tell the stories in the rest of the novels in this series.

I've included a brief explanation of the structure of a nocturne below, and an internet search for "Chopin nocturnes" will provide you with samples of his music. Let me know if you hear a nocturne playing quietly in the back of your mind as you read about Kate's and Jake's brush with nature and if I should continue the series using one of your favorite musical compositions. My email address is

norene@norenemoskalski.com.

The musical composition of a nocturne, developed by John Field in the 18th century and memorialized by Frederic Chopin, traditionally begins with a serenade to a beautiful woman or to a quiet scene in nature, designed to evoke a memory of a tranquil evening filled with beauty. Then the progression of the nocturne presents a theme with variations, adding harmonic contrapuntal interplay and counterpoint, casting the beauty of nature into perilous realms of discord, imbalance, and dissonance. Following a struggle to restore balance and a period of reflection, the composition returns to the original music depicting a tranquil scene in nature.

**In His Love,**
**Norene M. Moskalski, Ph.D.**

# Acknowledgments

My special thanks and gratitude to my husband Mike and my daughters Susanne and Lisa for their valuable advice and contributions; Genie and Fred Ray for sharing their knowledge of recreational vehicles and campgrounds for this novel; Dan and Dawn Sniezek for providing the correct pilot to flight tower dialogue and sequences in this novel; Anne Sniezek, Doris Moskalski, Priscilla Feir, Catherine and Bob Mesaros, Kathleen and Frederick Kloss, Barb and Nick Corbo, Marie and Denny McKnight, Barb and Bill Leary, Joan and Charlie Wagner, Pat and Howie Fyock, and DJ and Don Testa for their continuing encouragement and support; Patti Phillips, author of *One Sweet Motion*, for her insights, edits, and faith along with Terry McDonald, and Jeannie, Kelly, and Colleen Fida who shared my belief that God will guide us on our journey if we ask Him for His help.

# PROLOGUE



*Delaware Bay Estuary*
*Delaware, U.S.A.*

**Intricate colonies of** *Bacillus nocturne* **swirled** through the moonlit sea foam as she slid her kayak into the Delaware Bay. Unaware of the grave danger, she brushed the clinging sea foam from her calves, stepped into the kayak, and positioned her legs into the tight compartment stocked with the day's scientific supplies. She turned sideways and pushed her paddle against the sandbar, propelling the kayak into the bay. As dawn lit the night sky, she settled into a steady rhythm of paddling and headed north toward the marsh.

Tara Anderson welcomed the solitude. She listened to the sea grass rustling in the morning breeze, the fiddler crabs clicking out their soft cadences, the brown pelicans swooping and splashing . . .

Music surrounded her; every sound she heard added harmony to the constant stream of melodies in her mind. She could have written symphonies and majored in music, but her inquisitive nature defined her. She loved research; she loved discovery. She chose science. With a research degree in ecology, she would still be surrounded by music; but, with a music degree in symphonic performance, her opportunities to practice research would be gone.

Her paddle hit a clump of submerged reeds, reminding her to adjust her strokes for shallow water. A break in the tall grasses lining the shore signaled the entrance to the eastern sector of her testing site. She maneuvered a slow turn, careful to maintain her balance in the kayak. Its bow clattered through the reeds, revealing a saltwater pond drenched in sunrise.

Suddenly, Chopin's Nocturne in E Major flooded her mind. A surprising selection at first, but then she nodded, a smile breaking across her face as she acknowledged her inner musician's wit: Ecology Major. Her mind had found a balance between music and science.

As she paddled through the calm beauty of the pond, the nocturne serenaded her with its simple melody and dissonant undertones. Gliding carefully past a heron's half-hidden nest, she set her paddle across the top of her kayak. Leaning back, she dropped her hands into the water and trailed her fingers through the sea foam surrounding her.

She listened as the trills of salt marsh sparrows added counterpoint to the melody running through her mind. Closing her eyes, she relaxed her shoulders, calmed her breathing, and gave herself a few minutes to rest before preparing to collect the day's water samples.

Every morning she tested the water for a variant strain of *Bacillus nocturne*. Five years ago, the normally passive bacteria had suddenly gone rogue, killing eight people on bayside beaches. The first persons to die were Maria DeSanchez and Toby Hannah, graduate students whose water samples had indicated a high bacteria count in the bay.

Thousands of tourists had fallen ill that summer. Tara's own exposure had occurred during an international youth rally at Rehoboth Beach. After a few months, the strain faded away, as had most people's memories of it. Even Tara considered the frequent water tests merely precautionary. Now they had become opportunities . . . for quiet mornings alone . . . eyes closed . . . floating . . . on the calm water . . .

**The cry of a gull** startled Tara awake. She bolted forward, almost overturning the kayak. She caught hold of its rim. Her wet hands slipped off the edge. Frantically, she grabbed for her paddle as it slid into the water. Her weight shifted sideways and she fought to maintain balance. Bracing her thighs, while locking her knees under the forward cockpit, she tried to regain control by transferring her weight. Finally, the rocking slowed.

Tara's heart pounded. Her tousled brown hair hung over

her green eyes, blocking her vision. In a balanced move, she gripped the kayak with one hand and flung her hair away from her forehead with the other hand. In the quick movement, her wet fingers left a trail of sea foam scattered across her eyelids. It caught on her lashes, seeped through their ends and dripped into her eyes, softening the color of her irises to a pale foam green.

At first, Tara thought the clouding of her vision and the stinging along her eyelids resulted from the mixture of sweat, sunscreen and sea foam running into her eyes. Then the pain intensified to a fiery burn as the colonies of *Bacillus nocturne* embedded in the sea foam etched the surfaces of her eyes. Hungrily they began their search for the specific human proteins they had fed on in the polluted water of the bay.

The bacteria continued to navigate through the aqueous layers of her eyes, replicating as they absorbed the proteins scattered among their protective tissues. Blood pooled in the corners of her eyes as hundreds, and then thousands of rapidly multiplying bacteria swept across her lenses and eclipsed her vision.

Fighting through the excruciating pain, Tara struggled to turn her kayak around. Her fingernails gouged the soft wood of the paddle as she flailed it from side to side. Her splashes reverberated against the side of the kayak, and she lost all sense of direction. In desperation, she realized that her only hope was for the ebb tide to carry her back to the university's pier.

Terrified by the increasing pain, she slid down into the bottom of her kayak, her desolate cries for help the only sounds echoing across the marsh.

# Chapter 1

*Lido di Venezia*
*Venice, Italy*

**Nesting plovers and little terns stirred,** awakening as night turned into day on Lido Island. The scent of pine freshened the air, and ancestral plane and poplar trees spread their leaves to catch the morning's golden light. The changing currents and shifting sands of the Adriatic Sea laced the island's beaches with intricate patterns of sea foam and iridescent blue shells.

At the break of dawn, Dr. Kate Connors awoke to find three-year-old Crystal tugging on her hand, wanting to go to the beach to collect more sea shells. Ready to leave, Crystal had pulled on her lime green swimsuit, inside out, splotched 70 SPF sunscreen all over her body, wrapped her peach princess veil over her shoulders, and dragged a purple metal sand pail across the floor with a miniature red shovel jangling around inside. Kate and Jake Connors sleepily eyed their little girl and then broke out in laughter. In that moment of humor, Kate decided to reward Crystal's initiative with an early morning trip to the beach, instead of waiting for the resort's 9:00 a.m. water quality report.

Rising effortlessly, Kate navigated the pandemonium of sandy beach clothes, sandals, and sun hats strewn over the chairs and hardwood floor of their vacation suite, collecting everything that they needed for a morning at the beach.

Comfortable in casual white linen pants, white rope sandals, and a sleeveless yellow shell, Kate wrapped her long blonde hair into a chignon and secured it with a yellow hair stick. At the mirror she highlighted her flat cheekbones and straight nose with blusher, de-emphasized her wide jaw with bronzer, and added a touch of peach lip gloss. Then she corralled Crystal and gently brushed her blonde curls into a short ponytail and helped her find her green flip-flops.

Jake, on the other hand, rolled his muscular six foot four frame out of bed, grabbed whatever beach clothes were closest to the bed, slid into his sandals, and ruffled the top of his curly brown hair with his hands while proclaiming, "Ready to go!"

"You jest!" Kate laughed. "But then again . . ." She paused for dramatic effect, tilting her head to the side as she looked at him from head to foot, "Maybe that grizzled hair really does complement yesterday's wrinkled beach clothes." Their ongoing affable banter about his unmanageable hair amused both of them.

"Mommy . . ."

"We're almost ready to leave, honey," Kate responded to Crystal's tugs on her pants leg. "Just one more thing to do."

Kate grinned at Jake and then headed in the direction of the suite's third bedroom. On the way, she gathered all the brightly colored metal beach toys in the suite's living room, making as much noise as possible, and then dropped everything in a clanging heap outside her sister Julie's bedroom door.

"Sunrise in fifteen minutes, you guys! Meet us on the beach for breakfast in ten!" Kate loved waking up her night owl sister and her husband Luke Thurston as early as possible whenever they vacationed together. Julie would laugh it off and never complain. They were that close.

Julie, the youngest child in the Stafford clan, had always tried to imitate Kate, her oldest sibling and frequent babysitter. As the two grew older, Julie's facial resemblance to Kate deepened, and they developed playful rivalries over appearances, like who would have the better tan by the end of the summer. Julie always won. Her peach-toned skin, tawny hair and hazel eyes predisposed her to the deep tan that she knew her fair-skinned, blue-eyed sister coveted. Unlike some families, though, their sibling rivalry remained congenial and served to cement their relationship. They grew into a warm friendship, and Julie continued to follow Kate's lead in everything, including entering the premedical program at Kate's alma mater. Julie was intelligent, competitive, empathetic, and kind, and

Kate knew that she would be an excellent physician.

What pleased Kate even more was Julie's happiness with Luke. A good-natured, attentive husband with an unbeatable sense of humor, he fit right into their family. And it amused Kate that he often used his blonde hair and blue eyes as a ruse for being Kate's brother, whenever he and Julie wanted to set up another practical joke aimed at Kate and Jake.

Snarling like a *Tyrannosaurus Rex*, Jake stomped across the room with Crystal balanced high on his shoulders, clanging her sand bucket and yelling, "Auntie Julie, Auntie Julie! Unclie Luke! Wake-up! Dragons are coming!"

Grinning at Kate, Jake asked, "You know they're going to get even with us before vacation's over?"

"Yepper. But we'll be ready," Kate laughed.

Satisfied that they were not the only ones awake at this early hour, Kate and Jake picked up their beach bags and headed to the shore with Crystal.

**At sunrise, Crystal** had the entire beach to herself. As she filled her sand pail with shiny abalone and curly blue shells, her peach veil slipped off one shoulder and trailed behind her in the water. She knelt to examine a weathered sand dollar and giggled when she spotted a tiny seahorse hidden beneath it.

Kate and Jake watched their daughter play in the sand as they waited for Kate's sister and husband to join them in their private cabana on Venice's Lido Beach. Their two-week motor tour of Italy almost over, Kate relished a few more days of quiet luxury at the upscale AlbergoVenetian Stazione Balneare, one of the premiere hotels on the Adriatic Sea.

Kate hummed quietly to herself as she slathered sunscreen along her blonde hairline, over the bridge of her slightly tanned nose, and across her cheeks. As her hands spread the lotion down her neck and across her chest, she smiled at Jake, appreciating his smoky hazel eyes caressing the curve of her neck.

The soft sound of Crystal's laughter diverted Jake's attention. His eyes darted toward the beach. Every muscle in his body suddenly tensed, until he saw Julie and Luke laughing and waving at Crystal as they splashed through the waves with a huge green dragon float in tow.

"Ready for action?" Kate teased, pleased that double entendres just seemed to roll off her tongue. She knew Jake's SEAL training kept him alert to the slightest sound or movement, and she found that exciting.

"I remember the last time you reacted like that." Kate's mind wandered to an open piazza in Madrid, where recognizing his sudden muscle tension and hitting the pavement had saved her life. Her quick reactions, coupled with her Agency training, had paid off.

"Hasid," Jake nodded. "As soon as I heard Hasid's cackles coming from that rickety walk-up flat, I knew we were in trouble. One minute you're laughing and your blue eyes are sparkling in the sun, and then Bam! You're down! I thought he killed you."

Kate realized his anguish about endangering her life hadn't subsided.

"Can't get that memory out of my head. I've seen dozens of people die, but when it's someone you love . . ."

"It affects you differently."

"Seal excursions have a life of their own." He shook his head. "Every time we left someone standing, we knew we'd have to fight them again later. Hasid was no exception. But taking his revenge out on my family—that violated the code."

"We made it out." She regretted her light-hearted reference to the attack, unaware that it had affected Jake so deeply. She had thought Hasid had targeted her as payback for one of her Agency missions.

"We're safe now, Jake. Remember? We chose this hotel because it met all of our standards for safety—private security guards, private screening at check-in, private transportation by water taxi, private beach."

"No one's ever safe." His concerned look changed to a curious furrowing of his forehead and eyebrows, and then a broad smile swept across his face as he watched his daughter playing with her Aunt Julie.

He's resilient, Kate thought, and handsome when Crystal's antics light up his eyes and soften his chiseled jaw into a smile.

She turned her attention back to Crystal. I'm content, she realized. For the first time in months, I feel safe and happy.

Jake was right. We really did need a break from work, and inviting Julie and Luke to join us was a good idea.

Both Kate and Jake worked as research professors at the Institute for Public Policy and Safety, a think tank at Atlantic University in Dover, Delaware, dedicated to resolving the effects of climate change. They also served as covert operatives for the Agency, a secret subdivision of the Institute.

The Agency sent operatives to investigate and control environmental hot spots around the world, whether natural or man-made. As cover, the agents posed as visiting professors or graduate students at nearby universities.

The Agency maintained its secrecy through stringent need-to-know policies and prohibited the agents from disclosing their roles to anyone, including their spouses. Neither Kate nor Jake talked with each other about their missions. At times the secrecy stifled; at other times, it kept them alive.

Despite the Agency's rules, Kate had discovered Jake's identity as an agent five years earlier before they had started dating. On her first mission for the Agency, his research on contaminating an enemy's water supply was required reading. She never spoke to Jake about that mission or any of her missions, but she always wondered if he knew about her work for the Agency, too.

Kate sighed, the corners of her mouth crinkling into a frown as she thought about going back to work. She knew she worried far more than most people did, but most people didn't have husbands who were covert agents. And most mothers weren't agents themselves.

Kate's worries extended to her daughter's safety on two levels. As the number of excursions she and Jake made for the Agency increased, the number of retaliatory risks for her child increased proportionately. And as a researcher at the Institute, Kate knew more than most mothers did about the coming health hazards associated with climate change.

"What's wrong, Kate?" Jake finally asked the question she knew was coming.

"How do you always know?"

"Know what?"

"When my mood changes. When a thought shoots through my mind and triggers a landslide of worries?"

"Play enough poker and you notice things."

"What's my tell?" She needed to know all of her tells if she hoped to survive her missions, but this one escaped her.

"It's that quirky way you twirl your hair around your finger," he laughed. "You don't even know you're doing it, but it signals a change in your mood every time."

A little embarrassed by her childhood habit, she dropped her finger from her curls and worried about what other signals she broadcasted.

"So what's wrong, Kate?"

Hesitant to broach the subject again after all their discussions, she tried to find a new way to explain her concerns.

"It's the water. The quality of beach water. I'm working on improving it one pathogen at a time, but the progress is too slow. My colleagues attributed a 60% increase in bacterial infections last year to polluted beaches."

"Reclaiming the beaches. Isn't that what you always said would be your life's work? It may take awhile."

"But the data keep getting worse, not better. I think we'll see a waterborne pandemic before this decade's over. That's why I always check the beach water reports before letting Crystal play in the water. Except for today. I let Crystal go to the beach this morning without checking . . ."

"It's all right, Kate. Remember our discussion? A little germ exposure helps build up a kid's immunity."

She smiled at Jake, her way of saying thanks for trying to help, but she still felt apprehensive. When the lifeguard finally posted the water quality report at 9:00 a.m., she knew she would be the first person in line to read it.

Jake sprawled out lazily on his chaise, a bemused grin spreading across his face as he watched Crystal alternately throw fistfuls of sand and sea foam in the air, studying their unequal descent on her Uncle Luke's head.

"She's quite the scientist." His pride was evident in his voice. "Just like her mom."

Luke and Julie's antics with Crystal continued to hold Jake's attention. "They're really good with her, Kate." He grew serious. "They'd love her as their own."

When Kate saw him suddenly signal for the wait staff, she knew he could not dwell on that subject for long.

"Eggs Benedict with Hollandaise Sauce and Escalloped Escargot," he ordered for breakfast, savoring every word.

"Do you ever stop thinking about food?" she teased, easing the transition for him.

Jake stretched back against his chaise. In answer to her question, he held up a brochure featuring one of Italy's finest restaurants, and replied, "Which entrees should we order this evening?"

Jake interrupted his discussion as he caught a peripheral glimpse of his daughter's movement on the beach.

"What's Crystal doing?"

He sat up and then bolted for the beach when he saw Luke running toward Crystal and Julie.

Crystal's little arms flailed about, trying to untangle the peach netting that she had been dragging through the sea foam. It had caught on Julie's wire rim glasses. Julie gripped it tightly, trying to extricate herself from the stinging sea foam dripping through the mesh into her eyes.

At first, Kate could barely hear her sister's voice above the surf, but then her cries pierced Kate's heart.

"Crystal, run . . . run to your Mommy," an alarmed Julie yelled, her pitch increasingly higher with every shouted word. In one swift move, Julie ripped her glasses from her face, spun around, and inadvertently knocked Crystal backward onto the dry sand. Then Julie grabbed the bottom of her white tee shirt and furiously rubbed her eyes, all the time crying out for help.

Her muscles trembled and then stiffened, throwing her precariously off balance. Her body wavered for a few seconds as if deciding which way to fall, and then began a feint to the left, only to suddenly twist to the right. Her limp arms had lost all capacity to break her fall.

"Julie!" Luke rushed up behind her, swerved left and then right, trying to catch her careening shoulders before they hit the sand. She collapsed into his arms, but the unexpected force of her fall pushed them backward onto the beach. Luke eased her body onto the sand and pushed her hair away from her face. Blood filled her still eyes, running through her eyelashes, down her face, and onto the beach, forming red puddles on the coarse, white sand.

# Chapter 2

*Cape Henlopen State Park*
*Delaware, U.S.A.*

**Linda and Paul Henderson** had camped at Cape Henlopen State Park, near Lewes, Delaware, every summer since accepting their dual professorships at the Johns Hopkins University in 2007. Few would have guessed that these two were a pair: she, the popular, extroverted, thin nutrition expert with the fine features of an auburn beauty queen; he, the quiet, introverted, paunchy tech genius with a round face supporting a mop of dark taupe hair. But what they shared was no less precious because of its subtlety. They were devoted to each other and to the belief that a marriage should last for a lifetime.

After exhausting all their energy setting up their campsite, Linda and Paul collapsed onto their bed. Too tired to move, Linda blew a kiss in his direction, and in her sultry Louisiana accent asked, "Meet me at the Atlantic stand before sunrise?"

Paul smiled, remembering their annual morning rendezvous at the simple wooden viewing stand on the Atlantic side of the tip of Cape Henlopen. A weathered, abandoned lifeguard stand, its solitary silhouette had added to the intrigue of the early sunrises on that side of the Cape's beach. With the large, bird nesting dunes blocking the campers' views, early morning strollers on the ocean side of the Cape felt as if they were on their own private stretch of beach.

Linda always preceded him on this trek. She said she liked to begin her walk along the quiet Delaware Bay side of the Cape, enjoying the cool summer breezes just before dawn while mentally replaying and filing away the past week's medical cases. When she rounded the tip of the Cape, she would climb to the top of the old lifeguard stand, mentally refreshed and ready to welcome Paul with a relaxed smile as he jogged up the beach.

**Ambling through the scrub pines the next morning,** Paul found the deer trail that circumvented the asphalt parking lots near the rustic campsites, and he headed for the beach. On his northward trek along the ocean coast to the tip of the Cape, he noticed how the winter's beach erosion had eaten into the dunes, and along with the harsh winds blowing the dunes westward, he reckoned Cape Henlopen was beginning another cycle of topographical change. Since the late 1890's, the shoreline of Cape Henlopen had shifted inland 50 feet to the west with the tip which faced Cape May, New Jersey, melting back southwardly 70 feet. Someday the Atlantic Ocean would subsume his and Linda's private meeting place.

The quiet night calls of the nesting Least Terns and Black-billed Skimmers faded as dawn approached. Paul slowed his pace as his muscles relaxed, and the muffled gurgling retreat of the water beneath the sand drained his tension out to sea.

Ten minutes later, Paul was nearing the Cape's point, smiling and humming the Righteous Brothers' "Unchained Melody" and anticipating the sunrise flash of Linda's shiny red hair at any moment. He quickened his pace when he saw the outline of the deserted guard stand. The salty brine misted the air and settled back into the sea foam as each wave crashed upward against the crumbling grey boards that tentatively reinforced the bottom of the platform.

Linda must not be here, yet, he thought. He looked back through the path he had just traveled, and then he walked up to the life guarding platform, sloshing through unusually heavy waves that threw sprays of grayish sea foam up against his calves. Yesterday's weed-whacking nicks and abrasions stung as the salty brine penetrated his epidermis, jangling the surface nerves into a frantic alert.

The salt water hurts more than usual, he thought. Something is wrong. . . . The surfaces of my legs are starting to feel numb.

Puzzled, but not heeding what the nerves in his body were telling him, Paul pushed on toward the stand. As he neared the weathered wood steps, Paul laid a shaking hand on the flat platform edge, grasping it for support. His knees began to buckle and he struggled to maintain his balance.

Automatically, Paul looked around for Linda to help him. Knowing that she would always take care of him, as he in turn would take care of her, made him love her even more.

Slowly, Paul's eyes drifted downward through the swirling furrows of sea foam at the base of the platform. There, mixed among the grayish foam, strands of long reddish seaweed swirled around his lower legs. Then, as the wave subsided back to sea, a beautiful mass of auburn colored seaweed, no, something else, wrapped around his unsteady ankles. Before Paul's mind could register what his senses were telling him, he slid down into a roiling swirl of sea foam and saltwater.

Stretching his shaky arms out into the waves, Paul grabbed Linda's floating auburn hair, pulling her lifeless body across his chest and into his arms. He leaned back against the old lifeguard stand, tears flooding his eyes, as he fought to remain conscious.

Relentlessly, replications of *Bacillus nocturne* continued their voracious ascent through Paul's shanks, already six inches above their entry points on his calves. The toxins were carving lattice-like patterns in the fragile tissues of his blood vessels, and the resulting bleeds were decimating his body's ability to fight back.

**On the bayside of the Cape,** starting his early morning shift on beach patrol, thirty-nine year old Tom Delaney revved the engine of the Starboard XL 5 and let the four-wheeler purr through the mist that encapsulated the Cape.

Rounding the sandy bayside cove, Tom spurred the Starboard on, downshifting through the wet sand while he popped the clutch. The inherent jerking and sidling common to this maneuver tossed him off the seat and slammed his chest against the handlebars. Smiling, he could hardly keep from yelling a good ol' cowboy "Ya-hoo!" He loved his job. "For doing this," he would laughingly tell his friends, "they actually pay me money."

As the sea mist covered his protective glasses and the ocean wind whipped his straight brown hair across his broad forehead and nose, blocking his vision, Tom slowed his speed in a cautionary response to approaching the camping area. Never know when some little kid might be out wandering around pushing his parents' playtime limits, he thought.

Sighting the old lifeguard stand, Tom decided to approach it via the high tide mark's edge, hoping to avoid splashing the cool water up around his thighs if he trundled through the low-lying surf.

Barely visible through the mist, Tom caught sight of a crumpled figure leaning against the old wooden structure. Next to him lay a beautiful redhead, her long silver-highlighted hair wet and thick against the man's chest. He held her body tight to his, gently rocking back and forth, softly singing the opening lines from the Righteous Brothers' version of "Ebb Tide."

Tom's gut contracted and his throat tightened and dried, despite the moisture in the air. He knew immediately what had happened and grabbed his cell phone to dial 911.

**While they waited for the paramedics to arrive,** Tom gently covered the man's wet shoulders with his ranger jacket, still unable to remove the beautiful woman from his arms. Her red hair had dark red stains running through the wet strands covering every part of her face.

The man's large, thick hands gently held the hair over her face, as if to keep Tom from seeing her.

When the paramedics arrived, Gloria Goldenseal, a tall, calm Native American Physician's Assistant assigned to Cape Henlopen for the past three summers, recognized Paul, and then surmised that he was holding Linda in his arms.

"Paul, it's Gloria. I'm here to help you," she began softly.

Gloria realized that Paul didn't recognize her. She had secured her long, straight, ebony hair under her rain hat. Nor did he see her distinctive broad facial features punctuated by her teal blue eyes before he dropped his chin back onto his chest.

"It's time, Paul. Time to take Linda to the hospital. You can sit with her there for as long as you want. Come now, Paul, help us lift her onto this backboard."

Releasing his tightly curled fingers from Linda's auburn hair, Paul slowly looked up at Gloria and said, "It wasn't supposed to end like this. Not like this."

"I know, Paul. Let us help you." Trying to lift Linda from Paul's arms, Gloria watched as one of the other paramedics carefully brushed the auburn hair away from Linda's face. He jolted backwards two steps, nearly losing his balance. His lack of professionalism and lack of consideration for the husband's feelings unnerved Gloria . . . until she looked down at Linda's still, blood-soaked, green eyes.

"Tom, we have a problem here," Gloria clearly enunciated her words. "I think we may be dealing with a type of hemorrhagic disease."

Tom froze. "That would be highly contagious then, wouldn't it?"

"Maybe not. Paul is still alive and we have no way of knowing yet how long he has been sitting with her. We'll know more when we try to get him to stand up. Call the emergency room on my cell phone and let them know what we're bringing in," she ordered. "Tell them it's a Level 4 Alert." Her softness was all gone; the Physician's Assistant battling for everyone's lives had just taken over.

"Next, tell your boss to quadrant off the campground in case this turns out to be highly contagious," Gloria stated, "and notify the State Police that we think we have a Level 4 Alert here. They will want to set up barricades on all the access roads to and from the park. Ask them to have all the Cape Henlopen-Cape May Ferry pilots grounded, alert the Coast Guard to post barriers around the Point to keep small boats from landing here, and definitely stop any ferries, boats, or ships en route to either Cape. If this is highly contagious, we could be moving into a Level 5 Alert very fast."

Having secured Linda's body to the backboard, the paramedics turned toward Paul, who had now rolled over onto his hands and knees pushing himself up into a near standing position. "Easy, Paul, your legs are swollen," Gloria said as she grabbed for his waist to support him.

"I know. When I fell into the water, I couldn't move, and the tide just kept washing over my legs. I think it helped, as lavage often does. They're not numb anymore." But Gloria noticed the gaping wounds around his calves. She thought it looked like a knife had been twisted into his skin in several places, and all the sites, despite the action of the waves, were open and bleeding.

Nodding quickly to the other paramedics, Gloria ordered, "Let's go." Gloria's team had him pressure pointed, wrapped, and secured to the stretcher within a minute, ready to hustle him off to the ambulance. Rolling his head toward Linda's lifeless body, Paul broke into anguished sobs that racked his whole body.

Gloria thought, This is just the beginning. Just the beginning. Then she turned toward the frightened group of people.

"Everyone," Gloria swallowed hard, took a deep breath and exhaled slowly, "we all have to report to the Henlopen Emergency Room for observation and possibly isolation."

An involuntary cascade of twitches rippled through the muscles on the left side of Park Ranger Delaney's face, ending in a crooked grimace. Tom Delaney didn't love his job anymore.

# Chapter 3

*Lido Beach*
*Venice, Italy*

**Covered in crusty sand,** Julie shivered as Luke lifted her unconscious body off the beach and ran to the nearest water taxi for help. Julie's chest heaved and her breaths stalled in labored gurgles.

Kate scooped Crystal up and carefully checked her for any symptoms similar to Julie's. Crystal seemed well, but visibly shaken by the incident.

Kate prayed for help as she and Jake ran to the dock after Luke. Nearly breathless, she turned toward Jake as they ran, but like an episode from a nightmare, the only words coming from her throat were unintelligible garbled sounds.

Finally, she forced a few words out by heavily exhaling. "Oh, Jake, this has happened to Julie before." Kate's voice rose in near panic. "Rapidly cascading symptoms are a hallmark of *nocturne,* which Julie had five years ago when it hit the Eastern Coast."

Kate's disconnected phrases and her mention of *nocturne,* separated by gasps for air, drained the color out of Jake's face. He watched his wife begin to unravel. Jake froze for a second and stumbled as his feet nearly went out from under him. He recovered quickly and hurried to catch up with Kate.

"I interned at Atlantic Hospital that summer," Kate added, sucking in breath. "Several people died and many more fell ill and then recovered. Julie was one of the later cases with milder symptoms." Kate exhaled loudly as she ran. "This time her symptoms are worse, like Maria DeSanchez's."

"Maria? How do you know about her?" Jake was stunned. Maria had been an operative for the Agency before she had died.

"I was assigned to her case. She was the first case of *nocturne.*"

Gasping, Kate sucked in a huge amount of air and forced out her next words, "Julie will be dead in an hour . . . unless we get her to a ventilator."

Shocked, Jake raced to the edge of the pier. "Taxi!" he shouted, his deep voice echoing back to them from across the channel to the mainland. Rushing toward the nearest water taxi, Jake jumped into the small craft, helping Luke step in with Julie in his arms. Kate climbed in, cradling Crystal's head against her shoulder, as Jake yelled, "Nearest hospital ER," in

Italian.

The gray-haired Venetian revving the boat's inboard motor nodded solemnly as he looked at the sick young woman in Luke's arms.

"Kate," Jake yelled over the roar of the motor, "sit down, breathe deeply. . . . We need your medical training to get Julie through this."

"Yes," Kate nodded, forcing air into her lungs. Jake's right, Kate thought, I might be Julie's only hope. At least I've had experience treating this infection. I have to calm down.

Kate reached for the water taxi pilot's cell phone lying on the seat next to him. He looked up and nodded, giving permission as he repeated the words, "Ospedale. Ospedale Privato di Venezia."

As the water taxi sped off to the Ospedale Privato di Venezia, Kate called the operator and repeated the name of the hospital, asking for a connection. Though her voice sounded thick and rough from the adrenaline constricting her throat, Kate managed to ask for the Emergency Room supervising nurse.

"This is Dr. Katherine Connors, a United States' physician affiliated with Atlantic University's medical research Institute in Dover, Delaware. I'm bringing in a patient with a very contagious disease and will need ventilation support immediately upon arrival. We will arrive within ten minutes."

Kate heard the nurse alert the staff to be ready for the incoming emergency and then quickly return to the phone. "We will be ready for you," she spoke in flawless English. "Approach via the Red Emergency Dock only and enter through the Red Emergency sliding doors." A click, and then Kate's contact was gone.

Turning to look at Julie, Kate remembered Ambruster. Without hesitation, Kate dialed the cell phone number she had memorized years before while interning with Dr. Walter Ambruster. His family owned a summer villa in the Castello sestiere east of St. Mark's Square, his haven of retreat during summer break from the university.

"Walt," Kate cried out when someone picked up the call. A man's voice with a heavy Mexican or Guatemalan accent stumbled over a halting, Italian greeting.

"I'm sorry. Do I have the wrong number? Is Walter Ambruster there?"

After a pause, another voice answered. "I'm on the phone now. Dr. Ambruster speaking."

"Kate Connors from the Institute. Walt, *nocturne's* back. The symptoms are the same as the DeSanchez case, but the progression is rapid."

Kate shouted over the roar of the water taxi's old engine. "It's infected my sister Julie, again."

Kate choked on the word 'sister' and just barely held back a flood of tears. Trying to maintain her composure, Kate pressed on, "Walt, we'll be at the ER in Venice's Ospedale Privato in ten minutes. Can you meet us there?"

The graying physician on the other end of the connection had not spoken. The color drained out of his normally ruddy, handsome face, and the etches of stress, from years of intense medical research, creased deeper shadows into his clenched jaw.

"Not *nocturne*," Dr. Walter Ambruster finally said. "Not *nocturne* again. How did Julie come in contact with it? I thought your lab was the only one with clearance to study it."

"I don't know, Walt. She was playing with my daughter in the water on Lido Beach. She collapsed. We ran to her and saw she was unconscious and bleeding from her eyes. Her husband picked her up, and we all ran for a water taxi to take us to the closest ER."

"Is anyone else infected? Be careful, *nocturne* moves fast."

"No, no, for some reason we're all still fine."

"I have to call David Winters," Ambruster interrupted, "before he leaves for his morning rounds. I want him to come with me, Kate. You remember him. He works with me now. We'll meet you at the hospital in half an hour. Remember to put Julie on a ventilator as soon as you arrive in the ER and start the IV lines to keep her hydrated. Pietra Ambini is the Chief of General Surgery there—a good doctor, Kate. I'll call ahead and talk to her, too."

"Thank you, Walt."

"We can save her, Kate," Ambruster emphasized. "We know much more than we did when we treated Maria DeSanchez."

Kate almost felt hopeful as she ended her call with Ambruster, until she turned to look at her unconscious sister in Luke's arms.

Julie's frail, blue-tinged body began a series of convulsions, subtle at first, but escalating in intensity as her shivers began to fade. Her body was shutting down, pooling all its resources to maintain a steady state for the survival of her brain's basal ganglia.

"How could this happen?" Kate asked aloud. "We're nowhere near *nocturne*." Quickly, she dialed the Agency's emergency line and the familiar voice of its Director, Dr. Marlin Stafford, answered.

"Code Red. I repeat, Code Red. *Nocturne* is live. Emergence at Lido Beach, Venice, Italy. Advise dispatch team immediately. Ambruster treating victim at Ospedale Privato di Venezia."

Kate paused for a second, and then quietly added a personal comment before she hung up, "It's Julie. The rest of us are all right."

Jake's adrenaline level skyrocketed, causing his whole body to react to the surge with trembles perceptible only to Kate's trained eyes. He continued to stare at Kate as he lifted Crystal from her arms and hugged her protectively against his chest.

Jake could barely keep his shoulders from shuddering. "How do you know so much about *nocturne*?"

His accusatory tone evident, Jake continued, "What about

Crystal? Is she infected? Or Luke? Or us? How did it infect someone this far away from its source?"

Although Jake and Kate had never worked in the same Agency programs as Maria DeSanchez, they both knew *Bacillus nocturne* had killed her and seven others along the Eastern Seaboard five years ago. Thousands of summer visitors had fallen ill, too, but had survived because they had contracted a less virulent form of the bacteria. Kate and Jake understood the severity of the disease and its implication for Julie.

Kate nearly faltered hearing Jake's accusatory tone, but she kept quiet, refused to answer him, and focused on what needed to be done next. But, the fact did not escape her that Jake had no idea that the Agency, rather than the Institute, sponsored her research on water borne pathogens, including *nocturne*.

Within minutes, the water taxi approached the hospital's Emergency Room Pier, but Kate waved him forward towards the Red Emergency Dock. Jake held Crystal against his chest as he and Kate climbed up onto the pier. They followed Luke, who raced through the heavy red doors of the Emergency Room's Isolation Entrance.

"Julie Thurston, age twenty-three, respiratory failure. Vent immediately," Kate called out to the waiting staff while flashing her passport and physician's identification for them to see. She sounded like the confident doctor that she was, not the terrified sister hidden within.

Isolation Emergency nurses lifted Julie from Luke's arms

and gently settled her onto a ventilator-ready gurney. Immediately they began inserting the lifesaving intravenous lines upon which her life would soon depend. The emergency room nurses rushed to clean the crusted sand from Julie's body, carefully washing her eyes, nose, ears, and mouth. The supervising nurse ordered, "Lavage the epidermis. Sterilize the fingernails, hands, face, nose, mouth, and ears. Ready warming blankets and prepare ice baths in case her fever spikes."

The Head of Ophthalmology quickly examined her eyes and ordered an immediate and extensive eyewash, while the Head of Neurology worked to stabilize her seizures. Dr. Pietra Ambini, the sixty year old, silver-haired Chief of General Surgery, listened to the physicians' diagnoses as they treated Julie, and then she decided the order of primary care while prepping the young woman for a ventilator. Within five minutes, the staff had diagnosed, stabilized, and ventilated Julie. They rushed her upstairs with Pietra Ambini to an isolation suite where Ambruster and Winters awaited her.

No other hospital personnel entered the Red Zone, designated by huge red metal doors at every juncture with the rest of the hospital and multiple red Biological Contamination warning signs posted along its perimeter. From the arrival pier to the lone examining room, and from the rarely used connecting elevator to the specially outfitted isolation surgical suite on the third floor, no one, absolutely no one crossed the Red Zone perimeter except for the original receiving team, Ambruster and Winters, and the family.

"Walt, thank God, you're here," Kate said as the elevator doors opened and Walt Ambruster grabbed Julie's gurney and pushed it into the isolation suite.

"Tell me everything," Walt replied while visually examining the young woman as he pushed the gurney along. As Kate recounted the morning events, Jake's anguished face told another story. He was obviously aware that Walt's abrupt greeting and serious tone meant there was no time for civilities.

Finished with their examinations, Walt consulted with Pietra, his old classmate from the States, to ascertain the other department heads' opinions on the case. Satisfied, Walt and Pietra decided to start Ambruster's life-saving protocol that he had developed after the Maria DeSanchez case: respiratory support, intravenous lavage, and alternating combinations of antibiotics carefully titrated to Julie's weight and symptoms. Kate, a physician by training, but a research professor by vocation, could not accept the irony of the situation.

My sister, Kate thought. The one bacterium that I chose to study after the Atlantic Seaboard outbreak of *Bacillus nocturne* has reinfected my sister. And I'm no closer to a cure for this ruthless bacterium than the physicians were five years ago. She should have immunity since she had a mild case of it years ago. What is happening?

"Kate, Jake, nursing will set up a room nearby where Crystal can nap and all of you can get cleaned up. Luke, we'll set up a cot for you beside Julie's bed so you can stay with her tonight. You can help us monitor her vital signs," Ambruster said.

"Thank you. What is Julie's prognosis?" Luke's anxiety kept ratcheting upwards.

"We'll know more by tomorrow morning." Ambruster patted Luke's shoulder and then walked over to Julie's bedside.

Grabbing Jake's arm, Kate led him into the hallway.

"Jake, Walt means that Luke needs to be here in case Julie doesn't make it through the night."

"I thought that, too. Do you think Luke understands?"

"If he does, he isn't showing it. It's more likely that he's in denial or nearing shock."

"Does Walt think Crystal, Luke, you, or I need to be under observation?"

"No, I don't think so, Jake. If we had contracted it, we'd all be sick by now. But, I still can't figure out why Julie is the only one who is ill."

"Kate, I've got to make some phone calls to the Institute. I want to know if any other hospitals have reported cases of *nocturne*. I'll take Crystal with me. You get cleaned up first, and then rest until we get back. Then we can bathe Crystal and put her down for her nap."

After washing all the traces of sand from her face, arms and legs, Kate combed through her wind-blown hair with one of the plastic hospital combs the nurse had set out for them. She walked over to the window to see the canal below, and then slouched down in the green leather chair next to one of the two hospital beds in the small room. She fought back tears and forced herself to concentrate on a productive line of thought: reconstructing the events on the day the first case of *Bacillus nocturne* appeared. She hoped the answer to how Julie became infected would surface as she remembered the circumstances surrounding the Maria DeSanchez case five years ago.

# Chapter 4



*Oostende Beach*
*Oostende, Belgium*

**The usual gray morning clouds** hung over the North Sea at Oostende Beach, covering the rising sun.  Early morning winds, that whipped joggers' hairs into striated trails of colors, refused to calm.  The sea softly glistened with roiling gray sea foam, interspersed with small iridescent-rimmed charcoal shells.

Oostende, Belgium, one of the top rated chic cities to visit on the North Sea shoreline, hosted a rich clientele.  Trendy shops and restaurants lined the curving north side of the Visserskaal.  Early risers queued in front of Chez La Mer, observing the anglers at the Quai des Pecheurs while waiting for hot cappuccinos and croissants.

The black metal railings of the Albert I-Promenade, designed to prevent falls from the high cement boardwalk stretching along the beach, separated latte sipping foreigners catching their first morning glimpse of the Belgium coast from the local beachcombers searching for sea glass.

Near the water's edge, a group of twelve svelte twenty-year-olds from Bruges, Belgium's oldest medieval city, wandered among the algae-covered, black boulders that protruded at low tide. They remarked about the oddly colored gray sea foam, assuming that it had taken its hues from the dark morning sky.

Caught in the rock crevices among the bubbles of sea foam were tiny sea creatures attempting to burrow into the wet sand. Two young women knelt to scoop up the tiny wentletraps that were tunneling their way to safety.

As the women gently cradled the creatures, a huge wave generated by the passing Oostende ferry swept them backwards into the surf. Laughing, they stood up wiping the sea foam and salt water out of their eyes and long hair, shaking gobs of the sticky foam from their arms and into the faces of their surrounding friends.

Still gripping a sandy handful of wentletraps in one hand, one of the women rubbed her wet eyes with her other hand.

"Whew. I think that wave slapped its own handful of sand in my face," she laughed as she spoke in Flemish. "My eyes feel gritty and salty and sore all at the same time. Somebody throw me a towel! And why is this sea foam so sticky? Look! I can't shake it off my arms anymore. It's like it's clinging, no, attaching itself to me."

The sea foam did not cling to her, but the bacteria imbedded in it did. All night the bacteria had exchanged molecules, proteins, and genetic elements known as plasmids through their nanotubes. They were learning from each other. Learning how to attach to their prey.

Dropping the wentletraps into the surf, she tried unsuccessfully to rub the sea foam from her arms and legs. She squeezed her irritated eyes tightly closed and turned blindly toward her friends, groping for a towel.

"Steffenie, what's wrong?" Johanna asked. "Steffenie. Run up to the rinsing station. We've got to get this stuff off of us," Johanna yelled as the sea foam soaking her bangs clung to her forehead and then dripped into her eyes.

Trying to alleviate the stinging sensation, Johanna wiped her eyes with the palms of her hands, grabbed Steffenie's arm, and started running toward their hotel. As they stumbled along through the sand, Johanna rubbed her eyes across her upper arm, desperate to end the burning pain.

Steffenie, crying out for help as she staggered behind Johanna, yet trying desperately to keep up, lost her balance and careened to the right.

"Hey, watchit," an irritated middle-aged man yelled. The young woman had run right through the middle of his blanket, scattering his morning newspaper.

Unable to see well enough to avoid the next blanket, full of Bloody Mary-sipping couples enjoying a quiet breakfast on the beach, Steffenie and Johanna lost their balance and stumbled over several pairs of outstretched legs.

Falling forward into the arms of one of the surprised men, Johanna grappled to steady herself.

Steffenie veered left and landed in the lap of Dr. Ethan Holt. The doctor saw Steffenie's eyes seeping a bloody discharge mixed with salt water and sea foam. Wiping her eyes, Ethan tried to check her pupils, suspecting that drug usage may have dilated them, but instead they were puddling over with bright red blood.

Laying Steffenie down on the blanket, Ethan reached for his cell phone to dial 112 while carefully examining his bloodied hands for abrasions. "112, emergency. Oostende Beach in front of the Grande Hotel," he yelled into the phone in Flemish.

You fool, Ethan thought. Three years of practicing emergency medicine, wary of blood borne infection, and what do you do after three Bloody Marys? Wipe blood away from a stranger's eyes with your bare hands.

Ethan knew the blood soaking in under his fingernails could be as lethal as blood entering a puncture wound or an abrasion. He understood that he had a long waiting period of anxiety ahead of him. However, what he did not anticipate was the aggressiveness of the bacteria that had already entered his bloodstream.

When Steffenie's and Johanna's friends saw the young women fall, they began running to the water to rinse off the sticky foam that their friends had splattered on them. Their actions, of course, only splashed more of the bacteria-laden water onto their bodies.

Within minutes, twelve healthy university students full of promise and one slightly inebriated physician became the next victims of *Bacillus nocturne*.

# Chapter 5

*Atlantic University*
*Dover, Delaware, U.S.A.*

**At 58, Dr. Rachael Glass,** an elegant, petite brunette from Rhode Island, presided as the youngest President of Atlantic University and the first female. Her long list of accomplishments on her *curriculum vitae* read like a prestigious recommendation, or as she often said, like an obituary. Her staff, though, respected her vast experience and frequently commented that she was the visionary leader the university needed. She felt less assured. Once again, under her tenure, another inexcusable tragedy had occurred.

President Glass quietly gathered her Deans, Department Chairpersons, and Campus Security personnel together for an unexpected 8:00 a.m. meeting.

"Tara Anderson, a junior Aquatic Ecology major is missing," Rachael began. "Tara and her partner Jase Sirito have been gathering data for their marine biology research near the Thompson Island Preserve in the Rehoboth Bay. This morning Jase felt ill and could not cover his quadrants near the Preserve. Although it is against college policy, Tara decided to gather the samples alone."

"Arriving at the marina before its five a.m. opening," Rachael recounted, "Tara untied one of the University's kayaks, loaded her scientific supplies, and left a note tacked on the boathouse door saying she would be back in an hour. The Marina Coordinator notified me ten minutes ago that Tara had not returned and was three hours overdue."

"We have activated the University's Water Safety Quick Response System," Rachael soberly announced, "to search for Tara in Quadrant EE of the Rehoboth Bay. Hopefully, she is just overdue, but we have mobilized the University's search teams and notified the State Police and Coast Guard that we have a missing person."

Rachael could see that her colleagues were stunned. She pushed her charcoal bifocals down the bridge of her aquiline nose and peered over their top at her staff. Not again, they must be thinking. I imagine that their thoughts must be running like mine. . . . This is the third missing student at Atlantic University in five years. First, Maria DeSanchez and Toby Hannah, and now Tara Anderson.

Rachel overheard phrases from their conversations: "Maria DeSanchez's accident caused Toby Hannah's death." . . . "Was it really an accident?" . . . "A cover-up?" . . . "We could have all died." . . . "Such a brilliant mind!" . . . "A beautiful young woman." . . . "Tragic!" . . . "Unforeseen consequences of research . . . when you're not careful." . . . "The safety regulations came too late for them." . . . "Bacterial research without oversight!" . . . "It was Rachael's fault." . . . "No, Toby's fault." . . . "Both of them were too young." . . . "His war zone experiences . . . PTSD?" . . . "No, Mark was responsible. He was the professor-in-charge of the research." . . . "Thank God the bacteria depleted itself."

"Anyone," Rachael continued, "scheduled for research on the bay or marshes today must follow the Quick Response System Policy, reporting and investigating any unusual sightings in their Quadrants. Remember to hoist your boat's red flag to alert boaters and residents that a person is missing, and keep all communication lines open. Officer Gates will distribute identification flyers with Tara's picture for you to pass out throughout the morning. The University's website, the local and State Police, and the airport's advertisement planes will all be posting banners with her picture and last known position."

"I know that all of you are remembering what happened to Maria DeSanchez and Toby Hannah," Rachael continued. "They are the reason our Quick Response System exists; they are the reason we will find Tara Anderson before it is too late. Search thoroughly, search long, search hard. Bring Tara home."

# Chapter 6

*Tower Road Bayside*
*Rehoboth Bay, Delaware, U.S.A.*

**The heavy brown and white wood sign** posted at the entrance to the Rehoboth Bay side of the Delaware Seashore National Park had become a permanent fixture. Its ominous warning restricted even the hardiest of the local boat people from catching a cooling swim over the sides of their skiffs. The Bay wasn't for swimming anymore:

*"The waters of the Inland Bays may contain organisms that could be harmful to your health. Swimming could result in an increased risk of rashes, infections or gastrointestinal distress, especially during and after rainfall. For your health and safety, please swim at beaches with lifeguards where the water quality is tested weekly. For information on beach water quality or to report illnesses resulting from contact with these waters, please call 1-800-922-WAVE."*

The messages on the warning signs posted all along the inland bay beaches were clear: This water may be hazardous to your health.

**Ready to launch the University's small craft** into the Rehoboth Bay, Atlantic University's youngest Chairperson, Professor Mark Andrews, shuffled his water sampling supply kit into the galley, shoving his khaki jacket, first aid kit, GPS transponder, and cell phone charger into a storage drawer.

He centered his khaki baseball cap on his mass of dark brown curls, effectively concealing what women admired most about his appearance. Still a preppy dresser at 34, his expensive clothing had begun to look ill fitted on his slight frame. He realized that he had lost too much weight in the last five years. Even his emerald green eyes had faded away to a sad, opaque gray-green.

"Kristy," he called above board, "can you bring the filtering system down here, too? After last night's heavy rainfall and today's northeasterly winds, it may get a little choppy as the spring tide moves out through the estuary. This is the highest water level I've seen. Better to keep the expensive equipment below."

"Be right there, Mark," Kristy Lang yelled back. Lithe, polished, and bearing a natural suntan, apparent from the sun streaks highlighting her brown hair, Mark's graduate research assistant turned heads whenever she walked along a pier.

They had an easy relationship, both interested in understanding how the estuary affected the condition of the bay and vice versa.  In her third year of the Marine Sciences Ph.D. Program at Atlantic University, Kristy had developed a dissertation research agenda that paralleled and added to her mentor's research.  Together, they hoped to add new knowledge to the ecological field of inland water systems that drained into saltwater bays.

"We'll capture water samples from the central part of the bay at various water levels and along the eastern shoreline in the coves and along the mosquito control ditches that were cut into the marshes last week," Mark said.

"I hope we can locate the source of the bacterial contamination noted on all those signs surrounding the Rehoboth Bay's boat launch sites," Kristy replied.  "The locals say the warnings are really cutting into the tourist trade this year."

"I know.  We've been sampling the water quality of the bay for months, but still no evidence of its source.  We'll cover the EE Quadrant on the bay chart today."

"Okay.  Why did you leave EE Quadrant for last?  It seemed more promising to me than the other sights because of the old university pier up river."

Mark snapped his head and shoulders around to face Kristy, and she saw something wild in his expression.

"No reason."  He heard his voice scrape the air and waited for her to flinch as Maria had.

Kristy's expression remained neutral, but she stopped asking him questions.

He pointed at the boat's bow, and she dutifully helped him push the small craft away from the pier.

# Chapter 7



*Rehoboth Bay*
*Delaware, U.S.A.*

**Maria DeSanchez** kept flashing through Mark's mind. First, he would see Maria's image as if she were standing just to the left of his shoulder, observing what he was doing. Then he saw her face, framed in wavy jet hair, in front of him, her warm brown eyes watching his every move. Then he saw her sitting across from him at the dinner table. Then she was in his arms in front of the fireplace at the restaurant. . . . It had been five years since she had disappeared, but he still felt like he did on the last day that he saw her. Now, it seemed like that day was happening all over again.

**Five years ago,** Mark had met Maria in his laboratory at Atlantic University two weeks before September classes began. She was his new research assistant, assigned to him by the

Dean of the College of Marine Studies. Only a Master's Degree candidate, but extremely smart and a world traveler, the Dean felt she held great promise as a future researcher in the Global Water Ecology Program of which Mark was the Chairperson.

After one semester, Maria would enter the early admission doctoral program, earning her master's and doctoral degrees simultaneously. With a 145 IQ, an athletic build, and abundant energy, Maria would fare well in her studies, and the university's President, Dr. Rachel Glass, hoped she would become a renowned researcher at Atlantic University. Maria was Rachel's daughter.

Mark and Maria became immediate friends, he her mentor, she his devotee. She soaked up every word he spoke, asked him for opportunities to try every new piece of equipment, volunteered for mucky fieldwork, and worked long, monotonous hours in the lab, but nothing was monotonous for her.

Maria was curious, constantly curious about the workings of everything. Rather than ask, "Why?" she began each sentence with, "Is this because . . ." and she always knew intuitively the reasoning behind every scientific principle.

"What a gem of a research assistant! What a mind! What a beauty!" Mark heard himself repeat one day. He was falling in love, and he recognized it, as did Maria. Moreover, Rachel knew it, too.

Now, shaking his head to clear Maria's image from his mind,

Mark turned his attention to setting the GPS for Quadrant EE. His arm thrust behind his back, feeling for his weather alert radio, buried under his gear and his camel jacket. His fingers curled around the iPod-sized weather scanner, and he pulled it close to his eyes.

"These bifocals," Mark muttered. "Can't see a thing with them and can't see a thing without them." GPS and weather scanner in hand, he electric started the bay cruiser and yelled for Kristy to hold on.

Concentrate, Mark reminded himself before pulling the cruiser out into the bay. You can do this. It's just another water-sampling trip. Tara won't be found anywhere near where we will be working.

Despite his best efforts, Mark's mind slowly started to slip back in time again. He felt like a voyeur watching a scene through someone's lighted living room window late at night. His memories of Maria were still vivid.

**Mark had assigned Maria various duties** during her second semester as his research assistant. She was very bright and caught on so quickly that it seemed natural for her to take positions of responsibility. The Marina Director set aside office space for her so she could slip into the bay at a moment's notice and gather water data for Mark's grant projects.

At the time, Mark worked as the principal investigator on a prestigious $1.8 million grant from the Institute for Public Policy and Safety. It involved drinking water safety in the field of global ecology, and its monies funded the new department that he chaired. The grant also paid for Maria's graduate student salary and her travel to conferences. Remarkably, Maria was already an excellent researcher, and Mark had recently added her name as a co-author on a paper he sent to the *Journal of Water Ecology*.

Every day Maria's duties included predawn water sampling in the marsh, always accompanied by one of the marine research fellows, as policy demanded. She never complained, and through her gift for enthusiastic conversation, she capably managed the unwanted male attention her beauty attracted.

Five years ago, Mark and Maria culled water samples together at dusk. They were testing the bacterial content of the estuary after a heavy rainfall to see if any sewage leakage had contaminated the bay waters.

As night encroached, Mark and Maria realized that testing the water samples at night was just too difficult. For one thing, the fading light seemed to hamper their vision, and more importantly, the water samples were indicating unusually high levels of bacterial content. They both thought the aberration would correct itself if they had better lighting for reading the test results. Mark suggested taking the samples back to the lab where Maria could test them in sufficient lighting. Together, they decided to head back to the university's pier and discuss the day's activities over dinner.

**By 7:30 p.m., Mark and Maria** had settled in for a warm, comforting dinner in the authentically restored stone cellar of the Olde Forke, an eighteenth century restaurant on the National Historic Register, located just a half mile from the bay.

"Maria," Mark asked, "would you like your favorite wine tonight?" No matter how hard he tries, Maria thought, his sentences always come out stilted. She could tell that he was nervous around her. She sensed that he didn't want to spoil anything, as he probably had done before with other women.

"Yes, definitely." She was exhausted, cold, and apprehensive. Where is this relationship going? she wondered.

Maria rose from her seat and walked over to the huge cooking fireplace that lined the entire back wall of the room. She warmed her hands trying to eliminate the chill that had permeated her body while they had been out on the bay.

Maria needed time to think.

I've worked with Mark for half a year now. She began to organize the issue at hand. He thinks I am a student, not an Agency undercover agent ready for assignment wherever the Agency needs me. He doesn't know the grant he received from the Institute was not a competitive grant, but rather one to build my cover story and to fund my work here. I'm attracted to him; the way he looks at me tells me he's interested in me. I'm supposed to finish my degree here and accept the university research position funded by the Institute's next grant, a grant that Mark does not know he will receive in two years. Can a relationship be built around deceptions like that?

Mark approached her at the fireplace, and as she turned to face him, he wrapped her in his arms in a casual hug, pretending to warm her. To Maria, Mark's arms felt as if they had melted two inches into her body everywhere that they touched her. This unsettled her. She realized in that moment that this commitment would permeate her entire being, and she'd never be able to keep him separate from her work.

"Mark, please, don't," she said softly, keeping her eyes trained on the fire.

"Of course," Mark quickly responded as he backed away. "No problem. I just thought you looked a little chilled. No offense intended."

Maria recognized his half-hearted smile as a cover-up for his feelings. She believed that Mark thought he hid his disappointment well, but he had underestimated Maria's perceptive abilities.

Throughout the rest of the evening, neither one of them mentioned the scene at the fireplace. Instead, they kept their conversation focused on science. After dinner, Mark went home to his bachelor apartment alone, and Maria drove over to the lab to complete the bacterial testing of the water samples.

**Within a few minutes of setting up the water samples** for testing, Maria knew they would have to go out again and resample. All of the water samples showed incredibly high levels of bacteria.  Either she or Mark had accidentally contaminated the samples, or they had drawn samples from a highly contaminated area of water.  She decided upon the former, and began packing up more equipment for a second trip to the bay. Rather than asking Mark to join her again, Maria called the cell phone of Caleb Wright, her chemistry lab partner who often accompanied her on estuary experiments.

After the eighth ring, Maria knew Caleb was either busy or had fallen asleep, probably the latter.  She left a message saying, "Caleb, wake up.  I need you for a boat trip, again.  Call me back ASAP."

Two minutes later, Caleb returned her call.  "Hey, Maria. What's up?  I can't help you.  I'm in Connecticut visiting my parents. Just can't get there in time, but I would if I could."

"Caleb, I underestimated you!" Maria laughed.  "Thanks for calling back.  It's okay.  I'll find another way to get this done. Someone at the marina can accompany me.  See you, soon?"

"Yeah, I should be back tomorrow.  Have a great one!"

Maria decided she could still get the water samples, if she hurried out to the marina before dawn.  She knew that she could grab one of the people at the marina to help her.  If she arrived at the marina before daybreak, they could be out and back before the marina started to get busy.

Heaving her water sampling equipment into the back of her Jeep Wrangler, Maria climbed up into the driver's seat, keyed the ignition, flicked on the headlights, and headed for the marina. On her way, she called her roommate to tell her she would be water sampling on the marsh with someone from the marina, and wouldn't be home until 9:00 a.m.

As she approached the marina, Maria's thoughts focused on how she and Mark may have contaminated the water samples. She reviewed every step in the process, from selecting the containers to storing them in her supply kit bag. Yet, she could not recall how they could have contaminated any part of the process.

Usually very aware of her surroundings, as her Agency training had taught her to be, Maria's sampling conundrum coupled with her confusing feelings for Mark distracted her from the slight, shadowy movement around the corner of the well-lit marina office.

**Toby Hannah, a 6'4" blue-eyed blonde country boy,** in appearance only, thanks to his blue plaid flannel shirt and over-stretched suspenders, peered around the tall storage barrels lining the side of the marina office. Maria knew he was a freshman from the Bronx, and he worked at the marina prepping and repairing boat engines to supplement his financial aid package from the GI Bill. Her Agency report on him classified him as alert, bright, promising, and hopeful of earning a Master of Science degree in Oceanography Technology. After four years of Army duty in the Middle East deserts, he had decided that the only sand he ever wanted to see again would be at the ocean.

Maria could tell that her arrival both surprised and pleased Toby. He knew she rarely came to the marina before sunrise, and she realized that he would like to get to know her better. Perhaps the opportunity had arrived. Pushing his hair away from his eyes, he nonchalantly picked up a heavy crate of gasoline engine parts and walked to the front of the marina office.

"Mornin', Maria," he called out across the gravel parking lot. "What's got you out here so early in the mornin'?"

Maria smiled. She actually liked Toby, although most of the students felt he seemed a little rough around the edges. She had pegged him for an Army vet the first day she had met him. She respected him for that. She knew the Middle East drained a lot out of the troops, and the fact that many came back to serve their country through the workforce or by securing college degrees to attain government positions impressed her.

Grabbing her gear from the back of her muddy Wrangler, Maria called back, "Want to go for a little water sampling trip, Toby? I have to resample some of the water that Mark and I collected yesterday. It'll take less than an hour. We should be back by sunrise."

Toby gleamed. "Yep, sure thing," he casually replied. "I'll get the boat revved up while you sign us out."

Maria felt pleased. Maria felt so pleased that, when Toby

pulled the boat up alongside the pier, she flashed a smile at him rather than watching where to step down into the boat. Losing her balance, she tumbled face first into the water.

"So much for Lady Grace," she laughed, admonishing herself after she resurfaced, and coughed her way back to the edge of the pier.

Laughing out loud, Toby reached over and pulled her wet body back on board. Wiping the wet straggles of sea foam-covered hair from her shoulders and face, Maria laughed, emphasizing the first word of her comment, "Now, I'm ready to go."

Toby laughed as he slowly shook his head from side to side in mock disbelief.

"C'mon, Cowgirl, let's ride this motorboat out to the West range!" he chortled in his best John Wayne accent as he revved the motor, and they were thrown backward into the boat.

Maria liked Toby. His light attitude and raucous sense of humor always amused her. She decided the Tobys of this world would be better matches for her than her serious, professor friend. At least for now.

"Maria," Toby yelled over the roar of the motor, "a researcher by the name of Walt Ambruster came out to the marina just 'bout thirty minutes before you arrived this mornin'. Don't usually get too many of those types out here so early in the mornin'."

"That name sounds familiar," Maria said cautiously, realizing that it was a name she had heard at the Agency. "What did he want, Toby?"

"I dunno. Oh, yeah, he said he was gonna do some water samplin' at the edge of the pier. You know . . . stuff like you and the other students do for the university. Do you think I shoulda made him sign in like everybody else?"

"No, Toby, I don't think that would have been a good idea. You never know when he might be sitting across the desk from you in a classroom. But, thanks for telling me about him. If I ever run into him out here, I'll ask a few questions about his research. Profs always like that."

Toby nodded. As they crossed the bay, he pointed ahead to the Blue Crab Cove where Maria usually did her water sampling. "Same place as before?"

He turned to see why Maria had not answered his question. Maria still did not answer. Her hands were furiously rubbing her eyes, and when she finally looked up at Toby, he could see that she must have scratched them because drops of bright red blood lay scattered on her cheeks.

"Toby," Maria cried out, "My eyes. The wind is making them sting so badly, I . . . is it bothering your eyes this much?"

"No, I'm fine," Toby cut the motor just in time to feel the boat slide up onto the cove's sandy beach. He leaned forward and took Maria's face in his hands to get a better look at her eyes. They were bleeding along the outer corners. Dropping the cowboy accent, Toby promised, "You'll be all right, Maria.

Just a little blood in the corners where you were rubbing them too hard. My eyes are feeling gritty now, too. It must have been the salty spray we generated as we skimmed across the bay."

For all the reassurance that he offered to comfort Maria, she heard the same panic in his voice that she was feeling. They were both veterans of different conflicts, but each one of them received training on how to recognize the hemorrhagic fevers of the Congo. They began just like this.

"The pain, Toby, it's almost too much to bear," Maria clenched her teeth and tried to concentrate on a point outside her body, as she had been taught to do by the Agency.

Toby jumped out of the boat and tried to rock it back into the water, but the motor had dug itself deeply into the wet sand at the waterline. He couldn't move it.

"Maria, I've got to go get help. Lay back and rest. I'll be back soon," Toby said as he started out across the marsh, barely able to withstand the painful burning in his eyes, and the thoughts of what lay ahead for both of them.

# Chapter 8



*Captiva Island*
*Florida, U.S.A.*


**Breathless, yet still pushing herself to run as** quickly as she could, Claire circled back along the isolated running trail, finally catching up to her husband, Lance Martin.

"Jogged . . . 'round . . . charcoal . . . fire . . . pit . . . last . . . night's barb'cue . . ." Claire panted as she ran at top speed into his arms.

"Someone's . . . watching . . . me."

"No," she continued rapidly, catching her breath and starting to jog again, "not just watching . . . I could feel their eyes . . . on ev'ry muscle . . . in my whole body. . . ."

Lance watched her brown curls bounce in unison with her steps and had to concentrate to maintain eye contact with her amber-green eyes as they ran. It was the only way that he could maintain focus on what she was saying and not let his work assignments intrude.

"Felt like someone was sizing me up . . . then there was a slight rustling noise . . . like something crawling through the tall dune grasses . . . *Panicum amarum Elliot . . .*"

Lance worked hard to muffle his laughter. It was just like Claire, he thought, to use the scientific name for the marsh grasses. A marine biologist through and through. Just her and the tall grasses, he chortled to himself. Besides, it's 6:00 a.m., and I haven't seen a soul.

"Lance, are you listening to me?" Claire exhaled loudly as they continued their run at a slower pace.

"When I caught sight of the sunrise . . . reflecting off something aqueous like a lizard's eyes . . . I jolted around and sprinted . . . all the way back to you."

Lance Martin stared at Claire. He could see now that she was visibly distressed, pale and sweaty, cold and clammy, all at the same time. Lance stopped running and pulled Claire into his arms, burying her face into his chest. He stroked his fingers through her tousled hair, hugging her shivering body close to his, as if his 6'6" height could shelter her from any danger.

"Hey, Babe, it's okay. Probably just some locals gawking at those long legs," he cajoled, his onyx eyes crinkled by a reassuring smile.

"No," she was adamant, "it felt dangerous. Like something was hunting me."

"An animal?" He gently questioned her, realizing at last that she seemed genuinely afraid.

"We're on an island here, Claire," he said as he grasped her hand and purposely started walking back to the beach house.

"The only wildlife we have seen is that crazy four foot tall gray heron that strolls our beach every morning waiting for the fishermen to toss him their bait."

Claire hesitated, as her marine biology training kicked in. "Okay. Maybe I was just spooked. After yesterday's experience at the beach, I just don't know what to believe anymore."

"What experience?"

"One of the islanders yelled for everyone to get out of the water because he thought a group of manta rays swimming near the shore looked like an alligator heading up the coast."

Lance noticed she was talking even faster now. She seems shakened by that experience, too, he thought.

"Nothing. Nothing in my graduate school training had prepared me to believe that alligators would be swimming in salt water," Claire punctuated the air with her hands. "But other seasoned vacationers confirmed that it happens here. That was enough to make me stay out of the water for the rest of our vacation."

Lance wasn't certain that her fears were unfounded. Seven years of working for the Agency had taken him to numerous beaches where innocuous looking sand dunes and salt-water marshes hid bigger threats than anything Mother Nature had intended.

Yesterday, Lance thought, the local paper reported that owners of exotic reptiles were abandoning their pets in the island's swamps when the pets grew too large for safe handling. Nile monitor lizards were already taking over alligator lairs and sometimes surpassing the alligators in size. Then the alligators started looking for other ponds closer to houses to set up their new territories, sometimes attacking unsuspecting homeowners as they gardened in their own backyards.

Lance conceded to himself that it wasn't as safe on the island as people thought. I'll check out the beach and the nearby barbecue pit, he thought, after I settle Claire into bed with her favorite calming chamomile tea and this week's *Island Herald*. Well, maybe not the newspaper.

An hour later, Lance walked out of the cottage onto the sandy beach. His cell phone rang, but the ring tone wasn't the usual rap medley that accompanied his calls. It was a straight, 1950's telephone ring tone, repeated two times, and then after a pause, followed by four more rings.

The Agency, he thought. He quickly stepped away from the beach house before he answered the call.

"Lance, Kate's sister Julie contracted *nocturne*," Jake said. "She's at a private hospital in Venice. I've contacted the Director of the Agency. He is activating all the response teams. I need you to assemble your team, using the funds from the Ocean Waves Grant we wrote in March. The Agency wants to fly Kate to the Paris Institute to compare this strain of *noc-*

*turne* to the last outbreak. She'll need Claire's assistance in Paris ASAP. Our Agency teams will have to stop the person who released it, before they strike again. Worse, we need to know if this is their first and only strike or if there were multiple releases. We'll videoconference in twelve hours. Give your team members their regular assignments and tell them to be ready with full reports in eleven hours."

Lance did not have an opportunity to respond, nor did he need to. He knew what to do. Hurriedly, Lance dialed one memorized number after the other on his secure cell phone.

With each connection, the only words he spoke were "Stat Three Over" signaling the team would meet immediately at Base 3, Dover, Delaware, due to an overseas development. Then he repeated their standing assignment for cases like this one.

Within minutes, he had reassembled what the Agency called the Ocean Waves Grant Team, one of its secret, privately funded environmental emergency action teams at the Institute.

Next, Lance called General Joe Hatbourne, U.S.A.F., Retired, to arrange a private flight for Claire to Paris.

"Joe, Lance here. We are on Stat to Base 3, and I need to get Claire over to the Institute office in Paris. Can your private pilot be ready in an hour?"

"She's ready and waiting, Lance. That's what she's paid to do. Hangar 203, back entrance."

"Thanks, General," Lance replied to his old Agency mentor, a salute obvious in his voice. Lance knew he and Claire could hop the General's experimental titanium jet to Dover, and then she could land at Hatbourne's private field near Givenchy, France, within four hours. They had done it before.

# Chapter 9



*Rehoboth Bay*
*Delaware, U.S.A.*

**Kristy could tell something was bothering Mark.** Never jocund, but never morose, either, his normal demeanor seemed somewhat sad and thoughtful. She always supposed he had lost a great love and had not quite recovered from it. But today was different. He frightened her.

As they motored across the bay to the old university pier, she studied him. He edged closer under the roof, out of sight, when he saw her staring at him.

That was it. He's acting suspicious. Like he has some thing to hide. Like a dead body. Why did I think that? Was it his comments about the missing graduate student, Tara Anderson? This is frightening me. Maybe if I can engage him in conversation, it will help him return to his old self. That will make both of us feel better.

"Mark, how much longer until we reach the pier?"

"About five minutes."

She was thankful for any conversation. It kept her from thinking about Tara Anderson.

"We need to restock the storage room on the old pier. There are still a few projects going on up river. Water sampling and sediment traps on the marsh. Most experiment teams leave from the new Dewey Beach dock, now."

"Okay, I'll help you restock the cabin. I remember it as a cabin because one summer my family came here to rent boats, and it looked like someone lived there."

"We had several students with offices out there, and they brought a few furnishings from their homes to spruce the place up."

"Spruce the place up? Were they doing drugs there?"

"What? No!"

Recognizing the need to change the subject quickly, Kristy asked, "Where's the best spot for our sampling? Uh, water sampling?"

"Right where the largest tributary enters the cove. We get backwash there when the tide comes in, so any bacteria traveling down the streams tend to settle in there."

Kristy spotted the cove as they rounded the last shoal. The boat rolled a little to the right as its waves rebounded from the white sand bar. A quarter of a mile ahead, Kristy saw the weathered gray frame of the pier with its orange striped edge precariously dangling near the water's surface.

"Needs a little repair, doesn't it?"

"Needs a lot more than a little repair." Mark forced a laugh.

Angling the small craft to the stable side of the pier, he slowed the motor and barely brushed the edge of the pier as he pulled alongside it. Kristy jumped out and wrapped the rope around an old pillar, while Mark unloaded the supplies onto the creaking planks.

"Watch your step, Kristy. I'm not sure how well those boards weathered the last couple Nor'easters."

At last, Kristy thought, I'm getting the old Mark back. Safety is his number one priority.

She gingerly opened the door to the small storage room, expecting some wildlife to come scurrying out at her feet. "None today," she laughed over her shoulder to Mark.

**Mark stared intently through the small glass window** to her right, noticing the blue aluminum vase that Maria had always kept on her desk. The dried flower arrangement was a statement in time. He remembered when Toby Hannah had given it to her one day, filled with wildflowers. She had been genuinely pleased. With wildflowers. Mark had been terribly jealous.

He followed Kristy in, and as she restocked the shelves with water sampling supplies, he signed them in on the day chart. Just above their names was Tara Anderson's name.

What was she doing at this pier? Everyone thought she had left from the new pier down at Dewey. A chill zigzagged through his body. Sweat poured down his temples and dripped onto the dry wooden floor.

Kristy heard the sweat splat on the floor and gave him a curious look.

He went outside and slowly walked to the back of the structure. He didn't want to go there. It was a docking area made specifically to catch kayaks as they returned downstream without their occupants. First year graduate students always had a hard time learning the balancing act required to keep a kayak upright.

He cautiously turned the corner, and he inhaled the acrid smell of blood. A few green flies rose up and then settled down again on a small figure curled into the fetal position on the bottom of a kayak.

"Maria!" He ran to the kayak and rolled the young woman over into his arms. He was shocked to see that the hemorrhaging eyes belonged to someone else.

"I mean, Tara? Tara Anderson?"

A whimper, followed by a moan, and then movement. She stirred and began crying again as she awoke. He stemmed the bleeding by pulling his tee shirt off and wrapping it around her head and eyes. Lifting her gently out of the boat, he stood up, struggling for balance. Once he had her settled in his arms, tight against his chest, he started to run.

"Kristy," he yelled as he ran back to the front of the storage shed, stopping for just a second so she would see him heading for the motor boat.

"Is that Tara?" She wiped her belongings off the table into her bag with a long sweep of her arm and grappled together the ends of her carry bag with both hands. Reaching the end of the pier, her bag clanged down onto the dry boards as she grabbed for the mooring rope. She tossed the rope and then her bag into the boat.

Mark cautioned her, "When you get into the boat, don't touch her or any of the blood splatters. Sit up front on the deck. Upwind of her."

Kristy quickly complied, following Mark's commands explicitly.

Then he gingerly placed Tara on the cot below deck where she could still hear his voice while he sped the craft across the bay.

"Tara, you're going to be all right now. We found you. Try to sleep."

He didn't know if sleeping would be a good idea. She had lost more blood than he had ever seen, and she seemed to be very weak. If she slept, would she wake up again?

He didn't know what else to say. As a professor, he could lecture for hours without any notes, but outside the classroom, words often escaped him.

"Try to sleep, Tara." They were words of comfort from his

heart. He hoped, at least, that sleep might afford her some rest and provide a release from her pain. Like it did for him, when memories of Maria flooded his mind each night.

# Chapter 10



*Lido Beach*
*Venice, Italy*

**Sea foam,** sparkling iridescently in the early afternoon sun, piled up on the beach where the waterline met the sand. Children splashed through the shallow water, and their laughter intermingled with cries of delight as the waves tossed the sea foam around their legs.

Toddlers wobbled through the bubbly water while older siblings skidded boogie boards along the water's edge, flaying foam in every direction. It was a typical, happy day at the shore. None of the tourists had seen the Connors' early morning flight from the beach.

The hotel never did post a water quality report that day. The person responsible for sampling the water had gone home because of illness.

Suddenly, the sun dipped behind a graying storm cloud, and

the viperous shadows from overhead cast a darkened haze over the beach. Swarms of miniscule bacteria, alerted by the fading sunlight, stirred within their tiny capsules interspersed in the sea foam. Their unique genetic structures signaled that dusk was arriving; it was time to awaken; time to replicate; time to feed.

As quickly as the sky lost its brilliance, the wind picked up, frothing the sea foam high into the air above the gray shoreline. After a few seconds, the sea foam floated downward, piling upon itself, seeming to construct disjointed towers of off-white foam whose graying layers drooped over into toppled stacks. The scene delighted the families. Running through the shallow waves and splashing foam everywhere, the beachgoers laughed as they filled their arms with ammunition. They hurled armfuls at each other, as if they were commencing a snow battle.

Downwind of all the activity, a burly man, chest hair partially shaved to show a recent open-heart surgery incision from gullet to swim trunks, appeared covered in sea foam. He began a slow series of low, grumbling words as he swiped his hands across his chest trying to stop the stinging.

"Jelly fish!" he yelled, but there were no jellyfish tentacles clinging to his skin.

Little smiling faces quickly turned upward toward the man's loud protestations. The next gust of wind pummeled the stacking piles of sea foam, breaking their tops off and flying them into the startled faces of the little waders. Eyes wide open, the sea foam cuddled in under their protective eyelashes.

Adults, wiping the foam from their own faces and feeling the sting in their eyes, immediately bent to wipe the eyes of their crying, panicking children.

Chunks of sea foam seemed to blow maliciously along the water's edge, lifting upward five or six feet as if to avoid swatting hands and arms. Falling downward, the clouds of foam floated to child level, caressing faces, filling eyes with miniscule iridescent bubbles, and finding themselves sucked in by raspy breaths of panicked toddlers and grade schoolers alike. Soon the bacteria in the sea foam would begin colonizing the human respiratory track, exchanging information with bacteria already residing there. *Nocturne* would become an airborne pathogen overnight.

Panic swept the beach. Parents grabbed their children and blindly ran in the direction of the hotel cabanas and dressing rooms. Alerted by the screams, the poolside lifeguards and snack bar wait staffs grabbed towels and ran to assist the panicked guests.

Everyone thought that jellyfish had washed into the swimming area. No one understood what had happened. No one connected the stings to the sea foam. No one realized that the attack had begun as soon as the sky had clouded over.

# Chapter 11

*Ospedale Privato di Venezia*
*Venice, Italy*

**Kate slouched into the green leather armchair** in their hospital room and fought back her tears. No time to cry, she admonished herself. I have to think. Julie could die in three days if her body reacts to *nocturne* like Maria's did.

Why has *nocturne* surfaced on a Venice beach? What is the vector of infection? If it were the water, wouldn't we all be infected? Is this infection the same as Maria's? What can Maria's case tell us about Julie's infection? Kate hoped for answers as she mentally recounted the events surrounding the Maria De-Sanchez case.

**The first documented outbreak of** *Bacillus nocturne* started five years ago in the Delaware Bay estuary. In the afternoon, an emergency paramedic crew brought an extremely dehydrated and sunburned young woman to the emergency room, bleeding profusely from her eyes, unconscious, and with no identification. Search teams found her body in a beached motor boat on Ramee Point near Blue Crab Cove where the estuary met the Rehoboth Bay.

Dr. Walter Ambruster assigned David Winters to her case. Winters was a tall, trim, Scandinavian intern about whom none of us knew anything, except for the rumor that he had spent three years in criminal forensics at the Federal Bureau of Investigation. Winters discerned her age as 24 or 25 based on dental eruptions and growth indicators on a spinal x-ray. Ambruster assigned me, an ophthalmology intern, to culture and evaluate her hemorrhaging eyes and body fluids, and examine her skin for specks of environmental antigens and detritus from her recent surroundings.

What I found from the blood cultures stunned the entire emergency room staff . . . an antibiotic resistant strain of a highly contagious bacterium.

The host that the bacteria needed for survival was the protein in human body fluids . . . the moist layers surrounding the corneas of the eyes, for example. Completely antibiotic resistant, the bacteria continually replicated.

The only method that could slow down its reproduction was lavage, constantly diluting and washing away the bacteria as it replicated. In fact, I thought at the time that had the young woman fallen out of the motor boat and into the water, the massive dilution might have saved her life.

We tried extensive IV lavage to wash as many toxins out of her body as possible, but it was too late in the infection process to help. Ambruster carefully tried to balance the amount of liquid he used to wash her bloodstream and the amount of red blood cells that her body was able to produce. Overly diluted blood was deadly. Too few blood platelets and her organs would shut down. The level of dilution that we felt would be safe was not enough to offset the bacteria's rate of replication.

Ambruster struggled to get the balance right, but these bacteria seemed impossible to stop. Ambruster told us the bacteria traveled through her corneas and optic nerves to her brain. They attacked the basal ganglia and the brain stem, which controlled the body's basic functions such as breathing. Intubation and a life-supporting ventilator were too late to stop the toll the bacteria were taking on her life. Ambruster predicted that she would die from respiratory failure by evening.

As soon as the hospital staff members were alerted that a serious contagion had entered the hospital, all hell broke loose. Literally. Heliotrophic Enzymatic Lavage Leverage (HELL) aptly described the necessary scrubbing, cleaning, and disinfecting that had to take place immediately.

The hospital had instituted the program two years earlier when the Surgeon General mandated that every hospital develop a plan to handle exposure to antibiotic resistant communicable pathogens. By the end of the day, the staff at Atlantic

Hospital no longer joked about their humorous acronym.

Federal officials notified the local and state police about the situation, and cordoning began immediately. After setting in motion the hospital's emergency pathogen response plan and contacting the Centers for Disease Control, Ambruster charged David and me with discovering the young woman's identity and where she had contracted the deadly bacteria.

Ambruster insisted that the best way to help our patients was to discover everything that we could about the environments from which they came. Then and only then, he emphasized, could we put together a full picture of the patient and the origin of their illness. Together we examined topographical maps of the streams and estuary system feeding into the area where the EMTs had found the woman on a back bay beach.

"Working backwards," Ambruster taught us, "by accounting for the probable time of death and the tidal debris interspersed in the young woman's hair, we can extrapolate the tidal flow using the tide prediction charts to determine if her motor boat had been washed downstream or had motored upstream to the sandy beach of the cove this morning."

"Then, David," Ambruster continued, "you and Kate can contact the organizations up and downstream that may have had workers out in the field yesterday, the campgrounds, and the tourist bed and breakfasts and hotels to see if anyone is missing. Check police reports, too, for anyone filing a missing person report, or any other felonious activity that could lend itself to our investigation."

David and I understood that Ambruster meant "contact" by phone. No one who had worked on this case would be leaving the hospital any time soon.

By 5:30 p.m., just after the media began reporting the unusual case and workers were coming home for dinner, I got a hit on one of my inquiries. A student at a nearby university shared an apartment with an Atlantic University graduate student and had reported her roommate missing.

When I called the roommate, an expectant voice answered the phone, "Maria?"

"No," I said, "I'm sorry, this is not Maria, but I'm calling about Maria. My name is Dr. Kate Stafford. I'm an intern at Atlantic University Hospital. Could you tell me about the missing person report you filed?"

"Maria DeSanchez is her name," the weak voice offered over the phone. "She called me early in the morning to tell me she wanted to do some water sampling with Caleb Wright, her chemistry lab partner, but Caleb was visiting his parents in Connecticut. So she said she was going to go out with someone from the university marina since Caleb couldn't go with her. And . . ."

I couldn't stop the upset student's long rambling description of the probable events of the day. Finally, I asked, "What was Maria working on in the field? Did she often work alone?"

"Maria's studying the effects of stream turbulence on the reproductive cycle of the blue mussel, and no, she never took a boat out by herself. It's against university policy, and she'd never risk an insubordination warning in her academic record."

"Was Maria feeling ill lately?"

"She is the healthiest person I know."

"What . . ." but before I could ask my next question, the student volunteered more information. I kept thinking that she must not have very many people to talk to, or an often-absent roommate.

"Maria and her dissertation chairperson have been setting chemical snare traps together all week long in order to finish their data collection before the neap tide starts. She seemed a little tired, but that was mostly from long hours in the lab at night filtering the stream bed sediments and testing for medical and sewage waste materials."

"What is her dissertation chairperson's name?" I felt certain that I had found the person who could help us track down the cause of Maria's infection.

One hour and nine phone calls later, I finally made contact with Maria's chairperson, Dr. Mark Andrews.

"Dr. Andrews, this is Dr. Katherine Stafford from Atlantic University Hospital. I am sad to report that EMTs found one of your advisees, Maria DeSanchez, at Blue Crab Cove this morning, near Ramee Point, in critical condition. Sir, we believe she is dying, and we need to notify her family. Can you tell me who to contact at the university for information about her family?"

It seemed like Professor Mark Andrews couldn't process what he was hearing. He started to answer my question in a polite manner, as if nothing had happened.

"Of course, the Dean's office would have all that information, and . . ." It was beginning to sink in.

"Did you say Maria was in the hospital? We were just out on the bay two days ago collecting water samples because of a large fish kill in one of the streams that emptied into Blue Crab Cove. We ran into some trouble because of an unusual amount of sea foam fouling our water samples. We left and Maria said she'd go out again the next morning to resample. Did you say Maria was hospitalized? I thought you said . . ." The agony in his voice was palpable.

I remember that authorities reported subsequent cases of *Bacillus nocturne* along the eastern seaboard of the United States that summer, usually in back bay areas where housing developments had damaged the filtering capacities of the marshes.

The environment could not regenerate its filtering system fast enough to handle the increasing levels of bacteria-laden sewage that was washing down rivers and into the estuaries.

Making matters worse, the practice of flushing unused prescription drugs down bathroom toilets was creating a deadly cocktail of antibiotic-resistant bacteria that were washing up on Mid-Atlantic and bay beaches.

Ambruster reckoned that the young woman had contracted an antibiotic resistant bacterium that had fed on the proteins in wastewater draining into the bay.

Kate snapped back to the present.

"A bacteria indigenous to North America that thrives on wastewater suddenly appears in the coastal waters of Venice. . . ." Kate started her hypothesis out loud. Then her thoughts tumbled through her mind, forming chains of logic broken by images and formulas and vast numbers of people dying.

# Chapter 12

*United States Embassy*
*Rome, Italy*

**El Caldera Street** outside the United States Embassy in Rome received its name from the ancient myth that early Goth invaders had hidden forged metals, including gold and silver, in the hollowed out streambeds of the limestone caverns beneath the city. No one had ever discovered the bounty, but the hope of endless treasure survived even until the 1950's when the city renamed the street.

Today Skip Carpaccio, a 32-year-old Harvard graduate, found his work as the United States of America Liaison for Tourism just a bit more fanciful: two tourists in a row alleging negligence about the same cruise line, on the same beach, at exactly the same time, but describing completely different events.

Skip's day had begun with a belligerent, middle-aged woman

from Miami, Florida, bursting into his office saying, "I'm telling you, it scared me half to death. The cruise line is responsible; they sent us a printed document stating that it was their responsibility to provide the most reputable tour guides available. Imagine being left behind on an uninhabited Greek isle for ten hours before the cruise ship's porter reports you missing, and the concierge has to check his records to see what tour you had signed up for. I could have died out there. . . ."

Skip had heard it all before. Instead of interrupting her spiel, he thought he'd let her vent while he spent a dreamy moment imagining being left on that deserted island with Felicia.

". . . and then they found me lying dehydrated on the beach, burnt beyond recognition . . ."

Skip interrupted, "The problem, Mrs. Schooner, is that the cruise lines protect themselves from lawsuits by saying 'the best available tour guide.' Arguably, they can claim in court that your inexperienced tour guide was the only one available that time of day. Complaints like yours never make it to the courtroom because any lawyers worth their salt would recognize that you had a responsibility in this incident as well."

There, I said it, Skip thought. He often found himself treading a thin line of desperation from having to listen to ridiculous complaints all day. Yet he persisted in his work. He knew he owed his Uncle Pete at least the semblance of a job well done. Skip's uncle, Senator Pete Montelli, had arranged the embassy position for him, and he felt obligated to finish his term of employment.

Like every other complaint he had heard, this one was the result of carelessness on the part of the tourist rather than culpability by the tour guide.

Skip knew that tourists had to remember that it was their responsibility to return to the meeting place on time, or the tour guide might leave them behind.

"Well!" a very loud Mrs. Schooner said. "I never had this kind of treatment from a consulate before," she huffed as she slammed the door on her way out, rattling both his secretary and his next complainant.

Skip's second visitor that morning had been a beautiful, but slightly disheveled woman with striking brunette hair. Mary-Lynne Carlisle had entered his office tentatively.


**MaryLynne knew it was not like her to be timid** in front of authorities, but she was still trembling from the loud percussion of the door slamming as Mrs. Schooner left the office.

MaryLynne's usual, three-day migraine had uncharacteristically not resolved, even after taking her prescription medicine every twelve hours as usual. At least she wasn't nauseous with this headache, nor was she seeing electrical zigzags in front of her eyes.

The preliminary feelings of emotional distress followed by a migraine, MaryLynne thought, happened two days ago right after that moonlit dinner on the beach. She thought the food preservative MSG or the incoming cold front, both migraine triggers for her, had caused her migraine. She had learned over the years that if she took her migraine meds at the very first sign of head pain, her headache resolved itself more quickly. This time, however, her meds weren't even close to resolving her pain.

"Hello," MaryLynne had offered in a very subdued voice. "I'm here to report a murder."

"Well," Skip said, "you've got my attention, all right."

Following Embassy protocol, he had immediately called the police.

MaryLynne Carlisle, replete in a tight black crepe suit and white lace blouse with a diving neckline, was beautiful despite her furrowed brow and scrunched up eyes that were obviously trying to hide some inner pain. She appeared shaky, listless, forcefully trembling every few seconds as she slowly gave her deposition to the Rome police. Her voice dragged in between words, and the final syllables of her sentences muffled into obscure weak sounds. She still seemed dazed as she recounted the events on the beach.

"Jacob Courier and I had arranged to meet for dinner on the Grecian Isle of Nostrus, a candlelight dinner on the beach arranged by our cruise line. Several other couples had chosen this option, but the restaurant distanced all the tables by several hundred feet and interspersed them among the palm trees to provide privacy. Our table was at the end of the beach in the cove where the Marsh Wildlife Conservancy began. Dinner was quiet, romantic, and very pleasant. Small waves lapped at our sandals filling them with sandy sea foam. We laughed that our feet would feel too heavy to be able to walk back gracefully and in a straight line to our chartered van."

"After the dessert," MaryLynne continued, "we both felt a little unsteady and decided to start out for the van ahead of the others. We had trouble setting one foot in front of the other and held onto each other for balance, but neither one of us was laughing. Jacob complained that the salt water did a number on his tourist-blistered feet, and I complained that it had eroded most of the nail polish off my recent pedicure. After an arduous walk through the sand, we stumbled up the steps to the van, crawled to the back row of seats, and leaned against each other trying to maintain an upright position. That is all I remember until I woke up in the middle of the night.

"We were alone," MaryLynne said, "scrunched together on the floor in the back of the van, in a dark parking garage near the pier. Jacob was lying face down. He felt cold, and I couldn't hear him breathing. When I tried to lift his face from the floor, I felt something wet on my hands. Blood had pooled on his face, and his eyes were open and filled with blood. I panicked; I clawed my way to the front seat of the van and pushed the door open with my whole body."

MaryLynne's darting eyes betrayed the calm, organized façade her engineering training was still imposing on her.

Her disbelief that she could react so irrationally to an injured person jeopardized her forced composure.

MaryLynne continued speaking, despite a soft rasping interrupting her normally steady tone.

"The next thing I remember is standing in front of a mirror in my cabin, soaking wet, with the maid drying me off saying, 'You are so lucky the pier crew spotted you in the water. They saved your life.' "

"Then a ship's nurse gave me a sedative, and I slept until the next day. When I awoke, I discovered someone had packed my bags and laid out a new set of clothes on my bed, and within minutes, the nurse arrived to assist me in dressing and debarking. I never spoke to anyone and barely understood what was happening to me; I was rescued, drugged, and disposed of as soon as possible.

"When the mental fog began to lift," MaryLynne said, "I found myself in a taxi heading back to Rome. Through a series of rapid-fire flashbacks, each one providing more information about what had happened, I reconstructed the events of the previous evening, and then began to panic as I remembered feeling the congealed blood seeping from Jacob's eyes."

The rasping in MaryLynne's voice turned into hoarseness as she struggled to hold back her tears. She had deserted Jacob, and now did not even know if he was alive.

Sergeant Paolini expressed his condolences to MaryLynne as he turned off his DVD camcorder. "I am sorry to say, Ms.

Carlisle, that a body washed up on shore yesterday near the warehouse that you described. We identified the person as your companion. The autopsy showed that he died from a massive bacterial infection that began in the area of the blisters that he had on his feet. How have you been feeling, Ms. Carlisle?"

MaryLynne did not reply. The shock of losing Jacob, coupled with her fatigue, headache, and dizziness slowed all her reflexes down to a crawl. The officer's words about a bacterial infection were just now registering.

MaryLynne slid slowly down her seat and onto the floor. I don't care how I look, she thought. I just want to be with Jacob.

**Sergeant Paolini rushed to check MaryLynne's vital signs** as Skip called for an ambulance. MaryLynne's face burned with fever, and blood pooled in her eyes. Red subcutaneous streaks running up her legs from her partially polished, chipped toenails marked the deadly path that *Bacillus nocturne* had taken from her pedicured nails to her heart.

# Chapter 13

*Ospedale Privato di Venezia*
*Venice, Italy*

**Reconstructing the Maria DeSanchez case** had not stirred Kate's latent memories or helped her identify the vector of Julie's infection.

"I'm missing something," she said to no one in particular. "What had Ambruster said to David and me about solving Maria's case?"

"Kate!" Ambruster startled her as he called out her name while he strode through the isolation room doors straight for her room. "The hospitals in Venice have all been put on alert. Lido Beach is reporting more cases of infection. Several people have died already and dozens are very ill. We will be opening our Emergency Isolation Ward to the public within the hour. Jake called the Institute and they said there have been cases reported at Oostende Beach, Belgium, and Cape Henlopen,

Delaware. From the reports I've heard, there's something strange about this *Bacillus nocturne* outbreak that we didn't see five years ago."

"Three infection sites?" Julie's chances for survival just dropped, Kate thought. All the new cases would be competing with her for Ambruster's time.

"Julie was infected very early in the morning, right?" Ambruster asked.

"Yes. We went to the beach at daybreak. The sun was just starting to rise above the horizon. It was pretty cloudy and dark at first, but Crystal was in a hurry to collect seashells before anyone else came out."

"All right. The news reporters interviewed tourists staying in your hotel. They all said the sky suddenly clouded over around dinner time and the wind picked up, blowing large clumps of sea foam into the air, two or three meters above the sand. A few people said it was eerie. The sea foam fell on people, and they couldn't brush it off. Like it was clinging to their skin."

"That's not a characteristic of this bacteria. It doesn't produce secretions that would be capable of doing that." Kate was visibly shaken, and she could tell that this report bothered Walt, too.

"The lab reports aren't back, yet, Kate, but all the other characteristics and symptoms point to *nocturne*. Do you think this could be a variant?"

Kate collapsed into the leather chair behind her. If there

had not been a chair there, she would have fallen all the way to the floor. The possibility of a variant strain would make Julie's recovery unlikely.

Ambruster could see that he had lost Kate for a while. He rested a comforting hand on her shoulder and said, "I'm just about ready to titrate Julie's first tier of antibiotics. You rest, Kate. I'll call you if there's any change. After we administer the antibiotics, you can come in and sit with Julie and Luke for a while. She's sedated, but you may feel better being close to her. And I think Luke could use some company."

"What we learned from Maria's illness," Ambruster said, "and a series of similar cases that summer five years ago, may save Julie's life. The bacteria were waterborne then, too."

Ambruster turned and walked back to the isolation suite, in order to do his usual thinking out loud. He quietly recited *nocturne's* signs and symptoms aloud:

"Ninety-five percent of those patients infected with *Bacillus nocturne* had presented with severe irritation of the mucosa linings of the eyes, nose, mouth, throat, ears, or anywhere the bacteria could easily enter the body, such as a break in the skin."

"Ten percent of the infected patients had died within 72 hours of exposure," he continued, "due to the bacteria's colonization of the body's tissues, leading to shock and organ failure. The other ninety percent of the infected patients had lingered for days, nearly dying, but later making a slow recovery—sometimes six months to a year before they were well.

However, one common factor had prevailed—patients whose physicians had put them on ventilators within an hour of infection had the best chance for survival."

"Why the ventilator?" he questioned himself. "Was there an airborne component to the bacteria that caused it to be inhaled? Perhaps. Today's new cases involved sea foam. An unusual amount of gray sea foam. Sea foam tossed into the air could be inhaled."

"It took me five cases," Ambruster sadly recalled, "before I learned to ventilate, lavage, and then tier-treat the bacteria with combinations of antibiotics geared to the patient's and bacterium's genetic structures. But maybe I didn't fully understand the bacteria's attack on the respiratory system. I thought the patient needed the ventilator because of organ failures, when perhaps the ventilator was disrupting the replication of the inhaled bacteria."

Ambruster's antibiotic protocol to treat *nocturne* had succeeded, but it had been complicated. He believed the human body utilized the antioxidants in fruits and vegetables best when eaten in combination with other fruits and vegetables from the same geographical area. Then perhaps, he had thought, the body would respond best to combinations of medicines from the same geographical area as the bacterium's origin. Three years of clinical research had finally confirmed his hypothesis.

**Half an hour later,** Kate exchanged rooms with Luke. He was now watching the news broadcasts about the multiple outbreaks. Her drawn face showed her anxiety and grief as she waited for Jake to return. She presumed he had slipped away to call the Agency for any news about *nocturne* surfacing on other beaches. When he appeared in the doorway with Crystal asleep in his arms, she hoped he brought good news. He motioned to her that he would take Crystal to their assigned hospital room to sleep.

"Luke is there watching the news," Kate whispered. "He'll keep an eye on her."

When Jake returned, he looked more solemn than Kate had expected. "The CDC and WHO reported outbreaks of *nocturne* on beaches in Europe and along the Mid-Atlantic Seaboard this morning," Jake whispered as he sat down next to her. "I had a conversation with the Director of the Institute via Secured Skype at l'Universita Venezia. The Director considers *nocturne* to be a Class 5 Emergency, capable of producing a worldwide pandemic." Jake had also spoken with the Director of the Institute in the director's second capacity—Director of the Agency. The Director had activated the Agency's teams and met with all of their team leaders via secure communications links, detailing their missions. Except for Kate. The Director had asked Ambruster to deliver Kate's assignment to her when he felt she would be willing to accept it.

"Julie is stable," Dr. David Winters said to Kate and Jake as he slipped into Julie's room. "I spoke with Luke a few minutes ago."

"What happens next, David?" Kate asked.

"This will be a long process of careful lavage treatments. We have to dilute the toxins that the bacteria are producing. It's one of medicine's best tools; it's nature's method for handling intrusive substances. Already, Julie's body is overproducing cells in the mucous linings of her respiratory and digestive systems, in an attempt to wash out the invading substances."

"After the lavage . . ." Kate prompted.

"We have at least eight more hours to wait before the second phase of treatment could begin—administering the second round of multiple antibiotics tailored and titrated specifically for her," Winters explained. "She must remain heavily sedated for the next 72 hours."

Ambruster heaved through the outer set of swinging doors that separated the surgical suite from the hall leading to the waiting room. When he spotted Winters in Julie's room, he asked Kate and Jake to meet him in the waiting room in a few minutes.

Ambruster needed all the information about Julie's background that he could get, coupled with the current findings from Kate's experiments on the bacterium at her lab in the Paris Institute.

He wondered how he would deliver the Director of the Agency's assignment for Kate. He'd have to muster Kate into action, making her leave Julie alone in his care, while she returned to her lab to find the one key to Julie's case that he still needed—this bacterium's origin. If it were a variant, he needed her to tell him how it was different from the *nocturne* she had been studying.

"Kate, Jake," Ambruster called as he walked rapidly toward the worried pair. "Julie is resting comfortably, the ventilator is breathing for her, and she has been heavily sedated to prevent her from feeling pain or panicking if she awakens to a room full of intrusive medical equipment."

"Walt, will she survive?' Kate asked.

"This is a different bacterium than the Delaware strain that infected Maria DeSanchez. Something has altered its rate of replication. I'm not sure how well the human body can defend against something that replicates this fast.

"We still lack important information about this new strain's origin and how it reacts in different people. Julie should have developed an immunity to this bacteria since she had contracted it once before. Instead, she's more ill than she was the last time. That part of the equation is reminiscent of the complications from a second exposure to Dengue Fever. But this isn't Dengue."

Kate and Jake looked at each other, almost not recognizing the drawn, tight faces they saw. It was evident to Ambruster, from the expressions on their faces, that both of them knew what Ambruster's words really meant.

"What can we do?" Kate asked.

"Kate, I know you don't want to leave Julie's side right now, but with the ventilator and the sedation, there is not much comfort you can offer her. I need you to go to your lab to run tests for me on the samples you have been using in your experiments."

Kate's expression went from stunned to fearful within a matter of seconds. "You don't believe your treatment will work on Julie, do you?"

"No, I don't. I need to know how her strain is different from the strain in your lab . . . if it has mutated or been tampered with. I need to know what antibiotics can subdue the strain in your lab, and why they work. Then I will be able to tailor the antibiotics to Julie's personal medical history. I need you to fly to your lab and work on this now."

"But Crystal and Julie . . ."

"I arranged for Jake's mother to fly here from Paris to take care of Crystal and to check in on Julie while you work. She will be here within the hour. Luke will watch Crystal until your mother-in-law arrives."

"But Jake will be here."

"No, Kate. Jake has his own assignment."

"What assignment?"

Ambruster picked up Julie's chart and feigned reading.

Kate turned toward Jake, asking, "What assignment?" But Jake was already heading to Crystal's room where she had been sleeping. Still drowsy, she circled Jake's head with her arms and held on while he and Kate hugged her and explained that Uncle Luke would watch her until Grandma arrived.

Crystal turned to Luke and greeted him with outstretched arms, "Unclie Luke, I love you. Hold me now."

"Kate," Ambruster redirected her attention, "I've arranged for a private jet to be fueled and ready for take-off in one hour from the Venice Marco Polo Airport. A water taxi is at the emergency entrance dock and is ready to make the 45-minute trip to the airport.

"I'll fax the data I'll need from you this afternoon. We'll fly your colleague Claire Martin in to help you get started on setting up the new experiments." Without another word, Ambruster swung his large body around and headed for the double doors.

Kate's body stalled. She couldn't move until her mind processed what had just happened. Jake grabbed her arm and slowly guided her to the elevator. As he pressed the down button, her shocked expression gave way to tears.

# Chapter 14



*Ospedale Privato di Venezia*
*Venice, Italy*

**The hospital's water taxi** idled alongside the barnacled pilings of the emergency room dock. Kate struggled to keep up with Jake's outstretched arm as he raced toward it. Reaching the end of the dock, he swung her toward the arms of the driver who pulled her forcefully into the boat, just as a descending wave dropped the hull another foot. Her feet landed on the floor of the boat with a thud, and her knees crackled as they took the brunt of the fall.

Jumping into the water taxi behind Kate, Jake helped her move toward the last row of seats near the outboard motors. As the pilot revved the taxi's motors for embarkation, Kate and Jake looked over their shoulders to see where they had left Crystal, Julie and Luke.

"How are your knees?" Jake tried small talk as he gently lifted her legs onto the reversed seats in front of them. "Better keep them up so they won't start swelling. They took a hard hit when the boat dropped out from under you."

Kate just nodded.

Jake turned toward Kate, searching for eye contact. "Kate, I have something important to tell you. I work for the Agency, a covert operation at the Institute. Five years ago when I met you, I was one of their undercover agents. I served as a professor of biochemical engineering, at Atlantic University, ostensibly researching the effect of charcoal filtering systems on the biohazards draining into the East Coast drinking water aquifers.

"The Agency has a strict policy," Jake continued, "that no agents, absolutely none, are to reveal their true identity to spouses or family. I couldn't tell you what I did and keep my job.

"I was torn between loyalty to the Agency and being forthright with you," Jake said. "I loved you, Kate, and didn't want to risk losing you when you found out, but I also felt a strong responsibility to the nation I swore to protect and defend with my life."

Kate merely nodded as she listened to Jake's explanation.

"When Crystal was born," Jake continued, "my decision whether to stay with the Agency became even more serious. I knew that if I had to choose between my child and my country, my child would win out."

"Kate," Jake drew her attention by gently turning her chin toward him. "When you said Julie's symptoms looked like *nocturne*, I nearly panicked. Anytime an outbreak of *Bacillus nocturne* occurs in the environment, the Agency dictates that it must be isolated and investigated. The Agency knows how deadly it is and how quickly it can become pandemic.

"After this mission to find the people responsible for this outbreak, I will likely ask to be disengaged from service. It is the right thing for me to do; I know now I could never jeopardize Crystal's life, or yours, for the sake of any Agency assignment."

Jake grew silent, looking down at his heavy hands for a few seconds, and then looking back up at Kate's face.

Kate was crying. No huge tears rolled down her cheeks like in the movies. She had told Jake once that even as a child, her ancillary tear ducts rarely produced enough fluid to form tears that would roll down her face.

Instead, Jake knew that Kate had been a child who cried very hard but only grew red in the face. Consequently, few adults had understood the degree of sadness that was behind her tearless protests. However, Jake knew.

He knew that as strong and capable as Kate had grown, she could be reduced to utter despair at the first hint of a trusted friend's secrecy or rejection. She called it the "hole in her heart" that was never filled with the unconditional love most children receive from their parents.

Now, Jake thought, I've made that hole deeper.

"I'm stronger than you think," Kate spoke her words with a quiet measured rhythm. "I understand what we need to do to serve our country and love our family. I've done both, and I've never separated one from the other.

"But society asks too much of parents," Kate continued, "and when parents give society what it wants, the children bear the costs. I know what that feels like as a child, and I swore my child would never feel that loss.

"Jake, I knew about your undercover work with the Agency before I married you. I also knew that you would balance your roles as father and agent, just as I balanced mine as mother and agent."

Jake's upper torso jerked backward as if he had taken a small caliber gunshot hit. Kate's disclosure had caught him completely off guard.

"Shortly after arriving at the Institute," Kate explained, "Ambruster asked me to serve as a medical operative on one of the Agency's covert teams investigating a biological terrorism threat in Qinghai Province, China. They needed a physician agent with dual expertise—medical and water purification. Your last study on a model to combat hydrological bioterrorism was required reading. *Bacillus nocturne* was one of the pathogens you had studied. I was given your bio on a need-to-know basis since I might have to call on you for consultation."

Jake listened intently and learned about another woman he had never known existed.

Kate looked deep into Jake's eyes, and he felt as if she were searching for his reaction to her revelation.

"Did you know that I went on some Agency missions, too?" she asked.

No emotions clouded Jake's eyes, nor did he avert his eyes from her stare.

At last, Jake said, "I knew the Agency staffed its teams with Institute researchers, but they never told me which researchers. Everything at the Agency is on a need-to-know basis . . . as you obviously know."

"Jake, we can't fault each other for the secrets our jobs made us keep. We followed protocol because it was required of us. It's out in the open now, what we both do for a living. It's actually a relief to be honest with you."

"To be honest with you? Now there's a phrase we don't hear too often in undercover work. Okay, I admit I'm relieved we're discussing this. Keeping secrets from you has never been easy. And in retrospect, I should've figured that the Agency would want to use your talents for its missions."

"But we're in a lot of trouble if the Agency finds out we broke protocol."

"Let's just handle that on a need-to-know basis."

# Chapter 15


*Henlopen Medical Center*
*Lewes, Delaware, U.S.A.*


**Gloria Goldenseal gathered her syringes** and antibiotics, IV bags, antiseptics, bandages, and a hermetically sealed glass jar containing a grossly moldy piece of leather. She tossed them into her doctor's bag and ran to the waiting EMT vehicle.

She knew she was taking a dangerous risk by volunteering to accompany the next EMT squad out to the Cape campground where Paul and Linda had contracted the waterborne illness, but at 38 with no surviving family members, she decided that she should be one of the volunteers to go.

The lessons that her great grandfather had passed on through the generations of her family echoed around her mind among the years of medical training she had accumulated. He had always stressed the importance of revering nature. He taught the tribe that if a person must hunt to survive, they must honor the animal by utilizing every part of its body. That philosophy led him to discover how even mold on hides could benefit the tribe.

There is a seat at the table for every theory, Gloria thought, whether tribal medicine or traditional medicine, or a combination of the two.

The image of her aged great grandfather remained fresh in her mind, even thirty-three years after his death. She had been an impressionable five year old, called upon by tribal tradition to withhold her tears as she softly patted her g-pop's wrinkled cheek and pressed her little suntanned nose against his ceremonial robes for the last time. She thought he was just sleeping, but she sensed that he might not wake up this time.

As an adult, Gloria sometimes wondered if she were remembering his visage from childhood, or if the image, which came to her mind each time someone needed his medicine, was in fact his spirit visiting her. As soon as the EMTs started organizing teams to head over to the campground, he had appeared to her, just as many times before.

"Take the sandals," Gloria's great grandfather had simply said, but she knew immediately what he meant. The old leather from a worn-out pair of Indian sandals, kept damp inside a wrapper made from an old weathered cowhide, continued to produce a furry bacterium that flourished in those conditions.

In medical school, Gloria had researched native North American medicine and discovered that her great grandfather's stories of healing from the mold of leather were true. Specifically used for treating foot infections, the type of antibiotic produced from the mold actually cured a number of illnesses indigenous to the coastal region.

Gloria had learned that naturally occurring medicines were often superior to the manufactured versions produced by the pharmaceutical industry. Digitalis treated heart disease, belladonna alkaloids in plants aided anesthesia, quinine from the bark of cinchona trees cured malaria, and the common aspirin, discovered in the bark of the willow tree, became a wonder drug. Gloria remembered her grade school parochial school teacher translating to her class from the *Bible*, "Everything that you will need can be found in the plants and trees on earth."

Gloria kept the old leather pieces of sandals sealed in a glass jar whenever she traveled, and the accumulating moisture just replenished the moisture the bacteria needed to thrive.

She had injected patients with a serum from the leather's bacteria several times before, just as her great grandfather had done thirty years ago. Each time the patients had suffered from waterborne bacterial infections along the Delaware coast.

Today as the sun rose, the caravan of ambulances, EMTs, nurses, and physician assistants left the Henlopen Medical Center and quickly drove northeast on Savannah Road, making a right turn onto Cape Henlopen Drive near the Port Authority.

The offices of the Delaware River and Bay Authority bristled with activity. Uniformed workers erected barricades, and security guards staffed the entry lines. Activity in the nearby Cape May/Lewes Ferry Terminal had come to a standstill. The order to halt the ferry crossings arrived as soon as the emergency room medical staff had diagnosed a deadly and likely contagious disease on Cape Henlopen.

Speeding along past the Cape Shores bay front development, the emergency crew noticed barriers at the Cape Shores Drive West and East entrances, already manned by the Delaware State Police.

Entering the Cape Henlopen Park, the first vehicle veered to the right into the Park Office parking lot, alerting the Park staff to the expected emergency conditions likely at the campground.

Riding shotgun in the second ambulance, Gloria gripped the side door handle as they sped between the Park's two Welcome Kiosks. They entered the first camping area, and turned sharply left into the first row of parked campers. The other emergency vehicles fanned out, each one parking at the end of a blacktopped lane fitted with campsites on each side.

Gloria jumped out of the emergency vehicle, sprinted to its rear door, and bowled over her surprised team leader. At 36, John Gabbord righted himself in one swift move, and his smiling eyes met her face on.

"A little too anxious to get started, Gloria?" he teased. He had always liked her, and decided that if they survived today, he would ask her out for a late night dinner at Bethany Blues.

"Oh, John, I'm so sorry," she felt like blushing, but no blush came. His warm humor in the face of crisis made them both laugh instead.

"Okay, let's get started!"

John turned to see his crew hurrying out of the back of the van, medical equipment in hand, wearing protective goggles, breathing apparatuses, and gowned in the newest Hazmat protection suits bought with money from last year's Sea Grant. They handed him and Gloria two sets of protective gear, which they quickly donned and then headed to the first campsite to set up a triage area.

"Stay here, Gloria," John hurriedly said, "and set up triage cots, just like we did at last month's drill. We'll bring the sick to you, and you'll decide who needs immediate evacuation to the hospital and whom we can treat here. We will be running ambulances tandem style, and the hospital has arranged for the Lewes Ferry Trolley buses to manage the flow of outpatients to the emergency room and the temporary ERs at designated doctors' offices."

"How many may have been exposed?"

"We don't know. Eight of the park rangers on duty last night have not reported in this morning."

"Do we know how many people were registered to camp here last night?"

"Yes, 324 signed in," John said, as he hurried toward his colleagues who were awakening the sleeping campsite residents.

This is a nightmare, Gloria thought. And we don't know the pathogen, how it's transmitted, or its early symptoms. How can I make triage functional under these circumstances? Her hands trembled as she tried to set the cots and medical equipment up aligned with the entrance to the camping sites. Already, EMTs were ushering dazed vacationers to her triage center.

"Megan, Laura, and Todd Wainwright," retired nurse Stella VanDoren announced as she led the three toddlers to cot number one.

"Dr. Lorenzo is with their parents at Campsite 1. Ed and Jill Wainwright went for a late night swim, leaving Teddy, their fourteen-year-old son, in charge of the younger children. When they returned, the three youngsters were asleep and Teddy left to join his friends at the Teen Campfire and then to sleep-over at Campsite 16."

"Ed and Jill awoke several hours later," Stella continued, "with stinging eyes, general aches, stomach pains, and malaise turning into confusion. Jill is more coherent than Ed. He stayed in the water longer than she did."

"Doc wants them med-evacuated Stage 2 and the children sent to Peds for observation with Teddy as soon as we locate him," Stella related, as she turned to rush off to the next campsite.

Gloria's mini-camcorder had caught all of the details of

Stella's report and recorded the names and faces of the children while Gloria rapidly filled in the Emergency Evac forms.

Smiling at the three sleepy toddlers, Gloria turned to the voices approaching behind her.

"Goldenseal.  Addison and Steele here to assist," the two arriving Physician Assistant interns hailed her as they pulled their portable crash cart over the rough terrain.

They're so young, Gloria thought.  I wish they hadn't volunteered.  She smiled at them, acknowledging their sacrifice.  "Thank you.  Can one of you settle these children in Evacuation Vehicle 101 and wait for their brother Ted to catch up?  Then send them all to Peds for observation," she said as she handed Addison Copy 1 of the Evac forms while filing Copies 2 and 3 in her portable cabinet.

Steele joined her as retired EMT Emily Harrison led two female college students to the camcorder tripod.  The tousled haired women were wearing Yale tee shirts and striped Yale yoga pants with hurriedly tied running shoes, laces dragging in the dust.

"Carol Eisenrode, 19, and Melinda Haggerty, 20," Emily recounted.  "Burning eyes, contusions to the orbital bones, bleeding beginning.  Out for an early morning jog on the beach.  Had a water splash battle, but ran back for help when they saw a group of bodies lying on the beach. Team 2 set out to investigate and asked us to set up additional back-up with stand-by from surrounding hospitals."

Both women were weeping blood and tears, trying desperately to rub the stinging sensation away from their eyes. Melinda collapsed onto a cot while Carol wandered over toward the PA's vehicle.

"Steele, start IVs and med-evac STAT," Gloria ordered.

Steele had Melinda's line in immediately and called for the ambulance team to stretcher her cot to the vehicle while he settled Carol in the van with an IV. Both were on their way to the hospital in minutes.

The stream of campers and medical staff continued, growing heavy at times, but their practiced training kept them calm and efficiently matter-of-fact. Gloria data-recorded all of the cases for later identification and study, thankful that she had additional cassettes and back-up batteries.

"Goldenseal, get down here, STAT. Bring all available PAs and EMTs with you," an urgent rough voice crackled over her emergency band radio. "Call for back-up. Repeat. Call for back-up."

Startled, Gloria immediately recognized Dr. Ben Albright's voice. He was Team Leader 2, and he was following the lead that the joggers had given them about bodies on the beach. Grabbing her medical bag and every available medic along the way, Gloria phoned for more back up while she sprinted toward the beach.

Running up the sandy slope carved into the sand by two rows of weathered snow fences was not easy. Gloria felt her calf and leg muscles pulling tightly trying to ambulate her unbalanced body toward the crest of the dune. In stark contrast to the clear blue sky, white-capped waves, and sun-sparkled sand, dozens of still bodies with twisted limbs and bloodstained clothes covered the high tide line on the beach. Most of the victims appeared to be high school students.

Teddy, Gloria thought. This must be where they held last night's Teen Campfire.

No one had to tell Gloria what to do. She wasn't on triage, anymore. Every person here was Triage Category: Immediate Care, Life-Threatening.

Running to the nearest victim, a fawn-like tawny young female with her legs awkwardly splayed beneath her frame, Gloria started an IV while doing a visual examination.

Labored breathing, Gloria thought, shortness of breath, massive vasodilatation, increased heart rate, systemic swelling, jaundice, and lack of response to stimuli, in addition to the blood streaming from her eyes. Septic shock.

Gram-negative bacterial infections, Gloria remembered, and lately gram-positive bacterial infections caused septic shock. Also, but rarely, fungi or viruses.

Gloria rattled off just under her breath the rest of her training on septic shock, "The body reacts to the endotoxins, a structural component of the bacteria, and to the exotoxins released from dying bacteria in the bloodstream.

"The body's super-antigens cause an immune and inflammatory response so over reactive that it results in a cytokine storm which causes severe tissue damage. Body systems begin shutting down and the body is unable to thermo-regulate. The intestinal mucosae in the GI tract are invaded by the bacteria, causing massive GI bleeding, dangerously low blood pressure, and finally respiratory distress."

"Act now!" Gloria heard her great grandfather's command.

Like a reflex, Gloria reacted. Opening a glass jar from her medical kit, Gloria carefully removed a moldy mass and scraped a sixteenth of a teaspoon of mold from it. Dropping the mold into a vial of sterile water, she replaced the vial's rubber cap, and shook the vial vigorously.

Inserting the syringe through the cap, Gloria withdrew enough of the serum to administer a near lethal dose of the medication. The therapeutic index, used to determine the ratio of the dosage that would be lethal to her patient compared to the dosage that would be lethal only to the bacteria, guided her dosing.

"Too low of an index, such as 1.35," Gloria repeated her medical training aloud, "can be lethal because there is minimal difference between the patient's lethal dose and the bacteria's lethal dose."

Gloria cautiously talked herself through every step, not caring if any of the other medics might hear her.

"I'm mixing medical science with traditional Indian medicine, and I have to get it right," she cautioned herself. "Even if I save some lives, this will cost me my license to practice medicine." She surmised her decision to be her only choice.

Gloria administered a 1.5 index, understanding it was the victim's only chance for survival. She quickly added a vasoactive drug to raise blood pressure, mentally noting that the drug could also constrict kidney vessels, resulting in renal failure. Next, she completed the drug therapy with massive doses of corticosteroids to suppress the immune reaction and inflammatory response.

Any of the drugs Gloria administered at these high doses could prove deadly, and in combination, one would think they could kill. Yet, Gloria remembered her training from both med school and her great grandfather: where one drug may fail a patient, a carefully selected and titrated blend of drugs may surprisingly heal a patient.

From experience with her great grandfather's medicine, Gloria believed there was a third component to this formula: the medicines had the best chance of success when we compounded them from naturally occurring substances within the bacteria's indigenous geographical area. It was only her informal hypothesis, and she had never tested it in a clinical study, but in her mind, her great grandfather's experiences had confirmed its truth.

Rapidly moving to the next closest victim, a young sandy-haired male doubled over, gripping his stomach, face down in the sand, Gloria noted the same characteristics indicative of septic shock, as well as gastrointestinal bleeding from the esophagus and colon, and again the characteristic bleeding from the eyes.

"Definitely bacterial," she muttered as she started another IV and began implementing her drug therapy. "Where did this come from?" she asked aloud, mostly to herself, but also hoping for an answer from her great grandfather's spirit.

By the end of the morning, 42 teenagers and 10 adult Park Rangers had received medical care on the beach and medical evacuation to area containment hospitals. Twenty-five teenagers and eight adults died within five hours of hospital admittance, seven more died after 12 hours of extensive ICU care, and ten teenagers and two adults survived.

The survivors had been treated on the beach by Gloria Goldenseal.

# Chapter 16

*Henlopen Medical Center*
*Lewes, Delaware, U.S.A.*

**The sun barely peered over the largest sand** dune at Cape Henlopen State Park when the residents of Lewes heard the sirens of the first two ambulances racing back to the Henlopen Medical Center.

Early risers, grabbing their traditional hot coffee and the Americana Special at the Lewes Diner, merely nodded at one another, quietly acknowledging another early morning automobile accident.

Some bowed their heads in a silent prayer for the accident's survivors or the souls of the departed and their families. Others turned the pages of the morning newspaper, continuing their conversations with long time friends while glazing over the latest Town Council news.

Few were even surprised when two more ambulances passed

their quarter of the town.

What did surprise them was the sirens of vehicles five and six being surpassed by vehicles one and two racing back out toward the Cape.

Almost in unison, the patrons rose from their comfortable world and faced reality on the other side of the screened windows of the little diner on the corner of the town.

Down the street, the Henlopen Medical Center was overflowing. Physicians had designated triage areas at each entrance to the hospital, and already there were no other cots available for patients at any level of triage.

County hospitals and out of state medical centers had followed the Emergency Protocol for Biological Disaster, sending doctors, nurses, personnel, and well-equipped vehicles to the Henlopen Medical Center.

It was evident within an hour of the first ambulance's arrival that Phase 4 of the Protocol had to be called: "All resources bolstered at the designated disaster center, and no passage out of the emergency zone until the level of toxicity and mode of transmission has been discovered."

**Andrea Harbaugh, the veteran of the emergency** preparedness task force, a 25-year surgical nurse, was getting a little nervous.

"No one has determined the mode of transmission, yet, and we have a crowded hospital full of the best medical teams in the state. If they are all infected, who will be left to care for the patients?" she rhetorically asked her colleague Myra Burns.

Myra, fresh out of medical school at age 48, after fourteen years of biochemistry experience at Muirvex Pharmaceuticals, looked solemn.

"Forty have died or are near death so far," Myra whispered.

"The ambulances just keep coming, and we have no idea what we're treating. The lab reports say it's an unidentified, gram-positive bacterium with an aspect ratio of 20:1. Could it be gram-negative, too?" she asked, startled by her own revelation explaining why the first line of penicillin defense was failing.

Andrea jumped out of her seat and shouted, "Heywood, Carson, Burns, and Angiotole, to the lab STAT." She would put the best minds together and let them work out the unusual components of this disease. They were the best and the brightest, but her mind's ending to that phrase haunted her: They were the best and the brightest and the last.

# Chapter 17



*Venice Marco Polo Airport*
*Venice, Italy*

**When the water taxi pulled up to the dock** at the Venice Marco Polo Airport, Jake and Kate pulled close into a long hug, and together, arms wrapped around each other's waist, climbed up the boat's steps and into the frenzy of their new life together.

"Jake, how will we keep our secret from the Agency?"

"Anyway we can," Jake grinned. "We both seem to be pretty good at that."

"If they find out we broke protocol by sharing our Agency status with each other, we'll both lose our jobs, at the Agency and the Institute."

"I'm not ready to give up our only source of income right now."

"And we'd be sanctioned," Kate added. "Our references for future jobs would be ruined."

"All the more reason to make this work. What are our options?"

"We could find a way to get the Agency to put us on the same team. Then we wouldn't have to worry about slipping up and saying something about each other's role in the Agency."

"I could request a physician on my next assignment, or you could request a biochemical engineer," Jake said.

"That could work, but think about Crystal. Do we want both of us to be sent out at the same time?"

"Crystal could stay with your mother."

"That only works until she starts preschool," Kate said.

"Worse than making childcare arrangements, what if we both don't make it back after a mission?"

"Just the thought of that possibility . . . We can't risk that," Kate said.

"The risk of enemy retaliations after some missions would double, too."

"Yes. Other options?" Kate asked.

"I can request a desk job after this mission is over."

"Or we could resign and take new jobs elsewhere, before we slip up and make someone suspicious. That way we'd leave with good references."

"We hope." Jake stifled a smile.

"So no easy solution? I was hoping we'd come up with something more quickly than this."

"We can make it work for awhile. I'm confident we can pull

it off."

Rife with sarcasm, Kate produced a tight smile. "Great. I'm feeling better already."

**Navigating through the throngs of travelers,** Kate and Jake located their separate departure points in the small crowded terminal. A kiss goodbye and Kate ran towards the fueling area where the private plane to Paris waited for her.

Jake hustled down a short hallway in the opposite direction. He glanced over his shoulder for a last look at his partner. Then he ran across the tarmac to a revving helicopter bound for Barcelona.

Assembling the European half of the Agency's Quick Response Team at the secluded summer home of the Rodriguez family had been his idea because of its proximity to both Venice and Paris. The jet helicopter flight would land him on Barcelona's helipad in one hour, where he would meet an agent who would drive him to the Rodriguez residence.

# Chapter 18

*Venice Marco Polo Airport*
*Venice, Italy*

**Boarding the private plane** with nothing more than her over-sized Gucci handbag, Kate quickly settled into her seat and buckled her seat belt. No other passengers were on this flight, and within minutes, they were airborne.

What had just happened? Kate thought about her discussion with Jake. Our disclosures change everything. No more secrets from each other. What will that be like?

"Okay, kiddo," she whispered to herself as she curled a strand of hair around her index finger. Whenever she was stressed, Kate relied on her Dad's favorite phrase of encouragement. "Okay, kiddo," she repeated. "Think about that later. You've got a job to do now."

Get it together, she thought. You have to figure out how *nocturne* escaped your lab. Or if it has resurfaced naturally. And how it operates now.

Jake and Lance will help me, she thought, trying to calm herself. Their Response Teams were organizing as I started my flight to Paris. Within hours, they'll be scouring the coastal landscape, testing the waters for clues of the bacterium's origins in Venice and the cause of its advanced virility.

The New Jersey team will be coordinating medical reports around the world searching for other probable outbreaks and rushing teams to those locations to study the strain of bacteria responsible for . . .

With little food in the last fourteen hours, Kate's memory began to waver.

I have to eat something, and take care of myself, if I'm going to be worth anything in the lab.

Rummaging through her oversized handbag, she pushed aside her iPhone and very small Fujitsu Lifebook computer, revealing her stash of protein bars. These will hold me, she inwardly sighed, as she ate one after another. Sated, but not having sensed any flavors, smells, or satisfaction as she ate, she settled back into her seat.

Closing her eyes and concentrating on the hum of the jet's engines, Kate gradually let her heavy eyelids close. Thinking about Jake, she lulled herself to sleep.


**Those eyes. The first time** I looked into his smoky hazel eyes, I knew. He was kind, a deep inner kindness that would permeate his every action. Not a window to his soul, though; too much mystery surrounding him, layer upon layer covering his past, and I could only guess at his present. Yet, his eyes opened a window to my heart. He stared with such intensity that I felt he was reading my life script, how I came to be in Paris, where I was going. Obvious to both of us now, I was going with him.

Six years ago, was it six years already? I still remember how he sauntered through that hidden door into my life. In Paris during my internship, in general surgery in the ER at l'Hopital Americain. . . . I heard footsteps approaching the examining room, but they were coming from the back wall of the room. After a series of high-pitched tones, a windowless, nine-foot wall panel slid open, grating as it disappeared into the panel to its left. Jake Connors and Robert Smithson, the American Consul, walked confidently into the room, talking about North Korea. They had arrived via the American consulate tunnel connected to the hospital. When they saw the stunned look on my face, their conversation switched to the Washington Senators. "Baseball or Congress?" I wondered aloud, truly in shock. They smiled, as if they walked out of walls all the time. Then Dr. Peter Ligonier quickly entered the room, through a door. Still in shock, I actually giggled at that.

"Kate," Dr. Ligonier said, "I see you've met our back door guests. You might as well scrub in. We have a little repair to make, and then these gentlemen will be on their way."

He didn't have to add "and don't tell anyone what you saw."

I knew no one would believe me, anyway.

I merely observed as the surgeon sutured a ragged rip in Jake's skin just above and to the right of his left clavicle. An odd place for a wound, I had thought, but I was more impressed that he would not accept any sedation before treatment. I don't remember a thing the surgeon did; I just remember staring at those smoky hazel eyes until Jake swung off the examining table and followed Smithson through the opening in the wall. I just sat there, staring at the closed wall panel while Dr. Ligonier left the room smiling, and the nurses' aides entered to reset the room.

Later that afternoon while I reviewed my case notes, sipping green tea at one of the private atrium wrought iron tables, Jake surprisingly sat down next to me and began a lifetime conversation.

How he had known my name or where to find me at that hour puzzled me . . . our conversation . . . continued . . . on the water taxi ride . . . to the airport . . .

**Three hours later,** Kate awoke to the bump of the plane touching down on the crowded runway. Her memory stirred . . . something about our conversation on the way to the airport, she remembered, still half asleep. She sat up straight when it hit her: Jake's conversation in the water taxi about working for the Agency had explained a few of the mysteries that had existed when they first met.

The noisy sound of the plane's tires, buffeted by the asphalt concrete-filled cracks on the tarmac, reminded Kate that the plane had veered off the major runway toward the small arrival shed near the southwestern portion of the landing field.

As the plane slowed, Kate unbuckled her seat belt, grabbed her handbag, and walked to the front of the aisle. As soon as the door opened, she ran down the stairs and over to the awaiting private car arranged by Dr. Walt Ambruster. Within minutes, the driver had turned the car around, circumvented a hideous traffic tie-up, and swerved through the back streets of Paris, but not in the direction of her Institute laboratory.

# Chapter 19

*Paris, France*

**The cordovan leather in the back seat** of the hired car had a stale, coppery smell, and the Parisian driver didn't speak French.

Kate tapped on the gray glass dividing the front seat from the back, signaling the driver to slide the glass open. She yelled through the glass in French that he had missed their turn.

No response. She tried again, this time louder.

She saw him look into the rear view mirror, his toothy grin spread across his face like a Cheshire cat.

Why would Walt hire a driver for me who didn't speak French?

Looking more carefully around the back seat, she grew apprehensive. The worn leather had been stained in various places, and the inside doors showed scratches and scuffs half way up the doors.

*That is blood I smell. This is not the type of car Walt would have hired to take me across town from the airport.*

She tried one last time to get the driver's attention, banging loudly on the glass in English, demanding that he open the glass divider.

This time he threw the window open with such force that it startled her. But his words shocked her.

"Shut up, lady. You're going where I'm taking you. Eduardo has a little score to settle with you." He slammed the glass shut.

Kate jerked back. Eduardo Manuela, the Columbian drug lord that her Agency team had put out of business last year. They had sprayed the dense foliage and jungle surrounding his headquarters with an environmentally safe third generation Agent Orange defoliant, called Early Fall. When the overgrowth dropped their leaves, his set-up was an easy target to find via satellite. Her team had taken the compound in an unexpected firefight, and burnt it to the ground. She had thought he was dead.

Kate quickly assessed her environment, looking for the best method of escape. She knew she had a much better chance of survival if she had a confrontation with her kidnapper while they were still in the city. That way, if he shot her or stabbed her, someone would eventually find her. If she waited until they were in a more isolated location, the chances of someone finding her before she bled out were minimal.

The doors were locked and controlled from the driver's side

door. The safety glass would be difficult to break without the right implement. Kicking the door until it opened wasn't an option. How about pulling the back seat out to get to the trunk? I could kick the brake lights out, or there might be a safety latch that opens the trunk from the inside like in my Volvo.

She felt along the seams of the seat to get a handhold on the leather, but the seat fit too tightly into the back frame. Not enough room in this small backseat to pull the seat out anyway. Besides, who knows what I might find in the trunk.

Resources. Cell phone! She pulled it out of her pants pocket, ready to notify the Agency of her dilemma.

No charge.

I never let it run down, Agency rules. But I left the hotel at 5:30 a.m. and have been using it all day long. At least the GPS tracking device that alerts the Agency to my whereabouts will function independent of the phone's battery for a while. That's good. Eventually, they'll find my body.

She rifled through her Gucci handbag expecting to find the Agency kit she always carried on her missions. It held everything she'd ever need to get home safely, they taught her in training class.

It's not in my bag. I packed my handbag for the beach this morning, not for an Agency mission. In the zippered side compartment, I always keep my pepper spray. Yes, there it is. When the pepper spray runs out, I can always use the sunscreen sprays on his eyes. Better: use the sunscreen sprays in the car, the pepper spray outside of the car. This is going to be difficult.

She secured the two cans of sunscreen under the floor mat on the right side of the car. She tucked her iPhone in her top left shirt pocket, just in case she needed it to stop a bullet or deflect a knife stab. She readied the spray lid on her pepper mace, and slid it into her right pants pocket. She tucked her passport, driver's license, American Express card, and her currency in her left pants pocket. The next step was the hardest. With her red lipstick, she wrote *help* and *aide* on both sides of her white Gucci bag, and left some identifying cards in it. She looked out all of the windows to see if she could determine what part of the city they were in or their general direction. They were driving through back alleys, with very little traffic passing nearby. Then she hung her Gucci bag up by its strap's metal rings over the clothes hanger hook above the right door window.

That's all I've got?

She slid across the seat, behind the driver, and put both of her feet against the midsection of his seat. Then she pulled both feet back and kicked the back of his seat with all the strength she had.

The car swerved as she caught him off guard. She could hear him swearing as he looked back at her.

"Good! Keep looking at me!" She kicked again with such

force that he had to lean forward to keep the car under control. She kicked again with both feet and started a rhythm of hard kicks. It took twelve kicks, and then he was enraged. He slammed on the brakes and got out of the car.

Kate laughed, a huge relief of tension. It worked when I was a kid and no one believed me that I really did have to stop at a bathroom again.

She watched him unlock the car doors and push his door open in one swift motion. She grabbed the cans of sunscreen and spun onto her back like a cat ready to claw its opponent's underbelly. She kept her knees bent and her feet pressed tight against the door.

The slightest release of pressure on the door, and she was ready. He jerked the door open just as she kicked outward with full force, slamming the door against his body. It knocked him off balance, and she rolled up and out of the car, spraying his face with two cans of sunscreen. Then she grabbed her pepper mace and finished the job.

"I don't have time for this." She kneed him, and knocked him out with a blow to the neck. Scanning the alley, she saw no one. She could drive away in his car, but if he had stolen it, she risked being stopped by the police and languishing in a cell until the Institute rescued her. And who knew what the police would find in the car's trunk to complicate matters. She needed to get to her lab fast. Without a delay.

She ran out to the main street and searched for a metro entrance. Two blocks away she saw the familiar sign and ran to the ticket counter.

"Champs Elysees, s'il vous plait." She was on the west side of Paris. One hour's ride from the Institute.

"Merci, Madame."

"Merci, Monsieur." She found a phone on the platform and reported Eduardo's attempted agenda to the Agency. Four minutes gone. The driver would soon be looking for her. She'd have to call Jake later.

She blended into the crowd, picked up a discarded Paris newspaper, and just barely peering over its top edge, she watched the entrance to the metro until her train arrived.

# Chapter 20

*Paris, France*

**Kate edged her way closer** to the middle of the platform. Then she saw her opportunity. A tour guide had signaled to her group that it was time to board. In the flurry of bags and suitcases, Kate squeezed in behind two women who were studying a large, opened Metro map. When the train arrived, she blended into the middle of the group in one of the middle cars, just in case Eduardo's driver had followed her.

Satisfied that she had an avenue of escape to her left and to her right, Kate slid into a window seat behind the tallest man she could find. Safe. For a while.

She was exhausted and she was scared. The adrenaline rush that had helped her escape her kidnapper had taxed her energy levels to the maximum. She was hungry. She was sweaty. She was shaking. Would anyone notice?

The porter came through their car collecting tickets.

"Excusez-moi, s'il vous plait, monsieur. Will there be food service aboard the train?"

"Oui, madame. A vendor of light fare will be here soon."

"Merci, monsieur."

Food. Any food would taste great right now. Kate curled up against the window and waited for the vendor. And watched for the kidnapper. He could be on any of the cars.

A young woman dressed in a yellow frock pushed a cart into their car to offer lunch to the travelers. Kate felt famished.

At first, she panicked. She had no money. She had no handbag. Then she remembered. She had left her white Gucci bag in the kidnapper's car, inscribed with a cherry lipstick plea for help on it. But she had tucked her cash in her pocket. Good. She could eat.

She purchased a croissant box lunch and a bottle of iced tea, slid down low in her seat, and for a few brief minutes, everything felt normal again.

But she would really miss that Gucci bag.

**She wouldn't have recognized him** if she had noticed him. He sat three rows back in an aisle seat and blended in with his surroundings. He wore gray linen pants and a gray silk shirt with no insignia or crest, a gray sport coat, and a plain, charcoal, brimmed hat covering his black hair and pulled low over his narrow brow and dark eyes.

Eduardo Manuela's men knew better than to follow someone who had seen them. When the kidnapper regained consciousness, he simply called in for one of the back-ups who were strategically located along the route to Eduardo's meeting place.

Jon Smith, a disenfranchised, small time drug runner, got the call in the metro. He bought a ticket and followed her on board.

**When the train stopped** at the Champs Elysees, Kate exited only after looking all around her and on the street above the railing. The kidnapper had not followed her, she thought. She relaxed a little, fortified by her lunch, but still kept a wary eye on her surroundings.

Three blocks later, she climbed the steep steps of the Institute's façade and pressed her eye up to the retina scanner. Five seconds later, the tumblers in the lock made a quiet grinding noise followed by the sound of the lock being released. In! She was safe now.

**He continued around the building,** studying all four sides as he held his walking tour guidebook up, pretending to read about the architecture of the building. He enjoyed surveillance because he liked intellectual challenges; he found the other aspects of his job boring.

He looked for a way to get in. Delivery truck? Waste bins? Maintenance shift? Mail service? Window washer? Food service?　Floral delivery?　Falling down the stairs?　Crow bar? There was always a way to get in.　Getting out alive took a little more ingenuity.

# Chapter 21



*Le Beach*
*Monte-Carlo, Monaco*

**The gravel beach along Monte-Carlo's eastern** shore varied greatly from the other beaches of the Cote d'Azur. While those renowned sandy beaches ranked highest for beauty, pleasure, and natural settings, Le Beach provided only a foot of natural, multi-hued stones, replenished annually from the bay waters adjoining it.

Rarely did visitors lie on beach blankets at Le Beach. The uncomfortable pebbles covering most of the beach prohibited any such relaxation. Rather, chaise lounges and umbrellas for rent filled the small beachfront, every day of the year.

Hundreds of sun fanatics in their early twenties already lined the edge of the bay this afternoon, their chaise legs sinking into the wet pebbles. Walkers sloshed through ankle deep water, carefully avoiding a twisted ankle as they lost their balance from sinking deep into the loose gravel making up the shore bed. Cuts and bruises notwithstanding, the early exercisers plodded along the water's edge intent on clocking their five-mile runs once again.

Fourteen-year-old Calen Gallow splashed her way out to chest deep water, moving her graceful arms in treading motions, although her feet were still able to touch bottom. She enjoyed the deeper water at the beach because there were fewer rocks to walk over and some sandy shoals to stand on.

Looking along the beach as it wound toward Nice, France, Calen saw the sun peering through some dark clouds over the olive trees clinging to the rocky coastline.

How quiet, Calen thought. This is one of my favorite places and my favorite time of day. Gentle warm waves lapped at her neck as she lifted her feet from the sand and floated with bent knees treading water, while her arms smoothly circled along her sides. Then she noticed it.

Slapping up against the huge boulders to her left, in the shadows of the cliffs, unusually large amounts of sea foam gathered together and floated along the shoreline. The piles of foam seemed to topple over themselves, pushed by a slight breeze and the motion of waves, running crookedly in to shore over underwater sand shoals.

Funny, she thought, the sea foam seems to be creeping its way along the coast in the shade, spreading itself along the edge of the beach and interspersing itself under the beach pebbles.

As the sun dipped behind another large dark cloud, Calen watched the people on the beach through the dusk-like atmosphere. She could hear the vacationers' reactions when they noticed the sea foam intrusion. They seemed to laugh as they looked down from their chaises to see the sea foam bubbling up around their chaise legs, sometimes frothing up onto the plastic strips of their lounges.

Suddenly, a syncopated frenzy began, as if the people on the lounges were rehearsing a Moulin Rouge dance routine: one set of legs after another kicked high into the air, fell downward, and then quickly swiveled to the edge of their chaise lounge. Then the people pushed off their chaises and ran screaming back toward the hotels.

"What's happening?" Calen cried out. No one answered her; no one even heard her.

Near the water's edge, Calen saw screaming swimmers exiting the water. The shrillness of their cries increased as the seconds wore on. Sea foam clung to their backs, their faces, their arms, their thighs, their legs. Hurriedly, they tried to swat it off as if it contained stinging insects. Calen saw panicked people running, bumping into each other, falling suddenly, and failing to get up.

Calen backed up into deeper water. She knew that she could not wade through the sea foam to get to shore without suffering serious consequences.

Standing on her tiptoes, she nudged herself backward and

swam out into the bay. When she had reached the area where the water currents mixed the sediments with the Mediterranean Sea currents, she treaded water again. Watching the horror unfold on the beach, Calen prayed the sea foam would dissipate before the next tide change.

# Chapter 22



*Helicopter Flight*
*Barcelona, Spain*

**The Bell 206L-4 Jet Ranger helicopter's** orange and white pontoon skids skimmed the uppermost fringes of the olive trees as it lifted off the melded tarmac behind the Venice terminal.

Jake pulled his laptop computer out of his black travel valise and pushed his thumbprint against the brass locking mechanism's viewer. Within a few seconds, he made a connection with the Institute's server, hoping to get an agenda together for his meeting in Barcelona. Suddenly, a bright red Medical Alert Warning from the Agency flashed across his laptop's screen.

"All Personnel," it read, "Red Alert. US Mid-Atlantic Beaches and European Beaches Reporting Hundreds of Deaths. Cause May Be Water Contamination by *Bacillus nocturne*.

Avoid Exposure. Stand By for Orders."

What is happening . . . how many areas are affected? Jake wondered as he thought about Julie's exposure to *nocturne*.

Data, Jake thought, we need data now to answer these questions. He reviewed every one of his team members' bios, proficiencies and the reasons the Agency had selected each one of them for this team. Using one of the Agency's secure cell phone lines, he started calling each team member to give them their data gathering assignment.

Dr. Joshua Padrone, the leading epidemiologist of the Americas, had joined the Agency after his longtime veterinarian friend, Dr. Nash Taylor, invited him to a summer barbecue at Taylor's Wyoming ranch. Taylor had just solved the cause of a rampant form of hoof and mouth disease that had swept through the Bolivian and Peruvian slopes during their last rainy season. Knowing of Padrone's interest in the spread of disease, Taylor offered him access to the new computer program he had developed to track cases of insouciant strains of the disease among cattle. With that offer came the explanation of the funding available from the Institute. Taylor explained that Padrone and other researchers would receive grant money to use for developing new programs and building facilities to expand their research to areas that would benefit all of humanity.

A learned and compassionate man to begin with, Dr. Joshua Padrone appreciated the gesture, and moreover, shared the belief of the Institute and Agency that science should support the welfare of all humanity and nature combined.

"Josh, North and South American beach hospital stats," Jake said as he contacted Padrone on the phone. He had to neither identify himself nor explain the assignment. Each one of his team members had prepared well in advance for any type of emergency call from him or the Agency. They had availed themselves of ready access to the most sensitive data available in their field of expertise, knowing that some day it could be needed on a moment's notice by the Agency. "Time is of the essence" is the phrase they all lived by.

Dr. Sayed Yasmir, biological warfare specialist from the University of the Baltics, and noted author of *The Last Strike,* a controversial non-fiction bestseller detailing a failed attempt by terrorists to attack a neighboring population, accepted the Agency's offer of a position in 1998.

Through an unusual number of family ties in high security places in Africa and the Middle East, Yasmir had access to medical records in hospitals which did not usually submit data to the WHO or the CDC.

His valuable data would help Jake pinpoint the outbreak as localized to resort beaches in Europe and the East Coast of the United States, or as secondary infections resulting from the infusion of the bacteria into other coastal areas. Jake hurriedly called Sayed explaining the Red Alert and adding, "European and African coastal hospital stats."

Jake had worked with Dr. Jia Zhang in the Middle East during the Iraqi War for Independence. She had acted as a translator for the Chinese Special Forces working with the United States' Navy Seals, in which Jake's unit had participated.

When she had returned to Beijing to serve as a medical translator and president of international agencies, Jake encouraged her to join forces with the Agency, with the blessing of her government, of course. China, immersed in terrorist threats of its own from its western provinces, decided a collegial relationship with the Institute and the Agency would be beneficial if China ever needed international resources to intervene in terrorists' plots.

"Jia, Agency Red Alert. Please ready Asian beach hospital stats," Jake commented as Jia picked up his call.

Jake read the downloaded data on each continent that he had stored on his micro laptop, pausing frequently over data about coastal populations and tourism influx. Over half the world was enjoying warm summer weather now, filling the beaches with families like his.

Plotting his plan of attack, Jake coalesced the points he wanted to cover in his meeting, beginning with a personal introduction of Julie's experience and followed by the details of the first known death from *Bacillus nocturne*.

Current accumulated health statistics, followed by up-to-the-minute water quality reports, would determine where to set up the portable labs and the personnel staffing them.

Jake's mind buzzed through variables, players, politics, history, welfare, motivations. Where was the source of the contagion? Was it recurring naturally? If not, why would someone unleash it now?

# Chapter 23



*Barcelona, Spain*

**No one noticed the Jet Ranger helicopter** flying low overhead. As it followed the Barcelona coastline and lightly banked to the right, its crew and lone passenger watched an unplanned, mass exodus from the beaches.

Toddlers' heads bobbled wildly as their parents swooped their children off the sand and ran for their cars or hotel rooms, wiping off whatever trace of sand or surf remained on their children's faces and arms.

Children were screaming, fearful of the unknown thing that had so frightened their parents. A black iPhone half-buried in the trampled, tan sand displayed a news headline: Don't Go Near the Water—Beach Plague.

One young father, huddling around his children as he loaded them into their Audi, stood up and leaned back against the side fender of his car. Jake could see blood running down his cheeks, and he knew there would be no one there to help the children once the father had fallen.

Along the sidewalk leading from the boardwalk, deeply tanned local adolescents pushed their bicycles among the crowd of tourists, trying to avoid running over the outstretched limbs of those who had already fallen. It was a walking nightmare.

Jake peered out in horror. Thoughts of Crystal and Julie rang through Jake's mind as he watched the melee spread southward through startled groups of families and friends. For the first time in Jake's life, he felt truly afraid.

# Chapter 24



*Barcelona, Spain*

**"Jake, I've contacted the control tower** and requested permission to land at the far end of the runway, where fewer crowds are gathered. There'll be an experienced Agency driver, Art Baxter, and an equipped Hummer waiting to take you to Base 10. God's speed. . . ." The helicopter pilot's voice trailed off as he looked down at the crowds aimlessly wandering around the tarmac.

The helicopter descended, and Jake stood up, grabbed his bags, and moved toward the exit door. After a rumbling landing, Jake unlocked the door, ran down the folding stairs, and stopped on the tarmac just long enough to make eye contact with the pilot and nod his thank you.

As Jake turned toward the Hummer, a crowd of panicked tourists crushed him against the copter's retracting stairs and pulled him aside as they hurriedly tried to board the helicopter.

The pilot locked down and revved the rotors, causing the crowd to duck down and wince from the noise. In that instant, he lifted off before another person grabbed hold of the running boards.

Jake lay on the tarmac, trampled by adults pushing their children out of the copter's reach. Their panicked faces betraying their uncertainty about what to try next, Jake knew he had only a moment to board the Hummer and break for the open road.

"Baxter," he yelled as he scraped himself off the ground, grabbed his valise, and turned on a run toward the graying linebacker driving the Hummer. "Get me to Base 10," Jake called out as he raced the now alert crowd to Baxter and the relative safety of the Hummer.

Grabbing the door handle with one hand while swinging his bag backward with the other, Jake felt the sick thud of the case hitting the head of the closest person behind him. The young woman hit the tarmac face first, skidding her cheek across the rough texture of the hot pavement. Jake, nauseous and heart pounding, dove through the open door just as Baxter gunned the Hummer into reverse and shifted into first, then second gear, in what seemed to Jake to be one continuous motion. Righting himself off the floor and falling back into the passenger's seat, Jake sat up to see some men from the crowd still chasing their vehicle.

"Baxter, ol' buddy, it's been a real long time."

"Shut up and ride shotgun for me," Baxter shouted as he

slapped a Beretta against Jake's stomach. He wasn't kidding. With the panicked crowds milling in the streets, Jake wasn't sure how safe this trip was going to be, but if he had to make it with anyone, Baxter was his man.

Rounding the next corner too quickly Baxter plowed through a row of black, wrought iron café tables. Red-checkered table-cloths flew into the air and floated softly downward, settling on hastily moving passersby trying to escape the ravages of the Hummer.

"Sorry, Boss." Baxter fought to regain control of their ve-hicle. "Haven't been drivin' under these circumstances for awhile."

"How far to Base 10?" Jake's low voice groaned as his head hit the side window of the Hummer. If I can't get to Base 10, what will happen to Julie and all those other people? Jake stopped that thought as soon as it formed in his mind. Concentrate, he ordered himself. There is no time for theatrics.

Baxter's voice jarred him out of his thoughts, "Fifty minutes max, assuming the density on the street continues." Seeing Jake dazed was new to Baxter.

"Jake, watch our backs! I'm picking up interference on the three-way. Someone's blocking my transmissions to Base 10 for an escort. We'll have to get there ourselves, but this inter-ference . . ."

Jake and Baxter felt the Hummer vibrate and heard the loud rumble before they realized what had struck them.

"A heat-seeking missile right up our tailpipe!" Baxter yelled as the explosion rocked the Hummer's rear end up and over the top of its cab.

Small in size compared to normal heat-seeking missiles, the home-made rocket slammed into the back of the Hummer with enough force to flip the vehicle fifteen feet forward and over on its side.

Before Jake could clear the wreckage, huge rough hands reached in and grabbed him by the neck. They yanked him through the shattered windshield, raking his side over sharp edges of glass that clattered onto the pavement.

Jake caught only a glimpse of Baxter, face down on the pavement, bleeding profusely from a shrapnel-like wound to the back of his head.

In Portuguese, a huge voice boomed through Jake's consciousness as its owner shook him upside down while Jake recounted everything that dropped out of his pockets. . . . "Passport, visa, keys, Visa card . . . oh, I said that already," he halfheartedly joked through the fog of his concussion. Everything fell out except his miniscule Agency cell phone, which he kept rigidly enclosed in his left palm.

By the time Jake realized that his captor literally held his life in his hands, Jake's recall kicked in and the fuzziness started to clear . . . the Portuguese!

A leader in the Portuguese Revolutionary Front, Jake had made his acquaintance three years ago when the Agency had sent Jake in to disrupt efforts to bomb a section of train track near the Spanish border.

Jake had posed as a dissident Russian professor, joined the group, and constructed an infrared-shielded timing device for the bomb. When the bomb failed to overturn a tank car of hydrochloric acid, Jake quietly slipped into the forest and made his way over the border to Spain.

"Scum of the earth!" The Portuguese shouted at Jake as his compatriots righted the Hummer and loaded it with shawl-draped women and screaming children. Scooping up Jake's credentials, the Portuguese giant dropped Jake unceremoniously into a heap in the middle of the glass-strewn road and signaled the new driver of the Hummer to gun it forward.

Jake rolled himself out of the way just as the Hummer charged toward him with the clear intent of running him over.

Lifting his bloody head from the road, Jake saw the Hummer hit the brakes and start to turn around.

Through the broken glass of its windows, Jake could hear the high-pitched shrills of two women in the backseat urging the driver to get the children to safety.

A second for thought, and then the driver did exactly what Jake expected any father would do. He chose the safety of his own children over a Portuguese-American vendetta.

# Chapter 25

*Barcelona, Spain*

**A dazed Baxter awkwardly** made his way over to Jake, bleeding profusely from a head wound, his left arm dangling loosely at his side. He had been dumped out of the Hummer in the turnover.

"What was that all about, my friend?" Baxter asked.

"Old score that was never settled. A few years back in Lisbon. Seems the bloke remembered me . . . and somehow knew I'd be travelling to Base 10 on this route. I think someone compromised the base's communication system."

"Lucky for us that the Portuguese brought his family along on vacation as a cover. Their fear of contracting *nocturne* may have saved our lives today."

Opening his left hand, Jake showed Baxter the hidden cell phone. "Thought we might need this," Jake quipped as he called the Agency first and Base 10 second, warning them to be wary of visitors and to heighten security.

When he finished calling, Baxter grinned and said, "Thought we might need this," as he handed Jake the computer valise he had reached for and retrieved before being dumped out of the Hummer. Jake nodded, a very slight grin creasing his face.

Baxter and Jake scoped their surroundings. The street, now empty of wary pedestrians, and the homes, tightly shuttered against wind-driven contagion, left them few choices.

Four blocks down an orange cobblestone street, they spotted an old gasoline station with a red and white sign out front declaring, "Repairs, Trades, Sales." Searching the used car lot as they neared the station, Baxter walked over to a faded red Chevrolet Geo compact car, patted it on its hood, and said, "This is it. Old reliable." Eighteen hundred American dollars later, Baxter's American Express secured them their transportation to Base 10.

Throwing his gear onto the floor of the front seat, Jake slammed his door shut just as Baxter revved the motor and spun the vehicle ninety degrees to the right. Jake righted himself once again and wisely decided to fasten his seat belt.

Thirty harrowing minutes later, Jake's ride screeched to a stop in front of the main entrance to the Galleria, the Rodriguez family's home and the cover for the Institute's Base 10 operations, on Ronda del Litoral in Barcelona, Spain. Baxter threw open his door and spun around the back of the car to meet Jake on the passenger side, while Jake collected his computer valise and cell phone.

Then Jake fled up the travertine steps to the Galleria's ionic columned, tan stucco main entrance. Flashing his retina against the ocular scanner, Jake waited three seconds for the outer doors to unlock themselves and whoosh open into the suctioning airlock preceding the inner, fortified titanium doors.

As Jake leaned against the second ocular scanner, the outer doors closed, sealing him into a chamber-like stall capable of total decompression in three minutes, if necessary. Jake was always grateful when he heard the snapping clicks of the inner doors unlocking.

Once inside, Jake turned to wait for Baxter to enter. As he exited from the second set of doors, the two of them hurried down the ivory marble hallway to the Situation Room. There, gathered around a shiny granite conference table, eyes glued to three wall-mounted 60" LCDs broadcasting news from around the world, Jake's team members were anxiously talking among themselves about the reports on the screens.

"Hello, everyone," Jake announced himself. Without any other introduction or explanation of their blood-soaked, dusty clothes clinging to their injuries, or acknowledgement of his gathered team members, Jake began the questioning: "What's the total number of deaths so far?"

"Eighty in the United States, with 545 persons in critical condition," replied Dr. Joshua Padrone, leading epidemiologist of the Americas and the North, Central, and South American Liaison for the Institute. "Remarkably, most of the seriously ill are people in their twenties."

"And 324 deaths in Europe, with hospitals overflowing with patients in various stages of the illness. Again, most of the cases reported are young adults, 20 to 30 years old. A few others outside of that age bracket who became infected had weakened immune systems. The figures are estimated at 1200-1300 in critical condition. And the numbers are increasing rapidly this morning," reported Dr. Sayed Yasmir, Biological Warfare Specialist from the University of the Baltics and the Institute's European and African liaison.

"All right. Any new information about its cause? Why is it so suddenly virulent?" Jake asked.

Dr. Jia Zhang, President of the Biochemistry Institute in Beijing and the Institute's Asian Liaison, volunteered her latest efforts at finding concrete evidence about the outbreak.

"It is a highly virulent strain of *Bacillus nocturne*," Jia explained, "unlike any that we had experimented with in the Institute lab five years ago. The new DNA structure shows evidence of tampering on the 16SrRNA allele to produce exponential replication. *Nocturne* compensates for the high reproduction rate by rapidly colonizing suitable hosts: first, it colonized the waste products of amoebae living in sea foam; then, it colonized the human waste found in sewage and wastewater runoff; and now, it is colonizing human tissue."

"An important consideration has to be made," Dr. Yasmir said. "The variant strain was purposely engineered and developed to make the bacteria extremely aggressive. We could be looking at an accidental release of the bacteria, an act of one deranged individual, or a terrorist plot."

"I agree, Sayed," Jake said. "We need to find the source of the contamination and prevent *nocturne's* further spread. Hit the computers, everyone, and find the data we need to evaluate this strain of bacteria: how and when it was altered, where it was integrated into the environment, and its likely spread, based upon every variable you can think of, and most importantly, come up with your best analysis of how we can stop it. Make it fast. We don't have much time."

Everyone scattered, knowing exactly what to ask of the bank of computers down the hall. No one even slightly misjudged Jake for his veracity or his cold, calculated orders to them on how to attack this bacterium. On the contrary, every team member believed the seriousness of the present threat warranted Jake's abrupt commands.

# Chapter 26



*Fort Myers Air Force Base*
*Florida, U.S.A.*

**The damp, salty marsh wind** licked at Claire's long brown curls as the shoulder straps of her camera and carry-on bags entangled themselves around her neck.

She clutched her hair into a side ponytail with a five-inch section of red plastic-coated electrical wire that she had cut out of their Maserati's glove compartment. Her khaki shorts and safari jacket hung loosely over her bright yellow, stretch jersey T-shirt that she had thrown on just two hours ago.

Lance pummeled along loaded down with three duffel bags, two laptops, and her portable biochemistry lab equipment. The white outline of sweat stains were leaving their mark on his clothes as he hurried toward Retired General Joe Hatbourne's private plane, already humming on the tarmac behind Hangar 203.

Together, Lance and Claire had exited their beach rental on Captiva Island in record time, throwing all their beach clothing and snorkeling gear into two brightly colored duffel bags and their business clothes into an oversized, overstuffed black leather carry-on.

"Good morning, Captain," Claire offered as she climbed up the seven steps to the jet's entryway.

Captain Gladys Rainier nodded as she continued registering her flight plan with the control tower. Lance followed Claire up the stairs, dropping the bags heavily at his feet as he turned to close the lightweight titanium door behind him.

"Gladys, good to see you again," he smiled. Claire looked back over her shoulder at the two of them exchanging glances, and quickly registered Lance's reaction to the beautiful, lithe redhead.

"She's got to go," a quiet, whispery voice echoed across Claire's mind.

"Drs. Martin, welcome aboard," Gladys smiled. "We will be ready to depart in three minutes. Please settle in and buckle up for take-off. The pull-down side compartments under your windows already have hot coffee brewing and English muffins toasting with Eggs Benedict Remoulade a la Hatbourne. I hope you enjoy the flight. We will land at Base 3 in Dover, Delaware, in one hour, ten minutes."

Claire's adrenaline began its slow and steady surge as soon as she felt the plane start to move. Her fear of flying increased as they taxied to their assigned runway for take-off. "We're going to die," the voice in her head said. "We're all going to die!"

To control her rising panic Claire forced herself to concentrate on the events leading up to today's journey. Remembering the exact order of a day's events, even to the point of reconstructing her thoughts, her words, and everyone else's words had worked for her before as a form of self–hypnosis.

Claire prided herself on her vast memory. As a precocious child, she had never considered actors, who could memorize thousands of lines of script each day, impressive. She had repeated people's conversations in her mind all the time ever since she turned three. It had helped her to recognize when it was time to hide.

As soon as her parents began shouting their dangerous words, little Claire knew she had only a few minutes until they started to repeat the words about her. . . . "We were fine until she came along" . . . "I never wanted her" . . . "I doubt that she's even mine" . . . "She's no good" . . . "Go get her, or I'll beat the life out of both of you!"

When the last word was spoken and the silence started, Claire knew she had to run and find a safe place to hide. When she had exhausted all her hiding places in their old three-story house, all she could do was submissively roll herself into a tight little ball and take her mind to a faraway place where no one could ever hurt her again—a quiet, sandy cove near the edge of the sea.

Today, Claire decided to let her mind travel back a few days to relive the events and conversations of the days leading up to their vacation in Florida. She even managed to relax a little as she remembered how well her field experiment had gone.

# Chapter 27

*Two days ago*
*Beachwood Beach West*
*New Jersey, U.S.A.*

**Claire scrambled the four eggs** and fat free milk in a yellow mixing bowl, careful to prevent the raw egg from splashing onto the kitchen's Volga Blue granite countertop. "Wouldn't want to contaminate the surface with *salmonella*," she mumbled quietly to herself.

Lance was in the small but cozy living room watching her DVD recording of last night's rebroadcast of the "Mid-Atlantic States' Guide to Beach Water Quality." She knew he was listening for any details about the Captiva Island beach where they were planning to spend the next 14 days. Claire overheard the female newscaster begin her report:

"This is Late Night City News from New York City, presenting the Beach Water Quality Report. Beach closings and warnings doubled along our coastlines this year, according to the annual Beach Water Quality Report released today by the Mid-Atlantic Resources Defense Council (MARDC).

"Our source, "Testing at the Beaches: A Guide to Water Quality," the newscaster continued, "reported over eleven hundred closing and health advisory days along the Atlantic Ocean coasts of New York and New Jersey, including the beaches along Ocean and Long Island Sound this year, leading to a 98 percent increase from the year before. Other Mid-Atlantic states' closing and advisory days also increased, up an average of 88 percent since last year."

"Family summer vacations, and even weekend getaways, are being ruined by the pollution washing up on coastal beaches, and the local crowd hitting the shore for late night dining are complaining about the refuse washing ashore in secluded places," continued Jessica Loneto, director of MARDC's Beach Initiative.

"The source of this pollution" Jessica said, "is the extensive amount of sewage and contaminated storm water that are draining into our swimming areas. Redirecting this polluted water at its source to inhibit its transport to the shore is key to protecting our natural beach resources."

The familiar annual summer warning about coastal water pollution did not surprise Claire; rather, it caused a broad smile of satisfaction to spread across her face as she thought, "At last, progress is being made!"

She and her colleagues had already taken the necessary steps to make the public finally realize that their participation in stopping this ecological disaster was the only way they would survive.

**Every Saturday for the past five months,** Claire Martin and five of her colleagues from the Marine Biology Department at Peridore University had met at the corner table in the back of the Blue Heron Restaurant surreptitiously for lunch. Their dedication to engaging the public in their fight for pure water exceeded their culinary appetites, though, and their discussions always centered upon what they ambiguously referred to as Project Awareness.

"There!" Dr. Ahmed Azzizi, Claire's graduate school mentor, present colleague, and her co-founder of Project Awareness, slammed down a national newspaper on the lunch table.

Claire saw how much he enjoyed the attention he garnered whenever he made a grand entrance into other people's conversations, which he did quite often. She knew his reputation on campus leaned toward the passionate side in conversations and actions. When she was his doctoral student, she politely rebuffed his innuendoes, describing him to her husband as "tall, dark, and handsome, but not as tall, dark, and handsome as you, Lance."

"Look at this!" Ahmed continued. "We made the annual report this year, and no one ever suspected that the increase in beach closings had anything to do with us." Leaning against the scrubbed oak table, Ahmed picked up the paper and began reading:

"New Jersey Atlantic Coast and bay beaches had 1,192 closing and advisory days this year. Sixty per cent of those days were caused by rain advisories issued after heavy rainfalls that could carry pollution from land and overflowing sewers into the bays and ocean. But more ominously, the other forty per cent of those closings were due to documented, contaminated beach water. Bacteria levels exceeded the recommended safety level three out of every four times the beach waters were tested after heavy rains."

Ahmed fumed. "They're too lazy to investigate whether these bacterial levels might have been caused by something other than storm water."

Claire wasn't sure how to begin replying to her colleague's tirade. Her small group had decided to show the reticent public that something needed to be done quickly to stop the pollution of the coastal waters, but their plan had included releasing only small amounts of nonlethal *Bacillus nocturne* along the New Jersey waterways leading to the coastal zone. Just enough of a release of bacterial agent to get the presses' notice.

"Keep water pollution in the public's eye," Ahmed had always said, "and perhaps finally, the public will recognize that it's better to act now to clean it up than face the illness it will bring in the future."

Ahmed's anger was evident, but Claire wondered if he would be more angry or pleased when he found out what she had done.

Claire didn't know the answer to her own question. She decided not to tell Ahmed or the others that she had recently re-engineered *Bacillus nocturne* to be able to clean up the sewage pollution in the marshes. Nor would she tell them about her additional trips to release the bacteria in the estuaries near Cape Henlopen in Delaware, Lido Beach in Venice, Oostende Beach in Belgium, or the other resort beaches she had selected.

That can wait, Claire thought, and she turned her attention to the others as they rambled into the restaurant, lugging their field equipment with them in heavy green canvas bags.

Professor Ariel Tenmenson's bobbed, black hair with its white birthmark streak was covered in mud, as usual. Water and muddy sand always splattered her hair and variegated skin when she drilled holes for core samples to test the bacterium's concentration in the muddy banks surrounding the back lagoon.

Ariel and Claire had started to work at the University during the same semester, and their research interests led them to co-author two National Science Foundation grants to study the potability of estuarine water.

Ariel's research assistant, Eric Langdon, a tall, blonde junior from central Pennsylvania, trailed in behind her, arms full of computer printed graphs and charts, laptops, wireless printer, and field chemical samples. Splattered with mud like Ariel, Eric's hands and face were a montage of grainy sediments, white sunscreen, and yesterday's blistering sunburn. Their recent reports from the marsh indicated that the concentration of the bacterium that Claire had been dispersing was well within the 80-89 ml range throughout the water, increasing the total amount of contamination by only 38-46 per cent at the southern end of the estuary. Today, Eric could barely keep his voice low as he worriedly showed the group their calculations from that morning.

"Ninety-four percent." Eric said. "What could have caused such a high concentration to make it through the estuary?"

Ariel was somewhat calmer, but tenseness was evident when she spoke. "We'll have to go back to test all the banks in the lagoon near the effluvial flows. If the concentrations are that high everywhere, we'll have to report it to the EPA immediately so the local police can close the beaches."

"Sawyer Thompson went home sick an hour after we got to the site." Ariel continued talking about her graduate research assistant. "He was the first one in the water this morning, starting three hours before us. I have a bad feeling about this, Claire. I'm going back out now and will call you on my cell phone the minute I get my next bacteria reading."

Ariel glanced back at the table as she headed through the door, pointing forcefully at Eric to sit down. "No one else is to risk a second exposure. And someone, please call Sawyer to make sure he's okay."

Claire hadn't moved throughout the whole discussion, worried her facial expressions would give her away.

Too soon, still too soon to tell them what I did, she thought. Six more hours, only six more hours, and then everyone will know. I'm sorry about Sawyer, though. I liked him.

Eric looked down at Ahmed's printout. Some of Suffolk County's beaches had exceeded their safety levels for contamination one out of four times in the past year.

Eric exploded, "Today's readings are going to put the entire Suffolk County beachfront on alert. I knew I shouldn't have agreed to get involved with this activist group. Some group. A terrorist group, by the time the media gets done frying us."

Eric crumpled into the chair, head in his hands, crying in low, solemn moans. Claire had hurried to quiet him before he drew more attention to their already disheveled meeting. His wet forehead felt hot, and she could see the perspiration beading up on his brow. By tomorrow, he'll be showing all the symptoms, she thought.

Claire silently backed away from Eric, leaving Ahmed to tend to him as she sidled out the back door of the cafe.

Circling around to the front of the café, Claire clamored into her dust-covered red Toyota Prius, tossing her bulky field bag and waterproof laptop carrying case onto the passenger's seat as she slid her sunglasses down from her head and over her eyes. Starting the engine and shifting into reverse, she felt her state of mind shifting with the car. First, she was surprised that some members of her party had fallen ill, then she felt agitated that the team had documented the high contamination level found in the estuarine waters, and finally, she reviewed what that meant for the surrounding communities.

Claire felt pleased. She believed that her decision to alter *Bacillus nocturne* was justifiable, even ethically mandated, in order to convince people of the seriousness of the ecological disaster that was just waiting to happen.

# Chapter 28

*Four weeks ago*
*Peridore University*
*Beachwood Beach West, New Jersey, U.S.A.*

**On her first day of summer classes** in the United States, Ruthee Samayinathan, a sultry, twenty-two-year-old native of Maharashtra, India, carefully parked her shiny blue Jaguar Z56 convertible, which her father had bought for her, in the shade of one of the 200-year-old oak trees that lined the quadrangle of Peridore University.

Rathmanathan Samayinathan loved his youngest child immensely, but when she had insisted on attending university in Paris, he reacted with kneejerk certainty. No daughter of his would openly defy her father's wishes for her to attend medical school in the United States. He would put a stop to this foolishness immediately. And, he did. The shiny blue Z56 had greeted Ruthee as she stepped ceremoniously out of the airport limousine to begin her studies at a United States' medical school.

Yep, Ruthee thought, Popsa sure showed me where I would go to school. Ruthee ran her hand along the smooth finish of her new sports car. Popsa is just too easy to manipulate, she sighed. I'll have to come up with a better challenge. And, she did.

Ruthee's first class with Dr. Ahmed Azzizi mystified her, not because of its level of technical difficulty, but rather because of the esoteric manner in which Ahmed treated the female students in his class. He pampered the young women, treating them as if they were not capable of comprehending the theories supporting the classroom discussions. Some of the younger women swooned over their handsome, eligible professor and the extreme kindness that he exhibited toward them. Others, like Ruthee, resented his patronizing condescension.

Azzizi's classroom reminded Ruthee of a little boys' Tree House Club whose rules for membership were alluded to but never quite defined.

Ruthee recognized that Azzizi's attitude toward females was wrong; a professor, of all people, should be knowledgeable about academic abilities and model egalitarianism on and off campus. Regardless of Azzizi's lack of regard for women, Ruthee decided to play along in class. This could be a challenge, she thought happily. And Ruthee loved challenges more than life itself.

By the end of the second week of classes, Ruthee had inserted herself into Ahmed's psyche.  Acting like a distraught adolescent, she entered his office often, full of round-eyed innocent questions, feigning as much interest in his vast knowledge as she did in stroking her long black satin hair.  By the end of the third week of classes, Ruthee was seeing him after every class, just to make sure she had her lecture notes completely in order.

Carefully, during the fourth week of classes, Ruthee would slowly frame her question for the day, causing the entire class to moan with the absurdity of what she was asking.  But, not Ahmed.  He was flattered that one so stupid, and so rich, would try this hard to understand his every word.

This is just too easy, again, Ruthee thought. Time to add a new component to this game.

# Chapter 29

*Sutter Graduate Apartments*
*Peridore University*
*Beachwood Beach West, New Jersey, U.S.A.*

**The old 19-inch portable television's screen** quietly buzzed after every third word spoken during the newscast, its now soggy wiring feeding intermittent antennae signals to its sparking components.

Earlier in the day, Sawyer Thompson, Professor Ariel Tenmenson's graduate research assistant, had stumbled into his small, shared kitchen. He had caught sight of his roommates Raymie and Cole slouched on the couch, sucking bottles of Heineken, oblivious to the Beach Water Quality Panel Discussion on the screen. Had they looked up, they would not have recognized him. Dried marsh sediment clung to the top of his red hair and obscured his brown freckles. His retro over-sized glasses harbored grassy marsh debris, as if a weed trimmer had thrown tiny bits of reeds against his muddy frames.

Recognizing one of the speakers as his undergraduate ecology professor, Dr. Adrienne Esposito, Sawyer's confused mind couldn't help but hear Rocky's voice shout, "Yo, Adrienne! Wait 'til you see what I've done!" Angling toward the shower stall, Sawyer picked up the gist of the broadcast and marveled at how timely the newspeak was going to be.

Sawyer stripped off his clothes and dropped his dirty glasses into the sink while listening to the blaring report. Flipping the faucet to hot, he staggered into the shower.

"Whoa, shower stall," he muttered to himself as the shower stall tilted crazily to the left and then to the right. "This ain't right."

Sawyer had been feeling ill ever since he and Ariel Tenmenson had collected water samples in the marsh behind Peridore University for Project Awareness. Now, he felt dizzy. Very dizzy.

Grabbing onto the shower door handle, Sawyer attempted to steady himself. Leaning against the wall, choking back nausea, he let the water rush over his body. Slowly he became aware that scalding water was hitting his chest. He reached for the water spigot, and then grabbed for it as his vision spun out of control. Slamming his forearm against the showerhead instead, the scalding water furled over his forehead, burning the skin across his back.

Trying to turn quickly away from the scalding pain on his

back, Sawyer winced as sharp, searing pains flayed the surfaces of his eyes. No longer aware of the scalding water, his brain was registering only the excruciating pain encircling his corneas. As his face hit the steel edge of the shower door, Sawyer's legs buckled, and his one hundred seventy pound frame crashed through the glass door onto the bathroom floor. Blood, seeping from his eyes and the glass-filled wounds on his face and body, spread across the floor.

The water from the shower stall spilled over the shower's base, running across the blood-covered tan and white ceramic tiles on the bathroom floor, through the beige indoor/outdoor carpeted hallway, and under the small table in the kitchen, leaving a wavy, red, watercolor pattern in its wake.

# Chapter 30

*Peridore University*
*Beachwood Beach West, New Jersey, U.S.A.*

**"Professor . . ."** **Ruthee innocently began** as she followed Dr. Ahmed Azzizi into his office after their Monday morning class. "I noticed that when we were discussing the theories of aging today, the theories seemed to be divided into, like, two distinct groups. One group of theorists state that aging is, like, a result of wear and tear. The other group of theorists suggests that aging is, like, genetically programmed in the body. Which side of the contradiction are you on?"

Ahmed let a slight smile slip through his lips, but he caught it in time to regain his composure. The poor dear, he thought. Then he realized, I'm actually beginning to look forward to her inane questions.

"Ruthee, you may remember we also discussed combinations of these theories. Many new theories evolved which also contained elements of both of these ideas. Senescence may strongly be related to some adverse environmental factors which damage the ends of the alleles in our DNA, causing the body to malfunction."

Ruthee inwardly smiled. She almost had her planned conversation with Dr. Azzizi set up to the point where she could begin her new component for hassling him. *This is fun,* she thought, *and even more fun because of his condescending attitude toward females. I'll have to be careful not to let all those adolescent "likes" slip into my normal speech, though.*

"Do you mean, like, the factors in the examples from your field work you told us about? Like, when you are measuring and evaluating the levels of toxic wastes in the estuaries?"

"Yes," Ahmed said. "That is one way to study the effects the environment has on human health."

*Ready,* Ruthee thought.

"Oh. I want to try to sample the water, too!" Ruthee let her feigned enthusiasm bubble over. "What a great class project that will be! Like, I can go out with you this morning and learn how to do the sampling, and like, I'll help you with the daily sampling, and I'll help you record the results, and like, I'll help you analyze the data, and I'll help you write a new grant, and like, I'll help you . . ."

Ruthee's voice gradually trailed off as she tap-danced out of Ahmed's office, happily reciting her litany of assistance, all the way down the hall, inciting curious looks from Ahmed's colleagues and graduate students.

Ahmed suddenly realized he was in over his head. She was moving in on his private world, and he had led her there himself.

# Chapter 31

*Peridore University*
*Beachwood Beach West, New Jersey, U.S.A.*

**Dr. Ahmed Azzizi walked across campus** like a man condemned.

How did I let this thing with Ruthee get so out of control? What was I thinking? Was I even thinking at all? Yeah, I was thinking, all right. Thinking with my id.

What if she shows up at the dock today and someone sees us together? Undergrads aren't even allowed to accompany profs on fieldwork. Tenure, oh man, my tenure review is next week.

Climbing up the library stairs two at a time, Ahmed hit his stride as he bounded through the old oak doors and turned down the first hallway on his left.

The Cannary Room, a private meeting room reserved for faculty-student advising, was empty except for a lone figure weeping over a pile of documents spread across a table.

Ahmed could see Eric Langdon had collected more articles about terrorists contaminating water supplies. He's still distraught about Saturday's water analyses for Project Awareness, Ahmed thought.

Reaching over, Ahmed placed his right hand on Eric's shaking frame, hoping that the pressure would still the reverberating heaves and sobs which were draining the young man's body of anything remotely human and adult. His disheveled blonde hair fell over his sun-blistered neck, now ashen and raw.

Why was he crying? Ahmed thought. What was frustrating him? Didn't Eric say that he wanted to make a statement about water quality? Project Awareness had done just that, albeit a little stronger than anticipated, but still, Ahmed thought, they had accomplished their goal. People would respond now to the seriousness of the threats to our water supplies.

Ahmed had to admit that Project Awareness had overstated their cause. No one, he thought, was supposed to get hurt when the activists released *Bacillus nocturne* into the waterways behind Peridore University. Already though, one member of the team had gone home sick, and others affected by the water supply would probably get sick, too. At least they had not opted for releasing the more virulent form of the bacteria that Claire had recommended.

Anxious to complete his water sampling before Ruthee arrived at the pier, Ahmed grew impatient with Eric's refusal to talk. He could at least acknowledge my presence, Ahmed thought. Frustrated, Ahmed looked at his Rolex.

This delay will set my schedule back all day, Ahmed mentally protested. I'm going to be late for dinner tonight with Carla Blanchard, too. I need her to feature my research on one of her station's documentaries on the environment. The environment must be my platform for the Senate race against Pete Montelli. It's my best chance for winning the election.

Harsh gasping sounds refocused Ahmed's attention on Eric. Eric began heaving heavily, now barely able to catch his breath. He rolled his head to face Ahmed, hoping to say . . . but Ahmed's startled gasp and rapid movement backwards, interrupted him.

Blood pooled in Eric's eyes, overflowed his eyelids, and ran down the edges of his bristled cheeks.

Wiping his face with first his left hand, and then his struggling right hand, Eric realized that he could not stop the blood from cascading down his face.

Before Eric could question why he was bleeding, his head jerked back from the first onslaught of searing pain in the middle of his corneas. Whipping his bloody hair at a 45-degree angle to the right and backwards, Eric splattered Ahmed's forehead and upraised hands with his lethal bacteria-laden blood.

Reflexively, Ahmed reached for his face, furtively trying to keep the blood from running down his forehead and into his eyes; instead, his bloody hands drawn across his eyebrows left languid red trails that seeped across his lashes and down into the whites of his eyes.

Ahmed wiped his eyes with a handkerchief and rushed to the lavatory to wash the blood from his face. In the mirror, he saw the face of his father—worry lines etched by anxiety creased around his eyes and mouth.

Searching his pockets, Ahmed pulled out his cell phone and dialed 911.

"911. What number are you calling from?"

"That doesn't matter. Send a medic to the Cannary Room in Peridore University's library. A student is bleeding from his eyes."

Ahmed turned off his cell phone and rushed out of the library.

"If Eric has any blood-borne contagious diseases . . ." he muttered as he forced himself to not run down the library's white marble stairs.

"What if he has AIDS or hepatitis?"

Ahmed made his way across campus to the marina as nonchalantly as possible. He didn't want to draw attention to himself or have anyone know he was involved with Eric and Project Awareness.

That was close, he thought. If I want to run for the Senate, I can't be associated with any student problems like this.

Things are getting just too far out of hand. I better finish my research and get ready for my tenure evaluation before I plan my election strategy.

"And Eric?" Ahmed's conscience asked.

Ahmed's mind snapped back. He's just another dumb student who didn't take precautions while he was out on the marsh. It's his fault, not mine.

# Chapter 32



*Peridore University Marina,*
*Beachwood Beach West, New Jersey, U.S.A.*

**Ruthee arrived at the marine pier,** ready to help Ahmed with his water sampling, as promised. Parking her shiny blue Jaguar under a shady tree, she jumped out and scrambled together all of her belongings for the day's trip: wide-brimmed sun hat to flop off and lose in the water; greasy suntan lotion SPF 50 to apply to her palms before reaching for the engine starter; the sweetest smelling insect spray she could find; light weight gray nylon jacket for a cover-up after swimming in her very teeny polka dot bikini; very large woven picnic basket stuffed with hors d'oeuvres and bottles of water.

Yep, Ruthee thought. This should be a real fun day. How long will it take before he breaks?

Bustling her way through the weathered oak swinging doors that separated the motor boats from the kayaks, barely able to see over the bundles in her arms, she stumbled over a wet gym bag and fell face down, flat on the floor. Pushing her body over in disgust, she reached her wet hands up to her forehead to brush her hair out of her eyes.

"Ahhhh, no . . ." Ruthee gurgled as she realized her wet hands were covered with blood. Looking back at the soggy gym bag on the floor, she recognized the bloody shape of Dr. Azzizi, still clutching a bag of water sampling supplies under his arm.

# Chapter 33

*Late Night City News Studio*
*New York City, New York, U.S.A.*

**Carla Blanchard, the slightly edgy, beautiful** brunette news anchor at Late Night City News, welcomed her guests for the evening's follow-up discussion on the results of the Mid-Atlantic Resources Defense Council's beach water quality report. Everyone, that is, except for Senator Pete Montelli, who silently withdrew a seat at the end of the rectangular table, as far away from Carla as possible.

"Welcome, once again, to Part 2 of Late Night City News' discussion about MARDC's annual beach water quality report and what it means to our region," Carla addressed her television audience but caught Pete's movement away from her in her peripheral vision. "Dr. Rousche, what's going on with the city's sewer system overflowing after a storm?"

Carla angled her microphone in to catch the comments of

Dr. Benjamin Rousche, a silver-haired, septuagenarian, biological engineering professor *emeritus* from Princeton University.

"Most of New York City's sewer system is over eighty years old. One-fifth of an inch of rainfall can flood the system because it was designed to collect both sewage and storm runoff. Today after a brief but heavy downpour, this bacteria-laden sewer mixture overflows into the waters surrounding the city. There is a way to lessen the load on the system, though. Capturing storm water where it falls by incorporating 'green' solutions – street trees, green roofs, landscaped walls of buildings, and porous pavement – can prevent it from overwhelming our storm drains and flushing sewage into our recreational waters."

Carla just barely caught that comment with her microphone, distracted temporarily by the aggressive grin on Senator Montelli's face.

Picking up the speed of the conversation, Carla rolled through her fact sheet: "Nationwide, the MARDC counted more than 25,000 closing and health advisory days at ocean, bay, and Great Lakes beaches this year. Of those, sewage spills and overflows caused 1,473 beach closings and advisories, an increase of 508 days from last year. These may seem like a small percentage of the total closings, but they are the most dangerous reasons for closings. And many states require a second water quality test to confirm bacteria counts before notifying the public that a beach is closed. That can delay beach closures by forty-eight hours."

Turning toward Senator Peter Montelli, Carla looked directly into his Venetian blue eyes, framed by his ebony hair. Still a looker, she reminisced.

"Senator Montelli," Carla began. "As chair of the Bay Ecology Study Commission, what has the committee decided to do to protect our citizens from these increasing health hazards?"

**Pete Montelli recognized a trap** when he heard one. No way would Carla have chosen a question that centered on just one aspect of the pollution report on her own, he thought. He knew from experience that she was too perceptive of an investigator to narrow the whole problem down to one cause, effect, and solution. This was a political punch question, if he ever heard one, and he knew who was behind this question. Dr. Ahmed Azzizi, a medical research professor and leftist activist, had secretly stolen Carla's heart and openly announced he was running for Montelli's Senate seat.

Pete Montelli didn't want to think about when Azzizi had planted his question into Carla's consciousness. No, he wouldn't let his mind go there. Being cut out of her life was still too fresh of a wound.

Speaking extemporaneously had always been Pete's strong suit; now, he slipped into gear and proceeded with the apolitical answer:

"Aging and poorly-designed sewage and storm drainage systems are responsible for most of the beach water pollution in the tri-state region and across the nation. Unexpected record rainfalls caused by climate change strains an already overloaded infrastructure. Uncontrolled urban sprawl in coastal areas is devouring wetlands and eliminating the natural filtering of dangerous pollution. We can fix leaky pipes and design better infrastructure; we can require coastal developers to leave trees and meadows in place and plant additional trees and grasses to absorb rain; we can protect our dunes with replenishment; we can protect our filtering wetlands from salt water influx; we can create policies that require immediate notification of beach contamination. Waterborne health risks include gastroenteritis, dysentery, hepatitis, respiratory ailments and other serious health problems which disproportionately affect senior citizens, small children, and people with weak immune systems. All aspects of this problem must be addressed together to find a lasting solution, rather than singling out just one issue."

**Somewhat chagrined** by the Senator's clever response to her singular question, Carla wondered what Ahmed would say to her later that night. Did she help Ahmed's campaign or hurt it?

"Thank you, everyone, for joining us for Part 2 of our discussion about the water quality at our tri-state beaches."

As soon as the cameras turned off, Carla grinned, "It's a take. Everyone off to the beaches. Just don't go in the water."

# Chapter 34



*Late Night City News Studio*
*New York City, New York, U.S.A.*

**"Not so quickly, Carla!"**

Carla recognized Pete Montelli's baritone voice as soon as he spoke. Veering around to a close-up of his azure eyes framed by his sleek, black hair unnerved her, and brought back unsettling memories.

"How have you been, Pete? It was good seeing you here to-day." It was almost a lie. She side-stepped to her left to get him out of her personal space. Her day had been filled with apprehension about seeing him again after their break-up. Worse, she knew she would keep her promise to Ahmed and set the senator up for some on-air criticism.

"Carla, what was all that one-sided questioning about? You never cared much for political agendas. Are you suddenly supporting the other party? Or just any party that is different from mine?" He had trouble keeping the anger out of his voice.

"No, not that at all." Flustered, she tried to explain, "Just trying to liven up the conversation."

"Liven up the conversation? This is a public service program. There's no need to 'liven' it up."

"It's not just that," she stammered. "I have other people in my life now, and I want to please them, as well as my audience."

"You mean Ahmed, don't you?" Pete sounded threatening. Even saying Ahmed's name set him off.

"Ahmed plays dirty, Carla, you should know that by now. Look at how he tricked you into falling for him. He swiped you right out of my arms with that rotten little story he made up. None of it was true, Carla. You must know that by now."

"Look, Pete. I told you to stop following me."

"Following you! You invited me to be on this panel!"

"I had to. It was part of my job. I didn't invite your attention after the program was over. Now leave me alone!"

"You didn't answer my question. What was this all about? A political ambush?"

"Let it go, Pete."

"Just how am I supposed to do that, Carla?" His frustration shimmered across wet eyes.

"Let it go. I did a long time ago."

"A long time ago? Exactly 24 days and 3 hours ago." The senator felt his throat constrict, followed by an overwhelming crushing feeling deep within his chest. As he walked away from her, he knew it was not a heart attack. He already had one of those. This feeling was much worse.

# Chapter 35

*Base 3*
*Dover, Delaware, U.S.A.*

**Captain Gladys Ranier skillfully set the rear** wheels of the ultra speed jet onto the runway and smoothly lowered the nose of the plane until the front wheel touched the tarmac. Braking to round the covered corner of the fuel replacement shed, she angled the small jet into Retired General Joe Hatbourne's private hangar for a quick refueling and maintenance check before flying on to Giverny, France, with Claire Martin.

"All right, Claire. You made it." Lance smiled his encouragement to his wife. "Gladys will get you safely to Joe's private field, just east of Giverny.  He'll have a taxi waiting to take you to the Institute. He's already made arrangements with his wife Lenore to have their chef deliver meals for you and Kate at the Institute to allow you gals to work 'round the clock on the bacteria."

Claire barely listened to him. She felt like she was coming out of a stupor. Are we in Delaware already? she wondered.

Claire wanted to call Ahmed Azzizi to see how Eric had fared, but she wasn't ready for Ahmed's tirade if he had figured out what she had done. Instead, she debarked for a few minutes and accompanied Lance into the general's private lounge to freshen up, grab some of his infamously huge chocolate chunk cookies, a quart of cold milk, and a newspaper. Arms loaded with her sugar fix, she turned toward Lance to kiss him goodbye. A long, slow hug later, he kissed her and said, "Remember what I told you about getting your sleep. A person can only go for so long on four hours a night."

Claire knew he was right; she had not been sleeping well under normal conditions. Every day, she felt her restlessness rising. She sensed things were just going to get worse.

"Lance, I love you." Claire smiled at Lance.

Turning her eyes downward, she whispered, "Thank you for taking care of me these last two years. I know it hasn't been easy living with me some days, but I just don't know what to do about these racing thoughts I have. They seem to appear out of nowhere. I don't even understand what triggers them.

"Intellectually, I know I shouldn't respond to them the way I do. Emotionally, I feel drained and scared because I can't control my reactions to them anymore. It's like they belong to someone else, and I am watching that person from a distance."

She knew she had changed considerably since they first met

in Paris, but she was still at a loss to explain the reason for the change.  Lance had remained kind, tender even, throughout her angry flares, her anxiety attacks, and her paranoia, and she loved him even more than before.

As Lance hugged her, Claire felt her restlessness growing again.  She felt agitated, confined.  Suddenly, she broke away from him and quickly walked out onto the tarmac toward her flight.

Claire barely heard Lance call out after her, "I love you, Claire."

In a split second, which seemed like an eternity to her, Claire grimaced and silently mumbled back to Lance, "Oh, drop dead."

# Chapter 36



*Flight to Giverny, France*

**Claire buckled her seat belt** and then devoured the four huge chocolate chunk cookies and carton of milk she had taken from the Captain's Lounge. Ready for take-off, she thought. Her flight phobia succumbed to her body's flood of sugar-induced serotonin. Her racing thoughts scattered and then coalesced several times until they settled on Kate.

Claire had to admit that Kate's announcement had surprised her. When Kate said that she would be out of the lab for two weeks while she, Jake, Crystal, Julie, and Luke went on their long dreamed of Italian vacation, ending on Lido Beach in Venice, Kate had caught Claire off guard.

As a highly trained, brilliant marine biologist, Claire figured that Kate would still be safe. She really didn't want anything to happen to her best, and truly, only friend and her family. Kate and Jake had always welcomed her and Lance into their home and their family life. Jake and Lance had served together in the Navy Seals, and later both had accepted appointed professorships in their respective fields of biochemical engineering and chemistry at Atlantic University in Dover, Delaware, teaching and researching at its branch campuses in Paris, Venice, Barcelona, Warsaw, and Sydney.

It was at Kate's wedding that Claire had met Lance, who served as Jake's best man while Claire acted as Kate's maid of honor.

After the wedding reception, Claire and Lance helped the bride and groom load four suitcases into Jake's small Porsche convertible and waved good-bye as their friends headed to the Poconos for their honeymoon.

Claire and Lance then turned to each other and exchanged a high five hand clap as they laughed about what Kate and Jake would be doing that night when they opened up their four suitcases of white rice.

That night, Lance invited Claire out for dinner and drinks. Over a slow, two hour candlelight dinner, they discovered that they had more in common with each other than they did with anyone else. They started an enduring friendship that gradually turned into as close of a relationship as Claire had ever formed, except perhaps for the sisterly feelings she had developed for Kate. She and Kate had been college roommates and later graduate research assistants in the same medical program. Caught for a moment in a nostalgic daze, Claire quickly brought herself back to reality.

Claire questioned herself again: Should I have warned Kate away from visiting Lido Beach just two weeks after my experiment there? Probably not. After all, what were the odds of Kate or her family becoming infected two weeks later?

Her phenomenal mind answered her question incorrectly within a few seconds: 900 to 1. Her mental analysis had failed to account for one important variable.

Now she found herself on a flight to Paris in a race against time to help Kate find the cure for Julie's life-threatening waterborne infection.

Claire pondered how altering one gene in *Bacillus nocturne* had made it become so virulent. She had not meant it to be a killer, just an intestinal bug that would make multiple trips to the toilet enough to make any citizen reevaluate their drinking, bathing, or vacation water usage. Her purpose had been to educate the public about the effect sewage seepage had on their drinking water. Her goal was an activist citizenry that supported efforts to clean-up the waterways.

In a moment of utter clarity, Claire realized the gene she had altered to increase the bacterium's assault on the human digestive system also changed its preferred source of food. She had created a bacterium that thrived on the human waste contaminating its natural ecosystem.

The wetlands surrounding the bay and waterways were the perfect feeding ground for the hybrid bacterium. Claire's altered version of *Bacillus nocturne* was feeding on, and developing a preference for, the protein in human wastes. It was cleaning the coastal waterways of sewage now, but it was also replicating exponentially and soon would be colonizing any source of human protein it could find.

Claire felt chilled. As her heart struggled with the implications of her genetic tampering, her mind searched for a plan to escape the consequences of her actions.

Within a few minutes, Claire had thought of her justification for genetic tampering. She even liked the spin. The more she thought about it, the more excited she became. When *nocturne* completes its task of cleaning human wastes from the water, I'll simply genetically alter it again and reprogram it to clean up the previous strain.

Claire's manic thinking skipped right over the need to stop the current bacteria from continuing to replicate and killing people.

Simple, she thought. I'll bring some good out of this situation. I'll leak to the media that a renowned scientist's sister is infected with a super-annulated, deadly waterborne bacteria whose rate of replication is 10,000 times the normal rate of bacterial replication when it is exposed to human protein. I'll call a news conference, as a researcher at the Institute, present my research on bacteria-laden sewage tainting our water supplies, and pitch the need for clean efficient water treatment facilities throughout the world.

Claire felt the addictive rush of adrenaline that always accompanied her greatest ideas. What an opportunity to speak to the world to explain my ideas! she thought.

In her deluded mind, Claire thought she would be a hero. After the news conference, she would go to Kate's lab to solve the mystery of the devastating illness and produce its cure. Claire was convinced that she would become famous in a matter of hours because only she knew how to stop the bacteria from replicating.

"I'll figure out the cure, later," she huffed.

The image of her standing in front of myriads of microphones on the imposing steps of the Institute for Public Policy and Safety, announcing the cure that she had discovered, filled Claire's mind with eager anticipation.

A Nobel, at least, Claire thought.

Feeling her adrenaline rise another notch, Claire revved her thoughts to the next level. She loved the protective rush of adrenaline that she could call up at anytime. Her mind was in control. She could think a scene, create the scene, react to the scene, and resolve the scene, enjoying the rising surges of adrenaline at each level. She loved her work. How many people could actually say they loved their work? she wondered.

"Excuse me, Madame," Captain Gladys Rainier's voice over the airplane's intercom interrupted Claire's revelry. "We will be touching down at Giverny Field in eight minutes."

The announcement invaded Claire's thoughts, and she slowly

came to an awareness of her surroundings. Adrenaline still rampantly coursing through her body, supercharged by her feelings of eminence, and suddenly constrained in a narrow, low ceilinged jet, Claire reacted badly to the interruption of her planned rise to power.

In a burst of adrenaline, Claire shouted, "Shut up! Just shut up! You and your red frizzy hair and doting eyes . . . just keep away from Lance and me!"

Unbuckling her seatbelt, Claire sprung from her seat, the adrenaline propelling her through the aisle and to the cabin's locked door.

"You hear me in there?" Claire yelled as she pounded her clenched fists against the door.

"I saw the way you looked at him when we were boarding in Florida. I know your kind. Always after someone else's man, just for the rush of competition. Then you dump him and head after the next guy. All of you pretty faces are out to steal our men away."

Captain Gladys Rainer had been a pilot for thirteen years and had never had a passenger react negatively toward her. Now she could feel Claire swaying the lightweight titanium jet as she began throwing her body weight against the cabin door. Claire was trying to gain entrance to the cockpit.

Horrified, Gladys radioed the tower at Giverny Field.

"Giverny Approach, Hatbourne 6872 November Mike, 30 miles West, in bound with information Bravo. Be advised we have a passenger disturbance – working on it."

"72 November Mike, do you wish to declare an emergency?"

"72 November Mike, negative. Will advise if necessary. Request personnel assistance upon landing."

Gladys planned to stay safely behind the titanium cockpit door that could withstand over 1500 pounds of force until emergency personnel boarded the plane.

Remembering that Lance had warned her about Claire's fear of flying and anxiety attacks, Gladys steadied the plane and voice-dialed Lance's cell phone number.

"Lance, this is Captain Rainier. We have a problem."

"What's wrong, Captain?"

"Claire is reacting to an unknown stimulus and is attempting to break into the cockpit. We are both safe. The door is infallible, but the lightweight shell of this plane causes its computer system to overcompensate for any cargo imbalances or movements in the body of the plane. I am concerned about landing safely with Claire producing so much motion in the passenger cabin."

"Can you voice patch me over to the cabin's speaker system?"

"No, but I am putting you on speaker phone now. Claire should be able to hear your voice through the cockpit door. Perhaps that will calm her."

"Captain Rainier, thank you for calling," Lance swallowed hard. "I'm sorry. I didn't think Claire would have another panic attack like she did on her last transoceanic flight. I'll try to talk her down."

Within a few seconds, Claire heard Lance's soothing voice emanating from the cockpit.

"It's all right, Claire," Lance said. "Calm down. Everything will be all right. Just a few more minutes and the plane will land. Giverny is four minutes away. Everything will work out just fine. Sit down now and calm yourself. Just think about how close we are. . . . Just close your eyes and . . ."

"What are you talking about?" Claire snapped back. "How close you are? I thought you stayed back in New Jersey, and here you've been in the cockpit with her all this time!"

As her fury increased, Claire heard the little voices in her head repeat in singsong, "Kill her. Kill her. Kill her."

# Chapter 37



*Base 3*
*Dover, Delaware, U.S.A.*

**Lance strode into the Base 3 Conference Room,** confident that Captain Gladys Ranier had relayed his soothing message to his wife on the airplane. Claire will be fine, he thought. She'll adjust. Once again, he held her to the same high expectations he had for himself, as he did everyone.

Lance's team sat in the chairs surrounding the twelve foot long, polished mahogany table centered in the Base 3 Conference Room. Standing around the table were three of the best minds in politics, science and medicine that the United States had to offer:

Senator Pete Montelli, Chairperson of the Senate Bay Ecology Study Commission and leading Congressional proponent of the Safe Waterways Bill, had arrived a few minutes before Lance. Montelli taught a political science course at Atlantic

University as a guest professor every summer, and whenever the Senate would break session, Montelli presided over seminars for graduate students at the Institute. His expertise on the United States' political system remained legendary, and the Agency relied upon him to introduce legislation that furthered their means of operation. Montelli acted as the Agency's chief liaison with the President of the United States.

Dr. Paul Henderson, professor of biochemical analysis, Johns Hopkins University, authored seventeen books on the biochemical processes affecting the world's populated coastal areas. Shortly after accepting his position at the Johns Hopkins University Medical School, the Agency recruited him to serve as medical consultant, and often field doctor, to their teams traveling to remote coastal areas.

Dr. Benjamin LaTiera, a famous biological engineer, entrepreneur, and philanthropist, CEO of Genezene, an adult stem cell storage bank available for physicians and researchers worldwide, advised the Agency on all matters genetic. His past works defined the technological advances that made headlines in the media today. LaTiera served as a research professor within the Institute, advised the Agency, and donated millions of dollars to the Institute as one of its leading philanthropists.

The entire team worked in one way or another for the Institute and the Agency. They belonged to a covert civilian team who exercised great political, financial, and medical power. Their Agency work remained housed, subsumed, one might say, within the auspices of the internationally recognized Institute for Public Policy and Safety.

Lance was one of five co-captains in the Agency, team leaders whose responsibility it was to call together their teams for quick action responses. Lance had been working covertly for seven years, having made the decision to join the elite group after his longtime friend Jake Connors had convinced him it would be the ethically correct thing to do.

"Welcome," Lance began. "Today we face a potentially devastating environmental disaster that has erupted on the seacoasts of multiple European countries and along the United States' Atlantic Seaboard. I extend our deepest condolences to Paul Henderson whose lovely wife Linda was one of the bacteria's first victims. Paul, thank you for coming to our meeting today."

Exhausted, Paul Henderson slightly nodded his head, acknowledging Lance's condolences.

"I'm here to find Linda's killer and stop the massive murders that will result from this bacterium's release." He shook as he spoke, still reeling from the bacteria that caused Linda's death, yet determined to contribute to the bacteria's demise.

"At present, we believe the illnesses are caused by *Bacillus nocturne*, normally non-lethal estuarine bacteria that has mutated, or has been genetically altered, to replicate at an alarming speed when it comes in contact with human protein."

"Our team will disperse to the infection zones listed on these flight plans," he said, holding a stack of papers in his hand, "to gather samples, data, and begin analyses immediately.

"Biochemical dressing, everyone," Lance continued, "until we know what we're dealing with. We'll travel under the guise of CDC researchers and travel in vehicles marked with their codes.

"We have access to everything our CDC colleagues are investigating, and we will be sharing data and analyses with them round-the-clock. We need to know the mode of infection, the vectors, the strains, and the mutation or alteration, all within the next six hours. Lives are depending on us. Make every minute work."

The room emptied simultaneously with his last words as every person rushed to the locker room to suit up for their flights to their assigned sites.

Lance's team's first stop would be just ten minutes away by helicopter. His old friend and President of Peridore University personally requested that the Institute send Lance over to investigate another death on his campus.

Lance's interest in this case was personal, too. Ariel Tenmenson had worked with Claire in the Peridore University laboratories.

# Chapter 38



*Backwater Analysis Deck, Peridore University*
*Beachwood Beach West, New Jersey, U.S.A.*

**Ariel Tenmenson's body** puzzled even the best of doctors.

Today in addition to her variegated skin tones and white birthmark-streaked black hair, the Ocean Shores County Medical Examiner puzzled over her bloodstained body tangled among the heavy rope moorings on the Peridore University's Water Analysis Deck. Dr. Maureen Smith, her postdoctoral colleague, who had called 911, had discovered her body three hours earlier. The EMTs notified the Medical Examiner as soon as they realized they had found what appeared to be another bacterial death.

"Dr. Smith, I'm sorry for your loss," offered Dr. Ed Nguyen, Ocean Shores Medical Examiner, to a young, slightly overweight professor, dressed in field work khaki pants and shirt, the color of her hair. "Would you please answer a few questions to help us with our investigation of your colleague's death?"

"Yes. Anything to stop this madness. This is the fifth pathogenic death on campus this semester. Everyone is alarmed."

Nguyen politely hid his smile caused by her misuse of medical terminology. Less than 1% of the population has Ph.D. degrees, and most of them are experts in their field of study; perhaps it's just their love of research, but they often take a stab at speaking authoritatively on subjects outside their area of expertise, as well. Ha! He thought, just like I'm doing now, playing psychoanalyst. The little subtleties of life rarely escaped him. That was what made him a good medical examiner.

"Dr. Smith," Nguyen continued, "when you discovered Dr. Tenmenson, did you come in contact with her body or belongings in any way?"

"Yes, of course," Smith said. "I started CPR as soon as I saw she wasn't breathing. She was my friend. What else was I supposed to do? I continued giving her CPR until I could no longer catch my breath. I collapsed alongside her and cried and cried. Finally, a marina worker arrived, and she called for an ambulance. I'm going to be sick next, right?"

"No, probably not. If the pathogen that caused her death was still active at the time you gave her artificial respiration, you would be dead by now. It's a quick acting bacterium, and that means once it has used up its victim's resources, it must move to a new source of protein quickly or die out. But do stay out of the water until we discover the vector. So far, all of the deaths have been water-related."

Nguyen heard Smith's audible sigh. She had been waiting for her own death sentence. "Can you tell me about Dr. Tenmenson's closest colleagues? Her family? Her research?"

A little more relaxed now, Smith filled in some details. "Ariel had no family, except for a brother in Alaska whom she rarely saw. She considered her colleagues to be her family. Ariel became an excellent teacher because she truly cared about each of her students. She would work with them on the campus green for hours after classes, holding small group sessions on the lawn under the trees. She didn't stop the sessions, even right up to Finals Week, unless she knew all her students understood the coursework. Not too many faculty members are as diligent as she was. Obviously, her students loved her and would follow her anywhere. That is why the Dean became somewhat concerned when she started recruiting students to join an organization called Project Awareness. Dean Rackley felt Ariel exerted too much pressure on her students to join; just by the fact that she helped them so much, he thought the students might feel obligated to join her activist group. He finally told her to take the group off campus, and to stop recruiting undergrads."

"Were other faculty members involved in Project Awareness?"

"Yes. One of our colleagues, Dr. Claire Favore Martin, a marine biologist, started the group. Her doctoral mentor, Dr.

Ahmed Azzizi was a co-founder. He seemed to have a strong influence over her. She often said that Ahmed was the father figure she never had. Oh, and then there were several grad students involved—Sawyer Thompson, Eric Langdon. I think they're all dead now," Smith said, with little affect left in her voice.

"Yes, Dr. Smith, you are correct, except for Dr. Claire Martin. Right now, she appears to be the sole survivor of Project Awareness. Thank you for your cooperation. If you think of anything else, please call my cell phone number on my card," Nguyen said, pausing to carefully hand her his Medical Examiner's business card.

Smith accepted his card respectfully, holding it with two hands. "Thank you," she said as she read his title and cell phone number. Head down with shoulders slumped, Smith walked back to her faculty office.

Nguyen began directing his medical team to suit up in biological containment suits, in case he was wrong about the pathogen responsible for Ariel's death. As he decided the safest method to investigate the scene for the cause of death, Lance's Agency team arrived dressed in full bacteria containment suits, ready to respond immediately to the incident.

"Dr. Nguyen, Lance Martin. President David Cohen of Peridore University asked the Institute to send me out to investigate this death." Lance handed Nguyen the paperwork authorizing his team's investigation.

"Cohen wants to prevent a media circus since this is the fifth death in the College of Marine Sciences this semester. The Institute agreed to take responsibility for the investigation, with your approval, sir. We think our CDC trained team is better prepared to isolate the cause of death and protect against its possible spread."

One look at the hazmat equipment Lance's team had at their disposal and Nguyen graciously and gratefully stepped down from the investigation.

"Lance, I've collected samples and run data from the other four deaths," Nguyen said as he handed Lance reports on the other deaths. "Sawyer Thompson, Eric Langdon, Ahmed Azzizi, Ruthee Sathianathan, and now Ariel Tenmenson all died within 24 hours of each other. Everyone except Ms. Sathianathan was a member of Project Awareness.

"When we discovered Ms. Sathianathan's body, she was in the water near the university pier. From her bloody handprints on the boathouse floorboards, it appears she tripped over Dr. Azzizi's body, fell onto the bloody floor, and then tried to wash her hands and face off in the bay. At first, we thought she died from exposure to a pathogen in Azzizi's blood, but then we tested the water near the university pier several times. Each reading came back higher than the previous one. The bacteria count in the water is unprecedented and rising more rapidly than we thought possible."

# Chapter 39

*Backwater Analysis Deck, Peridore University*
*Beachwood Beach West, New Jersey, U.S.A.*

**"Where's Claire?"** Medical Examiner Nguyen asked Lance.

"On board a flight to the Institute's Paris lab."

"What's her recent connection to Project Awareness?"

"I'm not sure. She talks about the group a lot. I haven't paid much attention to what she was saying. She's always talking about water quality safety," Lance offered as a way of explaining his indifference to Claire's affiliations.

"Do you at least know if she's alive right now?" Nguyen's disgust with inattentive spouses set him off. "You do know, don't you, that 80% of crimes could be averted if family members would just pay attention to each other's behaviors?"

Nguyen's tirade accomplished what he had set out to do. Lance was chastised. He felt guilty. He knew he should have spent more time in conversation with Claire.

"Conversation with an obsessive person isn't easy." Lance could see his excuses weren't cutting it with Nguyen.

"Lance, you're a friend and an excellent investigator. But I have to tell you, you fall short on empathy."

Lance didn't like what he had just heard, but he knew Nguyen was right.

Claire, oh, Claire, Lance thought. Are you all right? How are you involved in this? You are the only survivor of Project Awareness. What happened?

The Medical Examiner's staff politely stepped back from the scene of Ariel Tenmenson's death, acceding to the Institute's request to conduct the investigation. Lance knew the two organizations were on good terms and had long-standing reciprocal agreements for teams sharing documentation. It would be only a matter of time before his questions would be answered.

Today, the Medical Examiner's team was visually relieved to pass on this case. Word among the medical community about the bacterial deaths was not encouraging, and each hour, the situation became more menacing.

"Let the Institute hazmat pros take over from here, guys," the Medical Examiner's team leader announced. "Pack it up, wash down, and motor on to the next case."

"Thanks, Lance, for taking over. We'll await your report on Dr. Tenmenson," Nguyen said. "In the meantime, we'll begin our investigation of Claire's activities during the last two weeks."

Lance gave Nguyen another stiff nod as his facemask and aerator pushed against his tensed neck muscles. Then he turned toward his team and motioned for them to proceed.

# Chapter 40

*Giverny Airfield*
*Giverny, France*

**It was the longest four minutes** that Pilot Gladys Rainier had ever experienced. After patching Lance Martin's phone call over the plane's intercom to calm Claire's panic attack, she had expected his soothing voice to reassure Claire that the flight would land without incident. Instead, it had set off a firestorm of anger.

Claire had forcefully thrown her entire body weight against the cabin door, yelling something about Lance being inside the pilot's cabin throughout the transatlantic flight. Gladys had fought to steady the small jet through four minutes of turmoil. Despite her years of experience, she had assumed that she would be unable to maintain control upon landing.

"Giverny Tower, Hatbourne 6872 November Mike, over the canal and the freeway, declaring an emergency. Be advised we have a passenger disturbance on board."

"72 November Mike, understand you are declaring an emergency. How many souls on board?"

Then just as suddenly as it had begun, Claire's hammering on the door stopped as they began their rapid descent. The sleek jet could make a calculated descent three times steeper than the average passenger jet.

"Giverny Tower, 72 November Mike, negative. Will advise if necessary. Request personnel board on landing."

That sudden angle must have jerked Claire off-balance, and she has fallen back into one of the rows of seats, Gladys thought.

Regardless of the reason for the lull in the passenger cabin activity, Gladys was thankful for the opportunity to land the plane safely.

Claire, on the other hand, had not fallen away from the door. Her athletic ability had immediately rebalanced her weight as she felt the floor fall out beneath her. Holding onto a seat back, she lowered herself into the second row of seats. By habit, she reached over to pick up the ends of her seatbelt and clicked them together.

When Claire looked up, she could not remember why she had moved herself up to the second row of seats in the small plane, but she was grateful that her flight was nearly at an end.

To mesmerize herself for the always-frightening landing, Claire envisioned herself standing alone in front of a microphone at a national press conference announcing her development of the new *Bacillus nocturne*.

**When four armed police officers boarded the aircraft** upon landing, looking for a wildly disruptive passenger, Claire demurely smiled up at them as she slowly unfastened her seatbelt. She was calm, again, but she still verged on insanity.

How nice of them to provide me with a security escort, she thought, as she quietly swept past the security guards' surprised faces while she politely exited the plane.

Safely inside the private terminal, she sent simultaneous text messages to all the international media correspondents stored in her Blackberry, announcing a press conference on the steps of the Institute for Public Policy and Safety by a well-known marine biologist addressing the disastrous waterborne plague about to decimate the world's coastal populations.

# Chapter 41


*The Institute of Public Policy and Safety*
*Paris, France*

**As soon as he saw her,** he knew he had found his way in. He could spot a delusional person three blocks away. It showed in the way they carried themselves. Self-important, staring past the peons of the world. Long strides, a heavy weight in every step. Never speaking, but conversing all the same. Ever aware, but paranoia free. Confident in their purpose.

Jon Smith had served as a psychiatrist in the military for twenty years until they had dishonorably discharged him.

All right, he remembered. I deserved it. No qualms about that. But if only they had waited six months more before investigating, I would've been home free. An army pension, an honorable discharge. Think about the scams I could've cooked up. Or better, a run for office. A mayor of some little town in the West. Work my way up to governor, representative, or senator. Yeah, but I blew it.

Jon Smith didn't deserve to serve as a psychiatrist for twenty years. A scam artist, pure and simple, he falsified his deceased brother's medical degrees and assumed his identity, volunteering for service overseas at a time when medical help was short and infantry were needed. When his ruse caught up with him, he walked away. AWOL. Never to be seen again. But he had learned a lot about the mentally ill. And he thought he may have done some good along the way.

Now he watched Claire. He saw the reporters asking her questions and noticed how she relished the attention. He figured out his way into the Institute. His boss Eduardo Manuela would be pleased with him.

# Chapter 42

*The Institute of Public Policy and Safety*
*Paris, France*

**"Ladies and Gentlemen,"** Claire began, speaking into her own handheld portable microphone on the white marble steps of the front entrance to the Institute for Public Policy and Safety. A crowd of tourists had assembled when they noticed a few reporters with video crews milling around. They were expecting an announcement from the Institute on the continuing health crises at the European beach resorts. Instead, they would be the first witnesses of Claire's increasing delusions of grandeur.

"I am Dr. Claire Favore Martin, a leading scientist at the Institute for Public Policy and Safety. On behalf of the Institute, I have an announcement to make. There is a deadly waterborne bacterium that is sweeping through the waterways of Europe and the Mid-Atlantic United States."

"What bacterium? What is she talking about?" voices from

passersby started asking each other. Then a few impatient reporters pushed through the crowd, addressing Claire.

"Dr. Martin, what is causing the epidemic along the coasts?" asked a writer from a Paris magazine. "Have any terrorist groups claimed credit for the epidemic?"

"Dr. Martin, is there a cure for the disease?" a reporter from Rome asked.

"Dr. Martin, when and where did the bacteria first strike the beach resorts?" inquired a British representative. "Do you know why the beach resorts have been targeted?"

Now Claire had the crowd's full attention.

Bolstered by the attention she received from the reporters, Claire continued her prepared speech, "This epidemic will awaken you to the severe consequences awaiting if you continue to allow the destruction of the ecological systems upon which your lives depend."

"Today," Claire pointed at the crowd, "you stand on the threshold of a continuum whose balance can swing in either direction. You can resolve to do the right thing or to do nothing at all. The easy way out is the route most humans have taken for thousands of years.

"Think of it . . . of the billions of people who have lived on this earth, less than one thousandth of a half percent of them made even a minor contribution to the world's progress. Where were the other 99.995% of the billions upon billions of people? Why didn't they act to propel civilization forward at the exhilarating rate possible if all had contributed?

"What have you accomplished in your lifetime to improve our ecology, our sociology, our anthropology, our pedagogy, our philosophy, our economy, our theology, our physiology . . ."

Impatient with Claire's rhetoric, news reporter Ashly Fromm shouted, "Dr. Favore, who is responsible for the release of this bacterium? How dangerous is it?"

Claire barely heard the shouted questions. Her thoughts were traveling through her mind at lightning speed; she felt exhilarated, like her heart was on fire. I'll tell them, she thought. They'll listen to my words, and they will act to save the waterways.

"Throughout Europe and the United States," Claire continued her speech, "you will see the self-righteous fall because they failed to contribute to the safety of the world. Today, you will witness on worldwide media what happens when individuals fail to act on behalf of humanity. Today, you will know how threatened we are when we refuse to stand up to protect our environmental resources, our air, our land, our water. Today you will understand how it feels to be an endangered species.

"Today . . . an extremely virulent version of *Bacillus nocturne*, a normally harmless brackish water bacterium, engineered to replicate exponentially upon contact with the protein in human sewage, will illustrate to the world the danger of pollutants in the world's drinking water supply. Everywhere you see frothy bacteria mixed with sea foam, remember that it fed on your sewage, in your waterways, on its journey to the ocean. And you . . . you never even cared enough to demand the purity of your own waterways."

"Claire? What are you doing?" Kate's weary voice intoned from the half-opened portico door of the Institute's main entrance.

Claire recognized the exhaustion in her friend's face as a combination of jetlag and emotional turmoil.

"Kate." Claire turned toward her, and then quickly back to her audience. "Dr. Katherine Connors, one of my colleagues who helps me at the Institute. We have serious work to do to stop the bacteria and critically little time to expend outside the lab. Please contact your local governments and health organizations and demand action to protect our waterways and drinking water."

Turning towards Kate, Claire wrapped her arm around her longtime friend's fallen shoulders and walked her quickly back through the portico doors, pushing aside many of the reporters who had hurried toward Kate to ask her questions.

One well-dressed reporter wearing a casual, navy French-cut suit and cream silk polo shirt, followed them in by extending his iPhone through the door, taking close-up pictures of Claire, not Kate. He fired intelligent questions at Claire in a polite, somewhat staid manner. Gentlemanly in behavior, he caught the heavy Institute door just before it slammed shut against her heels.

He let her step aside, but continued asking questions about the epidemic as if he had a biological or chemical background. Every question framed in flattery, he held Claire's attention just long enough to step entirely inside the door. He let the door close quickly behind him, satisfied when he heard the automatic dead bolt slide heavily into place.

Kate drifted down the hall, steadying herself by running her right hand along the polished marble chair rail lining the wall. It had been an exhausting day, and all she wanted to do was get back to her work in the laboratory.

"Claire, will you see that reporter out, please? No unauthorized people through that door, ever." Without looking back, she trusted her friend to escort the gentleman back out. She was just too exhausted to recognize that Claire willingly accepted his flattery and wanted to hear more.

"I'm sorry, Dr. Martin. I seem to have locked myself inside. I had so many important questions to ask you that I didn't pay attention to the automatic locking mechanism. Your premise about global warming affecting the bays, as well as the oceans, intrigued me. I wanted to hear more from an expert in the field."

"Yes. That is exactly what I was talking about. An aroused citizenry willing to take chances, act in new ways, and assert themselves to save the waterways. I'm glad you understood my message."

"Our paper is producing a double page spread this weekend

investigating the role climate change is playing on the proliferation of bacteria in European estuaries. I'd like you to be the lead scientist I interview for the article. May I come back tomorrow morning at 8:00 a.m. to talk with you?"

"Of course. Thank you for the opportunity to present my platform on water pollution. We will be working overnight in the labs, trying to identify the bacterium that is causing the epidemic. Tomorrow morning will be fine."

"Thank you, Dr. Martin. I interviewed the Director of the Institute last week." He scanned the antique bronze plaque on the wall behind her until he found the director's name and office number.

"I promised Dr. Stafford that I'd drop off a copy of the article I wrote before publishing it tomorrow. Professional courtesy. I'll make any changes he recommends. He's expecting me. I know my way to his office. I'm sure he'll see me out after we meet."

Jon Smith walked briskly away from her towards Marlin's office, calling out over his shoulder as he turned the corner, "Tomorrow at eight, then."

Claire checked to see if the heavy steel entrance door had clicked to its locked position. "Nice gentleman. He chose me over the Director for the two page spread," she said to the voices in her mind applauding her breakthrough with the media.

Feeling important for the first time in her life, she felt happy as she walked down the long, white marble hallway to Kate's laboratory.

# Chapter 43



*The Institute of Public Policy and Safety*
*Paris, France*

**"Why were you giving a speech** on the Institute's steps?" Kate's tired voice accosted Claire as she entered the laboratory.

"You're not even employed by the Institute. You've filled in for me while I traveled to conferences, but I've been subcontracting your help through grant money."

With no answer forthcoming, Kate was ready to ask again, but she didn't have to. Dr. Marlin Stafford, Director of the Institute and the Agency, walked quickly into the laboratory and joined them. His striking platinum hair, charcoal Armani suits with gem tone silk shirts and patterned ties commanded attention whenever he entered a room.

"Kate," Marlin said as he hugged her, "I'm so sorry to hear about Julie. I've called in all the lab personnel to assist you in whatever way they can. The Board and I are at your disposal,

Kate. I've set up a meeting in my office in forty-five minutes."

"Thank you, Marlin." Kate's downcast eyes spoke for her.

"Kate, no one is blaming you for this outbreak. You are our most precise, meticulous researcher. We all know you follow our security protocol to the letter. *Nocturne* is out there. So let us determine the best way to get it under control. Now, what was that fuss outside the building?"

"I arrived an hour ago, later than expected," Kate replied. "We'll have to talk about my trip from the airport to the Institute later." I can't discuss the kidnapping in front of Claire, she thought.

"I think I fell asleep on the cot in the back room. Then I heard the noise outside, too. What was going on, Claire?"

Facing the Director's stern gray eyes, Claire's voice wavered, "When I arrived, I really only saw some reporters in front of the Institute's portico. They asked me questions about the outbreak. They were really looking for you, Kate. I told them you were busy in the lab. I really didn't want them to bother you. I didn't want to let anyone know about our real work here today."

The longer Claire talked, the more fluent she became. "Did I do anything wrong? I'm sorry if I did."

"No, of course not." Kate felt sorry for her friend who always seemed apologetic about her work and less self-assured than most university researchers. "Thank you for deflecting the reporters."

Claire nodded to Kate, instead of responding orally. "Let's

get to work now," she added while setting her L.L.Bean travel bag on the floor next to the lab's door.

Kate nodded, too tired to analyze Claire's explanation. She turned toward Marlin and offered a weak smile. "See you in half an hour."

Together, Kate and Claire poured over Kate's experiment notes as she explained what happened to Julie on Lido Beach.

**As Kate described the circumstances** leading up to Julie's collapse on the beach, Claire listened intently for the details of Julie's reaction to the bacteria. She did not offer any possible explanations. Nor did she have any feelings of remorse that Julie had contracted *nocturne*.

*Nocturne* wasn't meant to be so virulent, Claire thought. When I took it to the International Chemical Conference in Venice, I remember carrying a dropper full of the altered bacteria down to the water's edge on Lido Beach outside my hotel. Just three milliliters. Why did it become so virile?

Oostende Beach in Belgium, she recalled, was only a three milliliters drop off, also. Yet, thirteen people died there.

Then on the Rivera, hundreds died. Was that because I released it at night? I programmed it to replicate faster during darkness.

Claire's research-oriented mind began generating a list of other variables that could have further altered the strength or replication rate of the bacteria: profusion of human waste matter in the waterways; competitive bacteria annihilated from antibiotics in wastewater; resistance developed from exposure to antibiotics; a more favorable environment due to the warming of the oceans' waters; overcast daytime skies . . . Claire's list continued. She was problem solving, enjoying the challenge that she had created. Never once did she give a thought to Julie's life hanging in the balance, nor the thousands of other lives affected by her reckless recombinant gene splicing.

# Chapter 44

*The Institute of Public Policy and Safety*
*Paris, France*

**Within a short time the entire laboratory staff** assembled in Marlin's huge office overlooking the well-lit grounds of the Institute. Phosphorus light filtered through the windows, which were covered by sheer silk drapes hanging from the ten-foot high ceiling.

The calmness of the atmosphere belied the restlessness gripping the entire staff. They had been watching the unfolding of a waterborne plague on their computer screens in the moments before assembling in Marlin's office.

Kate was still unaware of the impact the bacteria was having on the coastal plains in Europe and the United States, but the exchange of conversation among the Institute Directors and lab technicians quickly brought her up to the present conditions. Thousands were infected; 10% of them were dying.  Mostly young adults.

Like Julie, Kate thought.

"My friends," Marlin intoned like a eulogist at a funeral, "today we are challenged to identify the strain of *nocturne* causing this outbreak, discover how to stop it, and create a vaccine and treatment protocol for those already infected. What do we know about this outbreak?"

Among academics, all expert opinions are offered for solving a problem, followed by discussions until the colleagues come to consensus on what needs to be done.

Kate was the first to speak.

"I've seen this bacterium in action," she began. "It is brutal. Julie . . ." Kate's voice broke as she fought to hold back her tears. "Julie's eyes were affected first. I saw her rubbing them from a distance. Then she convulsed and collapsed onto the sand. Blood poured from her eyes. Her husband picked her up, and we all ran for the water taxi. We took her to the nearest emergency room, and Dr. Walter Ambruster met us there. He is using an experimental medical treatment that he developed during the last *nocturne* outbreak. More cases were coming in when Jake and I left the hospital. It is definitely *Bacillus nocturne,* but Ambruster believes it is a variant, faster acting strain than the one that caused the outbreak in the States five years ago."

An audible gasp arose among the technicians. "Are you infected?" several technicians asked at the same time.

"No, no one else from our group was infected. Only Julie."

Marlin continued, "You all know that Kate has been working on finding a cure for *nocturne*. That it has struck again is unnerving enough, but the bacterium is back in a more dangerous form, and we still do not know how to stop it. The death toll is rising on two continents.

"Kate," Marlin asked, "what could account for the virility of the bacterium? It is a normally harmless, backwater bacterium that feeds on algae and animal detritus. Has it mutated? Or worse, do you think it could have been tampered with, or altered genetically, again?"

"Again?"

Marlin's statement caught many by surprise. Their questions continued for several minutes.

"When was it altered before?"

"And why?"

Finally, Marlin interrupted the questioning. "Kate, will you update everyone on the Institute's earlier research program named Nocturne?"

"The Institute initiated a program that came to be known as Nocturne in the late 90's," Kate said. "Our researchers altered the replication rate of *Bacillus nocturne* to determine if it could be used to contaminate a terrorist country's water supply. The plan was to smuggle a single drop of *nocturne* into a country's main water source, and let it replicate during the night. Then the President of the United States would issue an ultimatum to the rogue state to cease and desist all support for terrorist cells within their country. They would have twelve hours to negotiate a non-proliferation treaty with the United States, or their water supply would be rendered useless."

"Once the country agreed to abandon its support for terrorist cells," Marlin continued, "we would provide the means to kill the bacteria. However, we discovered through our research tests that the bacteria replicated more rapidly in the environment than it did in the lab. We were unable to develop an antibiotic that could counter its rapid growth rate. We had to shut the program down. It was too dangerous. We knew that if a large number of *Bacilli nocturne* escaped into a nearby water system, we could not guarantee that we would be able to stop its spread."

"Since then," Kate said, "I've been working on a vaccine and testing antibacterial agents against its structure, but without any positive results. And now, we are dealing with a new strain of *nocturne*."

"I suspect," Marlin continued, "that someone or some group has chosen to release the bacteria after altering its genetic structure a second time."

"My thoughts, as well," Kate commented. "When Maria was infected, there was time for her to be taken to the hospital and to begin several days of treatment. From what I've seen today, that window of opportunity for treatment has been eradicated. Something drastic has changed. *Nocturne* is now a quick, efficient killer. We have to find out what is different about this strain of *nocturne* compared to the strain that infected Maria DeSanchez."

"Kate," Marlin's tone became a command, "tell our staff what you now know to be the source of Maria's illness." Marlin nodded at Kate, giving her permission to speak about previously classified Institute information.

Kate looked down at the floor, feeling the same shame she had felt in 2003 rise up again, flushing her face. She began speaking in a halting, soft voice.

"In 2003, after Maria's death, Ambruster invited me to join the Institute as a medical researcher. After working for one year as the sole researcher still studying *nocturne* to find its cure, Marlin called me into his office. The Institute's Board of Directors had given him permission to disclose to me previously classified information about Maria's case. They realized that I needed to know the truth about how Maria had become infected, in order to continue my research for a cure.

"I am ashamed to say," Kate faltered, "that the Institute's Biochemical Weapons Team tested *nocturne* at a Rehoboth Bay marina. They designed a study to test the effects of one milliliter of *nocturne* added to a remote section of the bay. They wanted to determine the replication rate of the bacteria in a natural setting, and see how much of the bay it would colonize before dying out. But the bacteria did not react to the natural setting as the team had predicted.

"The bacteria flourished in the nutrient rich bay, and at the concentrated point of insertion, the bacteria multiplied to deadly strength. The insertion point was the pier where Maria DeSanchez worked. In other words, the Institute was responsible for Maria's infection and the subsequent illnesses and deaths of others. Throughout that summer as the bacteria moved around the bay searching for new food sources, it became endemic.

"Even worse, that summer an international summer camp for teenagers was held at Rehoboth Beach. All of the campers fell ill, but thankfully recovered. What's shocking now is that most of the persons in their twenties who have died from this recent outbreak had attended that camp. My sister Julie was one of the campers."

"The Agency has been following those young people ever since the first outbreak to see how they fared," Marlin continued. "We thought they had produced antibodies to the bacteria and would be immune from future attacks. We were wrong. And we do not know why."

A stunned silence pervaded the room. Then everyone started talking at once. As the anxiety quelled, Marlin called the meeting back to order.

"We should never have tested the bacteria on the public. It was a time of great stress in our country, and we were trying to produce a non-lethal biological weapon that could be used against terrorist camps. We abandoned the program as soon as we recognized that the bacteria's virility had been enhanced by an unknown variable or variables in the environment."

"Why didn't this hit the news?" Jason York, a biologist, sounded incredulous. "I remember reading about a bacterial outbreak on the East Coast, but no one mentioned the Institute."

Carey Worthington, a ten year veteran of the Institute, added, "I was in the States that year, and people seemed to attribute the illness to water pollution. A water testing agency, responsible for testing the beach waters daily, didn't pick up on the problem or announce it to the public until three days later. So the public thought it must not have been an unusual condition."

"But what about the teenagers at the rally? Didn't their parents want answers?" Dale Thomas, seated at a computer bank along the wall, twisted uncomfortably around in his seat to face the others.

"Most of the students were from other countries, and the students went home reporting symptoms that were similar to a food borne illness. By the time they arrived home, many parents thought it was an isolated case of illness at the camp," Kate said.

"What about the deaths?" York wanted more answers.

"Those were more difficult to handle," Marlin said. "So, we created a cover-up for the deaths."

Silence. No one stirred. All eyes glared at Marlin.

"We floated news broadcasts," Marlin continued, unaffected by the judgmental stares, "using the high rate of polluted waste water in the estuary as our front. We flooded the media with research articles on the effect of sewage seepage and prescription drugs in our waterways and drinking water supplies.

"We offered huge grants for studying water quality management practices. Most people blamed the illnesses and deaths on poor water quality. Our cover-up succeeded."

Marlin paused. "I am ashamed, too. Had we exercised responsible management and good scientific method and principles, that crisis and the deaths that followed would never have occurred.

"Since then, the Institute has implemented tight control policies for all of our research teams. Our Board of Directors, as you see every day, now work side-by-side on teams with our researchers to promote knowledge through sound scientific practice and oversight. Not only in Paris, but at our labs in Warsaw and Sydney, too.

"Each Institute Director has created his or her own laboratory team," Marlin continued, "staffed by the most prominent university researchers in their respective fields of study. Each university researcher may select two promising postdoctoral researchers, and a bevy of lab technicians from a pool of scientists supplied by the intelligence agencies of their respective countries.

"Together, the women and men of the Institute have solved

or neutralized numerous threats to the environment and society, threats never noted in the media. Not because of our duplicity, but thanks to the quiet efforts of the Institute. The Directors knew that their work could never completely repay their debt to society for their lack of oversight on *nocturne*. Nor could they escape the tragic irony of the Institute's name: The Institute for Public Policy and Safety."

Marlin pulled the researchers' attention back to the present. "You have the right to be angry with the Institute for its ethical and moral failings. I am not proud of it either, but we have a more important task at hand. The lives of millions are in our hands. We must identify this strain of *nocturne*. We must find its cure. To do so, we will work around the clock until we have results. Please have a member from each research team report to Kate's lab to pick up a copy of her latest research on *nocturne*. Our Agency field teams are visiting outbreak sites now, collecting specimens that will be flown to our lab within a few hours. Please keep an open information protocol in effect throughout the night and coming days."

Kate turned toward Marlin as the Institute research teams talked nervously as they left for their laboratories.

"Claire's working with me in the lab. Is that all right? She's my friend, as well as a trusted colleague. She's substituted for me before in the lab when I've been called out for Agency duty. I asked her to join me to help find a cure for *nocturne*. If you would rather keep all the work in-house, I'll understand, but I could use her expertise."

Marlin nodded, fully understanding Kate's need for a close colleague at her side.  He, and many others at the Institute, battled similar personal problems over the years as their family members and friends had been affected one way or another by the work the group did.

"Kate, I have spoken with Claire a number of times before. If you've kept her clearances up to date, she can work with you. Keep her close by your side on this one, though."

"I will," she looked around the room to see if it had cleared and then moved in closer to him. "I need to talk with you about my trip over here from Giverny.  Can I come to your office after I get all the staffers set up with my *nocturne* research?"

"Kate, yes, of course.  You were in the hot seat at the meeting disclosing what the Biochemical Weapons Team had done. Thank you for taking the lead on that."

"It was a disgrace! I'm still bitter that you were involved in the cover-up." Kate barely contained her anger.

"Kate, if we had not done so, D.C. would have shut us down. It was better to pay our penance through positive environmental accomplishments than to have our scientists languish in jail." He was not backing down.

"Kate, I think it is time for you to learn who chaired that team and made the decision to implement the experiment. We can talk about it later in my office."

She hurried back to her lab, knowing the Directors' staffers would be lining up outside her door asking for her research data. Entering the lab, she signaled for Claire to join her at the lab's computer stack.

"Get ready for an onslaught! Researchers from the Directors' labs will be asking for data from my files. They are to have unlimited access. While you disseminate the data, I'll work on our analyses one more time. Maybe something will jump out at me."

Kate entered her office, closing the door behind her, and sat down in front of her lab computer. I'm tired, Kate thought as she refocused her eyes on the statistical program's screen.

What if we can't find the cure?

# Chapter 45

*The Institute of Public Policy and Safety*
*Paris, France*

**Kate liked the feel of the cold white marble** under her bare feet. Whenever she worked late at the Institute, she kicked off her heels and padded around the hallways like she did in her own kitchen. In the winter when the floors were icy cold, she would pull on a pair of angora socks, and enjoy a slide or two around the corners. Tonight she walked deliberately to the Director's office but did not enter.

Italy, she thought. If we hadn't gone to Italy, I wouldn't be standing here now, and Julie would still be well. But then again, she's in her twenties. Where would she be safe if this bacterium gets out of control? Or is it out of our control already?

She felt the garrote slip over her head before she realized he was behind her. On reflex, her muscle memory kicked in.

She tucked her chin and grabbed his thumbs, snapping them backwards as she bent forward and somersaulted him across her back onto the floor.

The loud clatter of his cell phone flying against the wall echoed down the corridor. Footsteps came running, and Marlin cleared the corner in time to see the man push past a disheveled Kate, and race out the front door.

"Security!" Two armed guards ran from opposite ends of the building and followed his pointed finger to the door.

"Navy suit, cream silk shirt," he yelled as they ran outside in pursuit of the attacker.

"Kate, are you injured?" He put an arm around her shoulder and helped her regain her balance.

"No, I'm all right. Hoarse. A little shaken, but all right. That's twice in one day."

"Twice? We need to talk! Who was this guy? Did you know him?"

"This is what I wanted to tell you about after the meeting." She exhaled in a long gasp and sucked air back in almost simultaneously.

He helped her into his office and guided her to a brown leather chair.

"It looks like Eduardo Manuela placed a hit on me after his kidnapping effort failed."

"You were kidnapped? Why didn't you tell me sooner? Manuela?"

"I called it in to the Agency from a pay phone before boarding the Metro. I thought the message would get to you. Besides, we haven't had time to talk alone."

"What happened?"

"I escaped from a car that I thought Ambruster had hired to drive me to the Institute."

"Ambruster?"

"Yes. At the hospital in Venice. He arranged for a car to pick me up at the airport. I got off the plane and the driver was waiting for me. I got in and he drove away from the airport. When I saw him head the wrong way, I questioned his direction. He made it perfectly clear that I was going where he wanted me to go, not where I wanted to go. Manuela wanted to see me, he said. I thought Manuela was dead."

"How did you escape?"

"I had to improvise. All I had was my beach gear, and a discharged cell phone."

He frowned.

"So I kicked the back of his seat until he pulled over and came to the back door. When he started to open it, I kicked it out at him, and applied a liberal dose of sunscreen and pepper spray to his eyes. Then I knocked him out and ran to the Metro."

"Good work."

"I don't know where this thug made me. I don't remember seeing him at all." She rubbed the reddening abrasion around her neck. "No, wait. I think he was a reporter. Posing as a reporter when Claire and I came in. I told her to see him out. I thought she did."

"Oversee Claire more cautiously. She obviously does not know all of our security rules, yet. Is she in your lab?"

"Yes."

He dialed the guard room. "Security, check Dr. Connors' lab to see if everyone is all right."

He waited a few seconds, and then he heard the shouts.

"Fire in Dr. Connors' lab!"

They raced to her lab and saw smoke billowing out the door. A multitude of extremely loud alarms clanged on, one after the other, as the alerts spread throughout the old building. Security guards grabbed extinguishers and laid down a foam path into the lab. Fire burned through the ceiling to floor draperies, and the painted woodwork around the old windows ignited, spreading flames across the room. The guards sprayed the bottoms of the draperies and pulled them off their rods. As soon as they fell to the floor, the foam extinguished their flames.

Then they sprayed the adjoining walls and ceiling, keeping the flames isolated to the wall of windows.

"Everyone! Out of the room. Go to the entrance door!"

Marlin ordered the frightened lab attendants to the doorway, cautioning them, "Stay inside the exit to the front portico." He wasn't sure it was safer outside if the killer was still out there.

Kate ran back to her office and found Claire already there, filling up Xerox boxes with computer hardware, software and disks. Together they carted four boxes out into the hall before Marlin ordered them to stop.

"Claire, how did the fire start?" He intended to ask every lab worker the same question, out of range of each other's comments.

"We were all working at our stations when something metallic sounding rolled from the hallway across the room. It stopped when it hit the base of the draperies and made a loud, crackling noise—like an explosion. Then flames shot up the drapes and the room started filling with smoke."

All the stories panned out. The guards' quick reactions had saved the situation from becoming much worse.

The fire department arrived in minutes and foamed the wood windows instead of using water to save as much technology as possible. Within an hour, they were gone and maintenance started to clean up the mess.

In the hall, Marlin listened to the report of the two guards who had pursued Kate's attacker.

"We followed him through the park for two blocks. Then he veered left and headed for an alley. He slipped into a back door of a home. By the time we got there, he was gone. Out the front door or the balcony on the side of the house. No one lived there. He may have rented it for an overnight stay, or as a good way to elude anyone chasing him. We alerted the police and they are sending a team here to check for fingerprints and interview you and Dr. Connors."

"Charlie, Scott, thanks. Stay with us because I'm sure they'll have questions for you, too."

"Kate, ask Claire to join us when the police come. She may have a better description since she had a discussion with him."

Marlin turned toward the crowd of scientists who had gathered in the outer hall, "Everything is all right now. Please return to your labs and continue your research on *nocturne*. I'll let you know if the police need to interview any of you. And, if you saw anything suspicious this evening, please let me know. Everyone, Code Black. Double down your security protocols and do not take any chances. We still have a killer on the lose."

# Chapter 46



*Base 3*
*Dover, Delaware, U.S.A.*

**Sweat poured down Lance's temples.** His hands shook as he read each page of his team's report. Every section fed into the recurring nightmare that had haunted him for the last six months. His instinct had been trying to warn him.

The pathology reports confirmed that the agent that killed Ariel Tenmenson was a highly virulent and aggressive strain of *Bacillus nocturne*. The bacteria had literally eaten away the corneal cells of Ariel's eyes and multiplied as it fed on her body's tissues. The young woman's entire body had become an extremely dangerous vector of infection, but with no other sources to infect, the bacteria had died out shortly after her death.

Multiple body system failures caused her death. While *Bacillus nocturne's* method of entering the human body had remained the same, its course had altered dramatically. The bacteria made contact with the conjunctivas or surfaces of Ariel's eyes, followed by massive infections of the corneas, irises, lenses, and optic nerves, resulting in painful blinding, and then the bacteria entered the bloodstream, attacking one or more body systems. This assault was inconsistent with the characteristics of Maria DeSanchez's case, five years earlier.

Maria's bacterial infection had spread slowly to her respiratory system over a period of several days. Lance was one of the few Institute agents who knew that Maria had survived in the hospital for five days before the Institute quietly declared her dead, and then moved her to their private treatment center in Sydney, Australia. Ariel's death, however, occurred within hours of exposure to the bacteria.

Recreating Ariel's scene of death, Lance's forensic team members agreed that Ariel's mud-covered hands, face, hair, and orange tee shirt indicated she had been working at some marsh water sampling stations. The team believed Ariel had dropped her field monitoring equipment into the marsh, splattering muddy water on her face, and then when she returned to the pier, she tried to rinse the mud out of her hair and off her face at the pier's outdoor shower.

The stinging pain in Ariel's eyes must have been immediate for they traced her erratic footprints back to the water testing deck where she then collapsed. Three or four minutes, they postulated. The corneal bleeding, shortness of breath, and immediate body systems failures indicated that she had died rapidly.

Testing for water quality at sites within the surrounding enclosed back bay, the research team discovered that the highest concentration of the bacteria occurred where the Tom's River emptied into the bay. Additionally, this was also the area of the bay most affected by backwash from the now unprotected, denuded salt marshes whose grasses were destroyed by tidal surges during the last major Northeaster. The water quality report from the mouth of the river showed extremely high levels of human sewage that would start to flow into the bay and then be backwashed by the incoming tide, nearly doubling the already high bacteria count in the bay.

Lance also recognized the chemical components mixed with the sewage: prescription antibiotics in sufficient quantities to render native bacteria lifeless and invading bacteria opportunistically viable.

How do I know this?

Lance furrowed his brow. He bit the inside of his right cheek to hold back his tears.

It was Claire's latest area of research.

Claire and Ariel were developing the set point at which the current lines of antibiotics would no longer be able to kill twenty of the most infectious waterborne bacteria.

What had Claire said about Ariel's water sampling? Lance tried hard to remember. Ariel was sampling the marsh behind the university to see if the recent flood of beach closings due to bacterial contamination had originated in the back bays where the salt marshes were failing to filter the water.

Thinking aloud now, as he often did when he was alone, Lance slowly put together several important facts about Claire.

"Claire believed that more researchers needed to study the effect that storm surges had on the water quality in the bays. Claire adamantly professed that rising sea levels produced more serious surges causing greater levels of bacteria in the inland bays. That was one of the reasons she was so interested in Ariel's research.

"Claire always recorded television news conferences on water quality, and she actually attended water quality conferences throughout all of Europe where researchers continually pressed for national funding to study the effect that sea level rise had on water quality.

"Recently, Claire had been to Oostende, Belgium, for the North Sea Consortium on Land/Water Surface Quality. Then she and Ahmed, her graduate school mentor, had attended conferences in Barcelona and Monte Carlo, presenting her doctoral research on beach water quality. Then she had traveled to Venice to receive the European Union's prestigious Balmaro Award for Promising Young Researchers."

Lance choked out the last, raspy words, not wanting to believe the path his analytical mind had taken. His nightmare had happened.

The nightmare's cloaked figure standing on a rocky cliff above the ocean, dispersing a liquid from a green vial while hundreds of bodies began washing ashore . . . was Claire.

As he grabbed his secure telephone line, sweat careened off his palms. He punched in Jake's code and immediately began speaking, knowing from experience that Jake kept his phone so close that he could pick up a call on the first ring.

"Jake, I need to know where Kate is." Lance barely controlled the panic in his voice.

"Lance, she's in Paris with Claire. What's wrong?"

"Tell her to get away from Claire immediately. Tell her to go home, no, better, to Marlin's office and wait for him there, alone, locked doors. Then call me right back." Lance exhaled loudly. He couldn't breathe. His adrenaline had skyrocketed.

**Jake called Kate's secure number.**

"Jake," Kate sounded exhausted. "Any word yet from Ambruster about Julie?"

"Kate, this is a Code Red. Go to Marlin's office alone. Repeat, alone. Lock yourself in until Marlin arrives. Do not take Claire with you." Jake knew Kate had to be versed in agency codes, and he counted on her quick reaction.

"Done," was all she said before she clicked off her phone.

Speed dialing back to Lance, Jake asked, "What happened?"

In an unusual rapid-fire recapitulation of the facts of Ariel's case and Claire's recent travels, Lance laid every piece of information on the line for Jake.

Lance paused. Then he asked the question that could change his life.

"How do you interpret these facts, Jake?"

"Why? Why would Claire do that?"

Lance's heart fell.

"What's her motivation?" Jake asked, as certain as Lance that there was a strong likelihood that Claire was involved in the biological disaster.

For his friend's sake, though, Jake hoped that they had both come to a faulty conclusion.

"Jake," Lance said, "I have to step out of this. I defer to you and Kate. Tell me what you want me to do."

Hearing the anguish in his friend's voice hurled Jake through a firestorm of emotions, ending with contempt for Claire and her dangerous disregard for her husband, friends, and the world.

# Chapter 47



*Base 10*
*Barcelona, Spain*

**Shaken by Lance's revelation** that Claire was responsible for *nocturne's* return, yet cognizant of his best friend's sorrow, Jake dialed Lance back and quickly decided what he needed to do.

"Lance, set John Bryden as your replacement as team leader, and have him continue analyses at the sites where the bacteria have been released."

"Then, Lance," Jake continued, "contact the United States' biochemical branch of the Institute, and the Agency's liaisons at the CDC and WHO. Relay all the information you know about Claire's research to them. Get them started on developing an antidote, or anything that will slow or halt the bacteria's replication.  After that's done, take the security jet to Paris. As you fly, run analyses of the predicted spread of the bacteria, based on its present locations, tidal changes, temperature changes, and every other variable you can think of. Let me know in mid-flight what the likely scenario will be if we do not stop its spread in the next 24 hours."

Jake knew that keeping Lance's mind busy on the flight out to Paris was the kindest thing he could do for his friend. He also needed Lance's technical expertise on this case. The urgency of the cause, coupled with the immediate need for analyses of the environmental and human impact of the disaster, would keep Lance's mind occupied by numbers instead of emotions.

"Lance, meet me at the Paris Institute in four hours," Jake continued. "And, Lance, I know you want to talk to Claire, but you know your voice will give away that we suspect her involvement. So, please, buddy, do Claire a big favor, and don't contact her. We don't want her to run. Lance, I feel for you, but please don't contact her. We will meet her at the Institute in four hours. Can you do this, Lance?"

"Yes," was all that Lance replied before he signed off, but Jake knew his friend was good for his word, even under these terrible circumstances.

Jake's throat constricted as he thought about Julie's life and the lives of thousands hanging in the balance. Had it not been for them, Jake would have been extremely concerned for Claire's welfare. Knowing Claire may have killed Kate's sister, though, and thousands more, motivated him to stop her by any means possible. Claire was no longer a family friend; she was the enemy.

# Chapter 48

*Base 10*
*Barcelona, Spain*

**No one commented as Jake's team members** reassembled themselves around the large mahogany conference table. The members' solemnity struck Jake's heart. It could only mean that their research analyses concurred with Lance's report.

"Lance Martin's team members have produced evidence implicating Claire Martin, Lance's wife, as the person responsible for releasing a genetically altered version of *Bacillus nocturne*." When no one from his team expressed surprise at his statement, he knew they had come to the same conclusion.

"Lance has stepped down as team leader, and he'll continue to work on data analyses until we are able to confirm his team's conclusions. Please present your entire report, despite this present disclosure. What has your team discovered?"

Dr. Jia Zhang, President of the Biochemistry Institute in

Beijing and the Institute's Asian Liaison, spoke first. "Fifteen university labs near the infection zones have completed analyses of the bacterium, and twelve of the labs report that the bacterium is *Bacillus nocturne*, the same bacteria that surfaced five years ago, with one exception. Someone has tampered with the bacterium's rate of replication.

"You remember," Jia continued, "that *nocturne* was being studied by the Institute as a biochemical defense against terrorist enclaves located along backwater bays on foreign soils or along United States' coastal areas likely to harbor terrorist infiltrators.

"At the time, the agent had been released in small doses where coastal sewage seepage was a problem. The thinking was that the sewage bacteria would mask *nocturne* during chemical analyses, and we could surreptitiously study *nocturne's* effect on the water supply.

"The program was called off after one of our agents, Maria DeSanchez, contracted a virulent form of the bacterium, and nearly died.

"We covered up her illness at a local hospital by having Ambruster fake her death and scurry her off to our private medical facilities in Sydney, Australia. Maria survived after three weeks of touch-and-go anti-bacterial trials, but the Institute's Nocturne Program did not survive. The Board unanimously agreed that it was too dangerous a toxin to let loose in any water supply."

Jia's report stunned Jake, but it also gave him hope for Julie. He, like many others, had thought Maria DeSanchez had died after contracting *nocturne* five years ago. Jake hated the Agency's internal secrecy. Its needless compartmentalization had caused extensive anxiety for everyone who knew Maria. But if she hadn't died . . . that meant Julie might survive. He wondered if Kate knew that Maria had survived.

"All work to alter *nocturne's* genetics ended soon afterwards," Jia continued, "and even researchers in the midst of studying *nocturne* had their funds pulled and their protocols called in.

"We housed the bacterium at only one site, the Institute laboratory in Paris, and only one researcher, Dr. Katherine Connors, had access to study it.

"Kate's laboratory staff have all passed our intensive scrutiny of their security clearances, except for one scientist, Dr. Claire Favore Martin, whom Kate occasionally asked to supervise *nocturne* experiments while she attended conferences or visited other campuses."

"Claire's psychological background checks are out of date," Dr. Joshua Padrone, leading epidemiologist of the Americas and the North, Central, and South American Liaison for the Institute stated.

"Claire's last psychological study occurred three years ago. The laboratory supervisors require researchers to send their staff's study updates to my department every year. That would be Kate, in this case."

Jake sat perfectly still. No one could read the emotions he blocked from his face.

Kate, Kate, he anguished. Why didn't you follow protocol? You could've prevented this whole disaster from happening if you had just followed Institute policy. Claire would never have passed a current psychological exam. She could've gotten help at the beginning of her psychoses, and with no access to *nocturne*, she wouldn't have been able to unleash this disaster on the world.

"Our chief suspect," said Dr. Sayed Yasmir, Biological Warfare Specialist from the University of the Baltics, and the Institute's European and African Liaison, "is Claire Favore Martin because she had access to the Institute's altered form of *Bacillus nocturne*, the biological and chemical knowledge to genetically alter the bacterium, and the opportunity to take the modified version out of the laboratory.

"We have also tracked her visits to Rehoboth Beach, Lewes, and Cape Henlopen State Park in Delaware, Oostende, Belgium, Venice, Italy, Monte Carlo, Monaco, and Barcelona, Spain. We believe she specifically targeted these beach areas because of their brackish estuaries loaded with decaying sea life and wastewater.

"The present analyses," Jia continued, "show that the bacterium has been genetically altered along the 16SrRNA allele, creating a necrophagous bacterium that subsists by eating dead tissue or carrion.

"We believe Claire had a motive for altering the bacterium, based on her last research publication, which ended with these comments: "These data confirm the author's belief that bacteria, natural life forms responsible for clearing detritus from the environment, can also be altered to attack and clear manmade pollutants from the nation's waterways."

"However," Zhang added, "we are unsure why Claire would release the altered bacterium on a wide-scale when she had to be cognizant of its potential to destroy living cells as well."

"My point exactly," Dr. Joshua Padrone interjected. "Claire may have been trying to make an ecological statement. She chose very popular beaches with high populations of summer tourists. If her aim were to alert the world to the hazards of water pollution, think of the media coverage she would get when her altered bacteria began infecting vacationers. I think she wanted to make people ill to draw attention to the need for cleaner waterways."

"I think she didn't predict," Sayed added, "nor understand the bacterium's potential for replicating out of control. She misjudged its virility. *Nocturne* has evolved from devouring decaying plant and animal life to feeding on human tissue.

"Five of Claire's colleagues, members of her ecology activist group Project Awareness, have died of the bacteria in the last forty-eight hours. Regardless of Claire's original motivation, once she altered the bacterium's genes that controlled replication, she regressed from eco-activist to eco-terrorist."

"Yes, I agree," Jia continued, "By selecting replication genes, her intent became criminal. Any trained biologist understands what an overflow of one species will do in a static environment.

"Moreover, as far as the mode of transmission, she had to know that any soft tissue available to the bacteria would be rapidly colonized, and the bacteria would spread throughout the blood system and vital organs.

"Most victims contacted the bacterial colonies in common beach sea foam splashed in their eyes or entering cuts or abrasions on their legs or arms."

"That explains how Julie contracted it, " Jake said.

"We know that sea foam," Jia said, "is composed of bacteria-laden decaying bodies of one-celled sea amoebae and particles of decaying plants whose decomposition mixed with salt water causes a foaming effect.

"Colonies of Claire's altered form of *Bacillus nocturne* floating down streams and through the estuaries appear to seek out the decaying bodies of the amoebae in the sea foam and colonize on their remains.

"The altered bacterium originally subsisted on decaying matter, such as plants or one-celled animals, but with the abundance of sewage seeping into our waterways, the bacteria adapted to being able to live on the sewage waste nutrients as well.

"This created large, reproducing colonies which developed resistance to the many antibiotics and other prescriptions flushed into our sewage systems by unwary consumers."

"In other words," Jake said, "*nocturne* turned deadly because of Claire's genetic tampering plus environmental pollutants?"

"Our data support that conclusion," Jia replied. "But the third variable involved with its toxicity is the warmer temperatures in the bays. This has been one of the hottest months on record, not only in the United States, but throughout Europe, as well. Call it global warming or climate change or whatever else you want to label it. It is responsible for the warming of the oceans and bays. Warmer water promotes greater bacteria growth."

"We have a fourth variable. The victims are in their twenties."

"Why is it killing people in their twenties?" Jake wanted to know. "Julie is twenty-three."

"We're analyzing that data, now. We're looking for common characteristics among those who have died. We're checking their medical histories, past illnesses, where they've travelled, the condition of their immune systems, everything. Everything our labs can think of, we're throwing into the computers. We don't know the answer."

Sayed continued with the analysis. "Our current analysis of the likely spread of this disease is based upon local reports where it has been discovered. Our data show that every time the bacteria strike, 10 percent of the ground zero population in their twenties die within 72 hours.

"Those predictions," Sayed paused, "cover the direct contacts with the bacteria in coastal settings.

"The data relating to the bacteria entering the drinking water supply indicate an initial death rate of 28 percent within 72 hours of exposure.

"The fault with our analysis," Sayed continued, "lies with the fact that there may be many more unreported cases occurring in remote beach towns which do not normally report data to the CDC or the Disease Control Center at WHO."

Dr. Joshua Padrone added, "We face the problem of demographics that Yasmir discussed, and it becomes compounded by the fact that even if a successful treatment antibiotic is developed, how do we transport it to every country affected as soon as possible . . . when we may not even know the breadth of the infectious areas?"

Jake rose from his seat at the table for emphasis as he said, "Ladies and Gentlemen. We face a far more dire problem than getting antibiotics to those who have fallen ill. We not only have failed to determine how to stop the bacteria from replicating and spreading, we have also yet to discover how to kill the *Bacillus nocturne* colonies currently infesting our waterways."

"Let us hope that Claire Martin will cooperate," Jia said. "If she doesn't, we'll be back to square one in our efforts to stop *nocturne*. We can't afford to lose that much time in our race to stop it from spreading."

# Chapter 49


*Late Night City News Studio*
*New York City, New York, U.S.A.*

**"We interrupt this program** to bring you an urgent news broadcast."

Carla Blanchard, Late Night City News correspondent, had never been this frightened. The news flashes kept coming in, and while the enormity of the danger from the first report caught her off guard, the following reports only served to frighten her more.

Staring into camera #4, ready to begin her statement, Carla felt her composure slipping away.

"Good morning," Carla began. "This is a highest priority announcement. The medical staff at the Henlopen Medical Center in Lewes, Delaware, reported 40 deaths among summer campers at the Cape Henlopen State Park, which is two miles east of Lewes and three miles north of Rehoboth Beach,

Delaware.

"The cause of death," Carla continued, trying to keep her voice calm, "appears to be a fast acting, waterborne bacterial infection. Police have cordoned off the areas of suspected contamination, and no entrance or exit from the area is likely until the Centers for Disease Control examine the patients and the environment.

"Veteran reporter Charlise David is on the scene outside the isolation area," Carla reported. "Charlise, have you interviewed any of the residents in the area?"

"Yes, Carla," Charlise replied, her graying hair damp with perspiration hung over her wide-eyed stare. "I spoke with several mothers who were at the Super Fresh grocery store buying their weekly groceries when they heard that there was a medical emergency at Henlopen Medical Center. All of them tried to re-enter the Lewes area to return to their families, but the Delaware State Police denied them entrance.

"One mother told me," Charlise continued, "she had left her two toddlers with a babysitter in the Cape Shores Development which adjoins Cape Henlopen State Park, and she was denied admittance to that area. She is still waiting for her babysitter to return her phone calls."

Charlise's anxiety visibly increased as she said, "Local radio stations first reported that a disaster had struck Cape Henlopen State Park, and later reports started clarifying that Lewes Emergency Medical Technicians found a large number of young adults dead or dying on the Atlantic Ocean beach at the Cape. Residents near the Cape reported hearing so many sirens early this morning that they were certain it was another hurricane evacuation drill.

"But, I want to tell you, Carla," Charlise continued, "a real, self-imposed evacuation is in progress. All three lanes of traffic on Route 1 North out of Rehoboth Beach are bumper-to-bumper as residents and vacationers are making a mad scramble to get out of town. I spoke with drivers as they stopped to fill their cars' gas tanks at the Wawa gas station north of Midway, and there was a sense of urgency bordering on panic. No one knows exactly what the problem is, but the number of deaths has certainly closed down this summer vacation area."

Charlise paused to listen to her earpiece, and then quickly announced, "Our latest report states a police barricade has gone up five miles north of here—blocking all traffic trying to leave the area. . . ."

"Charlise, can you get out?" Panic for her friend overwhelmed Carla's normal professional demeanor.

"I, I don't think so. Not now," she said, watching the traffic on Route 1 North coming to a halt.

"Charlise, please be careful," Carla said. Her distress for Charlise's predicament became more apparent as she read the next update handed to her by the news channel's aide.

"A second report of deaths along the Atlantic Coast occurred twenty minutes ago when Rehoboth Beach lifeguards discovered twelve nighttime anglers near death at a designated surf fishing area just south of the Cape Henlopen State Park."

Carla continued, "Early morning strollers on the Rehoboth Beach Boardwalk discovered five bodies of young adults in several locations under the boardwalk at the high tide line."

Carla had never reported this many deaths before. Her voice developed a sharp edge as she said, "Morning patrol officers at the Delaware Seashore State Park beach near the old Life Guard Station reported that a beer party and a campfire on the beach last night ended in the deaths of seven young men between the ages of 21 and 25 and five hospitalizations in critical condition. Shortly after assisting the ambulance crew who arrived in hazmat suits, two of the Park Rangers fell ill, and the EMTs transported them to the hospital."

Pausing to slow her breathing, Carla flipped her notes to the third page.

Her sigh was audible as she read, "Campers in the Indian River Inlet Campground awoke early this morning when five beachcombers returned to the campground carrying two 24 year old men whom they had found incoherent, huddled on the beach. Parts of the men's story emerged in bits and pieces until one woman on the scene, Denise Cordova, recognized the name of the small watercraft Isadora about which the men had been mumbling.

"Mrs. Cordova's three college age sons," Carla continued, "took the Isadora out of her moorings near the Indian River

Bay Inlet to leave for a pre-dawn fishing trip in the Atlantic Ocean to trawl for fish. The two men had helped the Cordovas launch the Isadora in the early morning mist by swimming out to the boat with the Cordovas. The 24 year olds said that they saw an unusual amount of sea foam around the boat's moorings, and it appeared to be washing up onto the shores surrounding the Indian River Bay Inlet as well.

The Cordovas, Juan, Tomas, and Carlos, have not returned from their fishing trip and are now considered missing persons. EMTs rushed the two youths to a nearby medical clinic when the young men's eyes began to hemorrhage."

Carla was shaking. Could anyone tell? she wondered. She thought she had her emotions contained and was covering them well, but she was scared.

Carla took a deep breath and continued, "Now we are getting reports of similar incidences along coastal shores in Belgium, Monaco, the French Riviera, Italy, Spain, and other European coastal towns. All reports have recently updated their death tolls and the number of beach areas quarantined. A list of those beaches is on the screen. We will continue to update as these data come in."

The camera turned from Carla to a large computer screen that pinpointed all the beaches reporting deaths. While the station's medical adviser discussed safety precautions, Carla slipped out of her chair and slowly walked past Charlie Gibson, the weather anchor, to the backstage alley exit.

"I need some air, Charlie," she said. Charlie Gibson nodded, acknowledging his nervousness, too.

Outside, Carla lit her nemesis cigarette, and tapped Ahmed Azzizi's speed dial code on her cell phone. Ahmed conducts research in the Delaware Bay estuary, she worried. Oh, Ahmed, please be safe. She would have to cancel their date for today, but more importantly, she needed to hear his reassuring voice.

After four rings, a stranger's voice answered, "Hello. This is Chief of Police Warren Adams. May I ask who's calling this number?"

"Carla Blanchard," she quickly replied. "What's wrong? Why didn't Ahmed answer this phone call?"

"Ms. Blanchard, I recognize your name from Dr. Azzizi's Favorites phone numbers," Adams continued after a brief pause, "and I am sorry to tell you that Dr. Azzizi has died. Ms. Blanchard, I am very sorry for your loss."

Carla's heart faltered.

# Chapter 50

*Centers for Disease Control*
*Washington, D.C., U.S.A.*

**"Ladies and Gentlemen,"** Dr. Anne Bodziach, the staid and still beautiful Director of the Centers for Disease Control, addressed her staff. "We are in a Red Alert."

Fifty-eight people attended her emergency meeting. All of them had watched newscasts the night before about deaths along the Mid-Atlantic Seaboard.

"Yesterday, doctors at the Henlopen Medical Center in Lewes, Delaware," the Director said, "reported 40 deaths at nearby Cape Henlopen State Park, followed by continuing reports of similar coastal deaths in Rehoboth Beach, Delaware, and all coastal beaches south. As of 5:00 this morning, the death toll on the Mid-Atlantic Seaboard exceeded 800 documented cases of this disease. Extrapolating for the number of cases that have gone unreported or still may be undiscovered, and the rate of infection since yesterday's outbreak at Cape Henlopen, the CDC Board of Directors and I believe we may have a death toll exceeding 3000 by noon today."

The Director observed her staff as she spoke. They are hardly breathing, she thought. This is the first true emergency for many of the younger staff. How will they fare?

"Throughout the night," Dr. Bodziach continued, "our staff members have been working in on-site portable laboratories at each of the quarantined sites where coastal deaths have occurred.

"The strain is a common, normally passive bacterium that has lived in the backwaters of the coastal bays and in the estuaries, which feed into the oceans. Our labs report that something or someone has altered the genetic make-up of the bacteria, increasing its virulence.

"It appears to increase in virility each day that it replicates. Its hosts are varied and some hosts appear to affect its rate of replication more than other hosts do. Until we can identify the strain, we will be unable to determine why some infected members of the population have survived the infection while others have not. It is predominantly affecting persons in their twenties.

"Once we have determined which factors are causing the anomalies, then we will be able to incorporate them in our treatment protocol.

"Hopefully, that will lead us to a better treatment methodology and then a vaccine. We continue to work around the clock to identify all of the effects of various antibiotics and combinations of antibiotics on this new bacterial strain.

"Public Relations is rushing to put out a health alert addressing the safety concerns of the general population," she added, "and specifically those living along the coastal zones of the United States. We have also alerted the World Health Organization, and they will be sending out similar alerts around the world."

Anne Bodziach took a deep breath and in a slow, flat, emotionless voice said, "It is critical that we stop the spread of this disease. Over 85% of the world's population inhabits the coastal range, which extends 60 miles inland and includes most rivers that feed into the estuaries and back bays. If this bacteria's march is not stopped, all river dependent drinking water sources will be contaminated."

Anne quickly walked away from the podium, surrounded by colleagues asking questions or firing data reports at each other.

The audience whom she had been addressing, however, sat still. Everyone in the room knew what the Director's speech meant.

The Centers for Disease Control had repeatedly used this worst-case scenario for emergency response practice drills. The steps that each one of them had to take were clear, yet no one in the audience moved.

The predictions of ecological disaster caused by climate

change and the concomitant spread of virulent diseases had turned out to be true.

It had happened, the audience immediately understood, twenty-five years sooner than had been predicted.

# Chapter 51

*Remote Beaches*
*U.S.A. and Europe*

**While *nocturne* continued its heavy toll** at the resort beaches in Europe and the Mid-Atlantic United States, environmental circumstances contributed to the bacteria spreading further and faster to other locations than had first been anticipated.

Ocean fishing boats, returning to harbor late in the evening, lowered their nets in the waters of the coastal bays, letting the force of the water wash away the ocean debris picked up off shore. But the nets also snagged the masses of bacteria floating in swaths of sea foam bubbling into the bays. At their next port, the trawlers' sailors pulled those nets up onto the piers for repairs, dripping colonies of *nocturne* around the docks' pilings.

During the day, typical vacation water sports contributed to the bacteria's spread. Sport fishers and water skiers splashed infected water into their boats and over their equipment, and vacationers riding the waves on inflated donuts and elliptical tubes dragged sea foam and bacterial colonies along with them to new beaches.

*Bacillus nocturne* flourished; it had everything it needed to spread: transportation, environments conducive to its needs, and unsuspecting food sources.

As the major news networks told the individual stories of dozens of people affected by *Bacillus nocturne* in the United States and Europe, other stories unfolded that would never be told. *Nocturne's* appearances on remote beaches equally affected tourists and locals, but often their deaths went undiscovered, and therefore, unreported.

*Nocturne* continued attacking all age groups and most of its victims who had not been exposed to it previously survived. However, anyone with a weakened immune system, substandard health care, or multiple exposures could fall seriously ill and not survive *nocturne's* onslaught.

**Eight-year-old Salaamed Perez and her neighborhood** Verando Street Gang ran their bicycles up to the breakwater where they always played Marco Polo. All of the children had recovered from mild cases of *nocturne* five years ago when Salaamed's oldest brother had returned home with it from a retreat in the United States. Slipping into the warm waters of the Gulf of Valencia along the Spanish Costa del Azahar, the children bobbed under the waves after calling "Marco," to one of their playmates, whose shouts of "Polo," echoed in response. The goal was to tap as many playmates on the head as possible before they responded to the call.

Pedro Sanchez was the "Marco" caller this morning, but after quickly tapping three of his friends on the head, the cries of "Polo" stopped. The other children were nowhere in sight. Panicking, the four remaining children hurried ashore, rubbing their stinging eyes as they fell breathlessly onto the sand. The sea foam splashed merrily around them, the sun glistening on its reflective proteins as the high tide undercurrents began tugging at the children's now still legs. *Nocturne* had struck them again.

Before anyone reported the children missing, the Verando Street Gang was lost to the sea.

**Careening along the Georgia coast dirt road,** Mavis Swaggart's dusty brown 1968 Cadillac convertible heaved to the right as the local Mobler's Pipes and Fittings truck veered to its right going in the opposite direction.

"Watch where you're drivin'!" Mavis yelled as he shook his fist over his shoulder at the passing vehicle. Still recovering from his second bout with pneumonia, Mavis felt a little feistier than usual. Shaking his head angrily, Mavis turned his head back towards the roadway just in time to see his front hood crumple up and the tree in front of him roll over.

No. I'm rolling over, Mavis thought, just before his car's final rollover before landing in the five-foot wide, six-foot deep mosquito trench cut out between the berm of the road and the edge the marsh. Coughing and spitting as he surfaced from his sunken car, he began a slow dog paddle to the edge of the trench. By the time he reached the bank, Mavis was heaving, barely able to catch his breath. Eyes burning ferociously, his cheeks running with blood, his last painful thoughts before he sank under the water were that the mosquito insecticide spraying must have fouled the water.

When Mavis didn't come home for dinner that night, no one paid much attention. They just figured he had gone out with the boys, drinking again.

**The young elementary school teachers** from Reggio Nell' Emilia had climbed aboard their chartered bus for their holiday to the beaches along the Rivieria di Levante near Livorno, Italy. Their last holiday together five years ago was along the Atlantic Coast in Rehoboth, Delaware.

Famed for their successful teaching methods, known in teacher education textbooks as the Reggio Way, the child-centered, dedicated educators embraced their vacation days with as much exuberance as they practiced in the classroom with their students.

They loved life. The natural world held for them their greatest joy. Laughing and singing, they ran down to the sandy beach, racing to see who could enter the water first and swim out to the first buoy.

Splashing their way through the drifting sea foam, Antony Rodini and Alicia Sponsera, hand-in-hand, dove into the surf, whirling chunks of glistening sea foam high into the air in their wake. Close behind them, Mario Mastronemi raced Loris Donatella through the flying foam, swiping it out of his way as he dove into the surf.

Loris smiled. Mario always beat him at everything, but Loris rarely minded because Mario was always a good sport about his wins. Laughing, Loris looked at his friend's arms flaying about, as if he were drowning.

"I'm not going to fall for that one," Loris teased his friend.

"Loris, help me," Mario called back.

Turning his face into the wind so his long hair would blow back away from his face, Loris smacked into a large chunk of sea foam that had been gravitating back to earth after Mario's forceful dive.

Alarmed at first by the density of the sea foam, and how thick it felt when it hit him in the face, Loris coughed out the bubbles he had inhaled. Then the burning began. His mouth, tongue, and throat felt like they were on fire.

Rasping as he tried to speak, Loris turned toward the others on the beach who were yelling something about Alicia and Emanuel.

"Where's Alicia and Emanuel?" they asked, as a frightened crowd began forming around the once happy group.

"They haven't surfaced, yet. Somebody get Mario out of there. Quick."

Loris turned back to ask Mario for help, but Mario was floating face down in a circle of red tinted foam.

Gasping for breath, Loris struggled to shore and fell to his knees, his eyes dripping water tinged with blood. His body spent, he sank into the warm sand, whispering his last prayer.

**Carlos Santiago pulled his last length of fish netting** into shore as the sun began to set across the Bristol Bay where he and his family had fished for five generations. Slowly gathering the net with his gnarled, arthritic fingers, the 82 year old fisherman felt a stinging sensation as the rough netting scratched over his knuckles. Nothing new. The rough acacia threads of the net always chafed his hands as he hauled in the daily catch. The stinging, of course, was from the salt water, but it would also cleanse his wounds, he knew. Now, at sunset, his thoughts were on his family—Carleta, his wife of 62 years, and the families of his sons, Carlos, Pedro, and Santana. Today's catch would feed them all nicely this evening and tomorrow, too. Then he would go out to fish again.

Rinsing the netting off one more time to try to remove some of the sticky thick sea foam attached to the ribs of the net, Carlos bent forward to grab the net and shake the foam loose from its webbing.

As Carlos freed the net from the water and shook the foam

loftily into the air, he smiled that smile of satisfaction that every good angler has when he has made an excellent catch for the day.

Turning into the wind and beginning to walk home alone along the dusky beach, his catch trailing behind him, Carlos' steps began to falter. First, he felt a tired heaviness in his gait, then he stumbled, then he had trouble righting himself when he lost his balance, and then he toppled over into the wet sand and scattered mussel shells.

Lying on the sand, his body reacting to the poisonous bacteria streaming through his blood, Carlos began to slip into unconsciousness. For a moment, he could see the last rays of the sun setting low across the water. The sun's rays glinted off the iridescent, silver lining of the dark blue mussel shells scattered near his eyes. Life glints like that, he thought. Dark blue and sad on the outside, but silvery and glistening on the inside.

Carlos remembered his father telling him when he was a child that what really mattered was what was inside a man. The soul never stopped glistening.

Carlos died soon after having these thoughts. In the morning when his aging wife came looking for him, not a trace of him, nor the netting remained. The nocturnal tides had claimed him.

**Throughout the night on numerous remote beaches,** *Bacillus nocturne* continued its toll, unknown to the beaches' inhabitants and unknown to the news media who were frantically reporting from the more densely populated beaches and beach resorts located around the world.

# Chapter 52

*Centers for Disease Control*
*Washington, D.C., U.S.A.*

**Health Alert Network**
Health Alert # 200: CDC Alert on *Bacillus Nocturne*

To: Health Alert Network
From: Mary Szuba, M.D., M.P.H. Secretary of Health
Counties Affected: Nationwide Distribution

This transmission is a "Health Alert," conveys the highest level of importance and requires IMMEDIATE ATTENTION.

HOSPITALS: Please distribute to all medical, pediatric, infection control, nursing, and laboratory staff in your hospital immediately.

FEDERALLY QUALIFIED HEALTH CENTERS:
Please distribute immediately.

LOCAL HEALTH JURISDICTIONS: Please distribute to all primary care physicians in your jurisdiction immediately.

PROFESSIONAL ORGANIZATIONS: Please distribute to your membership immediately.

The Department of Health is releasing the following information provided by the National Centers for Disease Control and Prevention:

CDC Alert on *Bacillus Nocturne*

The Centers for Disease Control and Prevention (CDC) is working collaboratively with the Mid-Atlantic Coastal Environmental Health Division, the FBI, and other public health and law enforcement agencies to investigate an outbreak of *Bacillus nocturne* along the Mid-Atlantic Seaboard. Preliminary results of environmental testing at laboratories in Baltimore have tested positive for *Bacillus nocturne*. *Bacillus nocturne*, first identified five years ago after a limited outbreak in New Jersey, is a potent bacterium that has infiltrated the waterways and seacoast beaches of the Mid-Atlantic states.

Clinical Description for *Bacillus Nocturne* Exposure

Infection with *Bacillus nocturne* typically leads to profuse bleeding from the eyes, nasal passages, mouth, and/or ears, followed by hypovolemic shock and multisystem organ dysfunction and/or failure. Patients may also exhibit weakness, dizziness, influenza-like symptoms, fever, myalgia, and/or arthralgia.

The CDC requests that public health officials and clinicians who encounter patients with symptoms consistent with *Bacillus nocturne* initiate immediate disease control protocols and report these cases to the CDC Emergency Operations Center immediately.

# Chapter 53

*World Health Organization*
*New York City, New York, U.S.A.*

**World Health Organization (WHO)**
Epidemic and Pandemic Alert and Response (EPR)
Disease Outbreak News

*Bacillus nocturne* reported in Europe and United States of America.

The European and American health authorities have reported 12,446 cases of *Bacillus nocturne* in the last two days. The countries of Belgium, France, Monaco, Italy, Spain, and the United States of America reported 8234 cases of *Bacillus nocturne* including 4212 confirmed deaths and 183 suspected deaths at remote island locations currently under investigation. The Ministry of Health (MoH) is working closely with the affected countries to implement the required control measures and identify priority areas for intervention. The MoH has already mobilized health professionals to the hospitals to support patient management activities, including clinical case management and laboratory diagnosis.

Additionally public health and emergency services professionals have been recruited to assist community-based interventions. Vector control activities were implemented throughout the countries especially in the coastal zones. The fire department, police, military, and health inspectors of each country are assisting in these activities.

For more information:
Emerging and Reemerging Infectious Diseases Update, World Health Organization

# Chapter 54

*The Institute of Public Policy and Safety*
*Paris, France*

**"This is a Code Red"** echoed through Kate's mind. The Institute's warning signal to agents to evacuate their immediate premises surprised and annoyed her. First, the attacker, then the fire, and now an evacuation, she thought. I don't have time for this.

Kate grabbed her secure cell phone, keys, and passport holder containing credit cards, money, and alternate identities. She knew the safety protocol. She had practiced it before and survived during actions in Sydney and Warsaw. However, to leave Claire and her staff behind, and not warn them, worried Kate. Why didn't Jake include them in the Code Red, she wondered as she left her office.

Kate could only speculate about the order, and that is what it was, an order. All personnel were to react to the spoken code as if the head of the Institute had delivered it. The philosophy of the Institute demanded it: they were all equals at the Institute, each person an academic who was outstanding in their area of expertise, governed by each other at different times, but with the understanding that the leader was one among equals.

Thus, Kate had to obey this emergency command signifying impending and serious danger, from any colleague, no questions asked.

Walking through her laboratory, Kate saw Claire cataloguing the computer software she had been handing out to the Directors' technicians. The lab staff calmly walked around the laboratory recovering equipment displaced during the fire, obviously unaware of the alert. It must have something to do with my safety alone, Kate thought. Perhaps getting me out of the lab will protect everyone else.

She slipped past Claire and the lab personnel without incident and walked quickly to Marlin's office. She saw his door slightly ajar, part of his open door management style. Gingerly pushing it open, she saw his empty desk with several chairs surrounding it. She sat down in the chair closest to his, and unconsciously ran her fingers through her long hair. One insouciant lock found itself being repeatedly wound and rewound around her index finger as she waited.

Within a minute, Marlin strode into his office, locking the door behind himself. He spoke softly to Kate telling her to retreat to the back of the conference room, which had housed his meeting with Institute personnel a short time ago.

"What is it, Marlin?" Kate asked. "What is Jake so concerned about? And you? What's wrong? Was there another break-in? Why a Code Red?" Kate couldn't stop asking questions.

"It's Claire," Marlin said flatly. "I'm sorry, Kate."

"But, what's wrong? What about Claire? What do you mean?"

"Within the last two weeks, Claire has visited every site where major outbreaks of the bacteria have occurred."

"But she's not sick. She's fine. . . ." It didn't take Kate long to figure out what Marlin meant.

"No! Claire's involved in this? How?"

"Working in your lab, she had access to your data on the bacteria's genome, and when she substituted for you while you were at conferences, she had the opportunity to alter its genetic make-up and remove samples of its hybrid from the lab. No one ever suspected anything was awry because all of the registered samples of the bacteria remained checked in at the lab."

Kate died inside. She felt half of her heart ripped away. Her trust in her longtime friend betrayed, her sister's life hanging in the balance, innocent people dying, her research about to devastate the world . . .

Kate struggled to gain control of her emotions before she spoke or made any decisions about what actions to take.

She felt her adrenaline begin its wild coursing through her bloodstream, smacking her artery walls and careening through the chambers of her tightening heart. She fought her adrenaline-soaked body for rational control over her extreme emotions.

She was losing the battle. Stand down, she thought, stand down. Everything she had learned in training as an agent came pouring back into her mind.

"Stand down," she repeated aloud, forcing herself to hear her voice giving the order, as if a repeated mantra would assuage her intense feelings. Instead, her emotions ramped up another level. Kate stood in a dangerous place.

Marlin recognized her attempts to control her anguish. He stepped backward a few feet to give the agent control over her own space. It did not help.

"Why?" Kate's voice was a raw hiss as she turned on Marlin.

"Why would Claire jeopardize lives? Why would she kill? Why would she set *nocturne* loose?"

Her tirade of questions, fired one after the other, coalesced the deep wrinkles on Marlin's face, spelling apprehension to Kate.

"Does Lance know?" Kate fired before Marlin had a chance to answer her last questions.

"What could possibly be her motivation?" Kate's anger rose another notch.

"Kate," Marlin spoke slowly, trying to calm her down, "We

do not know all the answers, yet. We have to question Claire." Marlin lowered his voice and his eyes in another failed attempt to calm Kate.

"Question her?" she shouted. "Arrest her! I'll bring her in for questioning one way or another! Who does she think she is!"

"Lance notified Jake immediately, as soon as he discovered Claire's complicity. Then he stepped down as team leader at Base 3. He told Jake that he would help the Institute in any way possible." Marlin's eye contact with his own hands attempted to diffuse the situation. The mention of Jake's name made only a slight difference in Kate's demeanor. Marlin tried using Jake's name several more times, attempting to calm her.

"Jake has Lance flying in to meet with us and Claire. Both Jake and Lance should land at General Hatbourne's private airfield. Jake will be here within a few hours."

As Marlin finished his last sentence, Kate barely listened. She had focused on one word that Marlin spoke—"Claire." Suddenly, a slight change in her facial expression turned into a convulsion of muscle activity, rapid eye movement and reddening capillaries.

Before Marlin could stop her, Kate sprung out of her chair, charged out of his office, and headed for her laboratory. And Claire.

# Chapter 55

*The Institute of Public Policy and Safety*
*Paris, France*

**Kate swung the laboratory door open** with so much force that it cracked the marble wall next to the reception desk where Claire sat. Everyone in the room reacted, nervous about the meaning of the loud intrusion into their normally quiet working quarters.

"Out!" Kate raged. "Everyone out! Now!" Then Kate directed her low, gravelly voice toward Claire, pointing menacingly at her, "Except for you." Kate's adrenaline-roused body caused her strong, firm pose to end in a shaking forefinger. Already her fingertips were beginning to feel the numbing effect of the rapid release of adrenaline. Kate adapted to its effect by positioning the back of her hands to administer or defend against a first blow.

The laboratory emptied in seconds; each lab assistant and

postdoc rushed to be the first person through the door. No one looked back or asked any questions. Kate's strained expression warned them to get out quickly.

Kate slammed the door shut, hitting the wall-mounted automatic locking device with her elbow as she spun towards Claire. Claire remained frozen in place, just as she had been when Kate's facial expression had tipped her off that Kate knew.

Claire's adrenaline surge could have triggered any of the instinctual responses: fight, flight, or freeze. Mercifully for Claire, her body's sensory response recognized the impending danger if she were to fight, or flee and be pursued by Kate. The intensity of Kate's anger coupled with her hand-to-hand combat experience triggered an inescapable conclusion: Kate could easily overcome her. Freezing in place saved Claire's life.

"How could you?" Kate's voice scraped like gravel thrown across the marble floor.

"How could you harm my family? After all the time we've spent together! We treated you like family."

Claire stared at the floor.

"You knew we were vacationing at Lido Beach." Kate dropped her voice half an octave and then a full octave. Her slow, deliberate intonation frightened Claire. "Was that part of the plan? Get rid of us and the *nocturne* research would be yours?"

Claire did not respond.

"Look at me!" Kate grabbed Claire's chin and snapped her

neck backward, forcing eye contact. Claire's pupils enlarged with fear, just as they had every time her abusive parents approached her.

"You betrayed me! You betrayed my trust!" Kate remained livid. "I was responsible for you at the Institute. I trusted you. I gave you access to my research, and you . . . you used it to create a killer bacteria."

Kate could not hear the malice in her own words. Nor did she recognize the voice that spoke with razor-sharp harshness, signaling extreme danger. She felt rife with revenge. She had lost control.

In that moment of rage, Kate decided how she would kill Claire. It was but a few short steps to the refrigerated glass cases where all the samples of *nocturne* were kept.

"How appropriate," Kate said, glaring at the samples. "Live by the sword; die by the sword."

# Chapter 56



*The Institute of Public Policy and Safety*
*Paris, France*

**Kate measured the distance from Claire** to the glass cabinets where the laboratory stored its samples of *nocturne*. In her heightened emotional state, Kate wanted immediate revenge. Yet, another strand of thought kept surfacing, despite her efforts to tamp it down.

Her adrenaline flow was lessening. Claire had not fought back. She offered no resistance. She just sat still.

Shocked by her own tenacity and vitreous revenge, Kate slowly realized that Claire had not set up any defensive postures nor had she attempted to flee. Claire simply sat still. Perfectly still. Staring at the floor.

Finally able to recognize Claire's defeat, Kate forced herself to stand down and cancel her attack. She could hear her father's voice echoing through her mind. He was teaching her the difference between a soldier and the enemy: the enemy is ruthless and the soldier is rational.

Startled by her own vicious reaction, Kate fought to regain control of her emotions. They had ignited because a friend had betrayed her trust and endangered her family. But they would not help her learn what Claire had done. And her planned revenge would have made isolating the new strain of bacteria virtually impossible.

As Kate regained her emotional balance, she started thinking rationally, again. She needed answers. She needed to interrogate Claire.

"How do we stop *nocturne*, Claire?"

Claire did not respond, move or speak.

Kate forced Claire up and started her walking in the direction of the office computer reserved only for their usage.

"Show me how you altered the bacteria, and then how to stop it from replicating. Show me, Claire," Kate ordered, as she shoved Claire down into the wooden computer chair. "What have you done?"

**Claire reacted like an automaton.** Barely cognizant, she heard Kate's voice asking her a question, but the words didn't register.

The buzzing noise was back again, louder than ever. Claire had grown accustomed to its gradual increase after each beating her parents had inflicted on her. Sometimes the noise ebbed, but it always came back, louder than before. And with it came the muffled sounds, muffled voices of relatives past and friends lost. People who knew, but never reached out to save her. They were trying to speak now through the static droning noise, and Kate's voice finally surfaced as the loudest: "Show me, Claire. What have you done?"

"I think . . . do you want me to get *nocturne* up on the screen?" Claire asked hesitantly. Through the droning buzz, she barely heard her own voice.

"Is that right?" Claire fumbled with the keys a few times, but then her muscle memory kicked in and she started typing. Her rapt concentration on the rhythmic strokes on the keyboard blocked out the haunting voices in her mind. She stared, eyes transfixed on the computer screen, her fingers sliding across the keyboard entering numbers and letters more rapidly than seemed possible.

Suddenly lighting up Claire's LCD screen in bright red letters appeared the words "Program: Nocturne. Highest Security Level Needed" cycling around like a screensaver.

"Claire, what are you doing?" Kate asked while Claire busily entered every security code requested.

"I'm in!" Claire gleamed. "Now to find our little show stopper."

Clicking on a series of tabs, Claire finally pulled up a software program similar to the program Kate had used to dissect the bacterium.

Kate stared at the screen. This program designed recombinant DNA, too, and an altered chemical structure of *Bacillus nocturne,* outlined in bright green, blue, and yellow, filled the center screen.

"That's not the *Bacillus nocturne* that I've studied for the last five years. You've unlocked a high level security file containing what looks like a weaponized version of the bacteria." Kate stood in shocked silence. She had no idea that such a file existed, nor did she know who had created it.

Claire's expression glazed over; she was in a world all her own. She rustled through the sub files on the screen, finally settling on an inanely named file. "Here you are, 'My Little *Bacillus* Baby'," Claire murmured. "Isn't she beautiful, Kate?"

Kate had never heard Claire talk this way before. The transformation in Claire's facial features, tone of voice, and body posture made Kate uneasy. Claire, the smart, collaborative friend that Kate knew, had been superseded by a strong, determined, hacker activist intent upon creating her own signature bacterium from a stolen version of *Bacillus nocturne.*

But, why? Kate wondered. What had happened to cause Claire to act this way? Dissatisfied with herself for overlooking or not seeing Claire's transformation created too much of an emotional impact for Kate to deal with now. I have to find out how she altered this version of *nocturne*, first, Kate thought. Motivation and blame, later.

Calmly now, Kate cautioned herself. Don't set her off. Her mind is in another place right now. I have to start her talking about *nocturne* without irritating her.

"Claire, let's look at *nocturne's* genetic structure," Kate began, forcing her voice into the soft, lower register that she used with Crystal. "You've done such good work on reprogramming it."

"I know," Claire said. "I reengineered *nocturne* and made her mine. She's my baby now, not yours. And she's a beauty."

"Claire, will you show me how you created this little beauty?" Kate strained to smile, feigning admiration, hoping to coerce Claire's cooperation. And hoping that Claire knew how to stop *nocturne's* high replication rate.

Referring to Claire's hybrid creation as anything close to Claire's offspring, rankled, but Kate realized she needed to play on Claire's delusion to get answers.

"It was really quite easy, Kate." She triggered the arrow across the computer screen to the end of the formula.

"I dissected out the last allele and replaced it with this allele."

Such a simple rendition of allele conversion, Kate thought. Anyone with basic genetic knowledge could have created this same hybrid, if they had access to its original sequence. Few would have thought it could be as harmful as it turned out to be.

"Claire," Kate countered, "Why did you alter *Bacillus nocturne?*"

"It was necessary." Claire's voice flattened, all modulation gone. "Ahmed knew that I had access to it through your lab. He said he remembered seeing you there the weekend the coed died."

"Ahmed who?" Kate's expression remained stable as she ransacked her memory. She finally remembered him. He was an intern when Maria DeSanchez fell ill.

"When everyone on the case returned to the hospital that night, they were told that the young woman had died. No one ever mentioned the case to Ahmed again until I told him I was working with you on the bacterium." Catching her breath, Claire continued, still failing to answer Kate's question.

"Ahmed grew increasingly interested in your research, and together we developed a plan to set a modified version of *nocturne* lose in river tributaries leading into the back bay marshes."

"But why?" Kate interrupted. "What did you two think that would do?"

"We planned unleashing the bacteria," Claire said, "right before the summer beach water testing cycles began. *Nocturne* would spike the contamination levels upward and draw the attention of the public to the inland and seacoast water contaminants."

"What about the beach populace?" Kate challenged, but quickly softened her tone. "Weren't you concerned about their safety?" Julie's pale face flickered through her mind like an electric shock.

Claire laughed. "Oh, no, never. We knew I could alter the bacteria so it wouldn't be deadly. The massive dilution and the huge amounts of saline present made it relatively safe. The worst that could happen would be a few upset stomachs and some diarrhea. Nothing to worry about!"

Kate stared at her friend through narrowed eyes.

"Nothing to worry about unless it's your child who falls ill. Or your sister!" Kate had bridged the gap between controlled questioning and a tortuous desire to get the information she needed anyway she could.

Kate slowed her breathing and isolated her next question from her emotions.

"How did the bacteria become so virulent?"

Claire appeared unfazed by Kate's growing agitation with her disclosures. Except, Kate noticed that Claire never answered a question directly. She rationalized first, almost as an excuse for her behavior.

"Ahmed insisted that no one was paying any attention to the water quality readings," Claire said. "He wanted to take the bacterial dispersion to the next level. None of the team members thought that would be safe or effective, so we decided not to pursue his line of thinking."

"And . . ." Kate fought hard to remain calm.

"So," Claire added, suddenly cheerful, "I decided to further hybridize the bacterium without telling anyone on the team. Not even Ahmed. I decided to test it on the back marshes. It really spiked the bacterial counts. People became alarmed and several activist groups formed to fight for better water quality.

"My plan finally was working." Claire's expression brightened. "Single-handedly, I spurred the public's concern about water quality."

Claire's delusionary boast, coupled with her pride of accomplishment, caught Kate off-guard. It signaled a major personality change.

"That explains your motivation, Claire. But why didn't you stop with that success?" Kate watched Claire's every move. She sensed danger. The passive Claire wasn't there anymore.

"Because I knew I could do more," Claire announced. "I was going to several European scientific conferences near coastal resorts. If I released the bacteria at a few more sites, then the European community would get involved with water clean up, too. I could start a world-wide movement!"

Delusions of grandeur, Kate thought. Feed the delusions to get the answers I need. Watching Claire's slightest movements, Kate tried a new line of questioning.

"Claire, I need your help. I have a problem."

Claire looked up from her computer screen, incredulous. "What problem?"

"I don't understand how to alter *nocturne's* rapid replication rate. How would you halt *nocturne's* replication?"

"First of all," Claire was indignant, "I'd get rid of all the water pollution it has been feeding on. Clean up the decaying organisms from the sewage wastes that pour into our waterways, and it will starve. But, every scientist knows the easiest way to stop it, Kate. I'm surprised that you don't know the answer to your own question."

"And that is . . ." Kate nodded, pretending awe to persuade her to complete Kate's sentence.

"Sunlight, of course." Claire said. "Pure unadulterated sunlight. Stops it right in its tracks. I reprogrammed *nocturne* to replicate wildly in the dark or in shaded places. Not in the light. Irradiate the waters with ultraviolet light, natural and manmade. Weaken *nocturne* by limiting the protein pollutants that it feeds on, and the sunlight will do the rest."

"Claire, you seem especially proud of yourself."

"Especially since I knew something you didn't know." Kate thought Claire sounded like a needy, petulant little girl.

"Claire, have you been listening to the news the last few days? Have you heard what is happening along the coastal plains?"

"No." Claire's voice was flat, devoid of emotion. "I don't have time to listen to the news. I'm too busy planning press conferences. I have to respond to people's questions about the increased bacterial contamination in the world's waterways." Claire speeded through her conversation, never pausing long enough to give Kate a chance to comment.

"People will want to know how they can help clean up the water. I have activist groups to advise. I'm planning a huge rally in Yankee Stadium for the American kick-off campaign called Clear Water. I'll be its CEO and chief fundraiser. I'll need a staff of hundreds. Then in Paris we'll rally at l'Arc de Triomphe. All Europe will be yelling Clear Water! Clear Water! Claire Water! I'll be famous."

"I see," Kate said cautiously, as she edged her way over to the laboratory door. Eyes still on Claire the whole time, Kate crossed her arms and casually leaned back against the wall where the door locking mechanism was located. Kate's right shoulder blade pressed hard against the door release button, and she heard the deadbolt slide quietly back into its door plate.

Marlin immediately opened the door, followed by three armed guards. Kate nodded in the direction of her private office where Claire was still sitting at the computer. The guards rushed toward Claire and lifted her from her seat, adjusting her arms behind her back while slipping plastic band cuffs over her wrists.

"Claire, watch the news today from your cell." Kate's words even tasted bitter.

The guards led Claire out of the laboratory and down the hallway to the Institute's holding room.

"Kate," Marlin said. "What just happened?"

Kate collapsed into the nearest chair.

"I got what we needed, but I almost killed her."

"What?"

"I went in there because I wanted her dead. I wanted revenge," she shuddered, "for Julie, for everyone she's killed, for betraying my trust. I didn't go in there for answers. I was so angry; I wanted to kill her."

Defeat edged creases in the white flesh above her lips. "I'm no better than she is."

"Kate, you are an Agent, trained to kill in an emergency."

"I made the emergency. I charged into the lab and accused her. My emotions were totally out of control." Exhausted, she leaned forward, resting her elbows on her thighs and burying her face in her hands.

"Why so emotional?"

"I couldn't separate my feelings from my work. My emotions took over and . . ."

"Kate, you had to fight back your emotions to regain your ability to think and act rationally. Your instincts had kicked in, fueling your emotions. Self-preservation. Preservation of the lives of your family. They were all threatened."

"I was so angry. She betrayed me and my family. And she may have already killed my sister. I'm getting angry again just thinking about her!"

"Are you also angry at yourself? Were you transferring that anger onto her?"

"No! Not at myself, but . . . well, yes, maybe . . . Yes, I am angry at myself. God forgive me, if I had exercised responsibility and not depended on trust, I'd have updated Claire's Psychological Review. Then none of this would have happened. I'm responsible for Claire's behavior."

"No. You are wrong. You are responsible for your employees' work, not their psychological behavior. That is influenced by outside forces over which you have no control. These criminal actions lie solely on Claire's shoulders, not yours. She crossed the line. You did not."

"But, I . . ."

"Were you negligent on the psychological reporting? Yes, you were. Don't let that happen a second time, or I will have to fire you."

Kate could only nod in assent.

"Kate," Marlin's entire posture softened, "you may have felt like killing her, but you didn't. That's what separates you from psychologically disturbed persons like Claire. Your rational thoughts kicked in as soon as you exercised control over your emotions."

"But I came so close this time. What if next time I can't pull myself back?"

"You will."

"How can you say that? You don't know what I'd do. I don't know what I'd do."

"But I have known you a little longer than you have consciously known yourself. You are not a killer, Kate. Yes, you would fight to the death to save Crystal or any child. You would not hesitate to defend Jake or a stranger. But you would not kill if someone's life was not immediately in danger. You would find another way."

"And you know that, how?" Her challenge showed him she was unconvinced.

"You were three. Precocious for your age. Gifted in ways I had never seen in a child before. The easiest thing for you to have done, when you saw the black snake in the ash of the fireplace, would have been for you to scream for your mother. You did not. You saw me carrying wood in for your mother and said, "Don't call Mommy. I'll put him out. He didn't hurt nobody." And before I could reach you, you grabbed him by the tail, pulled him out of the firebox, dragged him wiggling across the yellow carpet, opened the patio door, and put him out."

Her eyes widened as the memory came back to her.

"You have a very strong sense of justice, Kate, and compassion. You demonstrated that today. You got what we needed from Claire, and then you put her in a safe place. That sense of compassionate justice at a young age is what we look for when we interview prospective agents. It is not a characteristic one loses in adulthood."

"But these emotions I have. They well up uncontrolled, and . . ."

"Kate, your mother was very emotional, but she thought of it as a gift. Her compassion and empathy made her an excellent counselor and advisor for many of us here at the Agency, and for you girls."

"I remember. Here I am, all emotional again remembering

Mom. I miss her so much. She died too young." She twisted a lock of hair around her index finger.

"She thought that was cute—a barometer of your emotions, she called it." A smile lit his face for a moment. "I miss her, too, Kate, but we will see her again. I do know one thing: if she could master her powerful emotions, you can master yours, too. You had a good outcome, today. What brought you back from your emotional cliff?"

"Claire's psychological state. She transformed in a few seconds into a person I didn't know."

"You had compassion for her, like your mother would have felt." He smiled and placed his hand on her shoulder. "Next time your emotions confront you, it will be easier to control them because of today. You'll use them to help you evaluate people, especially people in crisis."

Kate felt her self-confidence renewing.

"Thanks, Dad."

Taking Kate's hand, Marlin pulled her up from her chair and said, "Now, let's get the best minds around here working on the information that you extracted from Claire."

# Chapter 57


*Ospedale Privato di Venezia*
*Venice, Italy*

**Ambruster administered the third in a series** of five antibiotics that he was adding to his patient's intravenous drip. Fifty-two patients in various stages of *nocturne* infection crowded the rooms and hallways of his small epidemiology wing. The scene repeated itself in hospitals throughout Europe's coastal plains and across the Mid-Atlantic seaboard in the United States.

Ambruster had searched every medical record file on Internet 3 that were available to physicians worldwide, and he had poured over his old notes and those of his colleagues who had attended Dr. Genek Snyrzek's Summer Institute on combined antibiotic usage in post World War II Poland.

Shortly after the discovery of penicillin, American army medics began administering the wonder drug to the battlefield wounded in the foxholes and the civilians on the plains of battle-worn Europe. Ambruster thought the drug contributed to the Allies winning the war.

So precious was the antibiotic that once its powdered form was mixed with water to form a serum, it was often salvaged by collecting it from patients' urine to be refined and used again on other patients.

A young, brilliant Polish-American doctor, Dr. Genek Snyrzek, recognized that many of the villagers were making quicker recoveries using the antibiotic than were the soldiers in the field. Curious as to the reason, Dr. Snyrzek hypothesized that the native vegetables and plants added to the families' stews and salads aided the antibiotic's ability to overcome the bacterial infections. Many of the ingredients, like garlic, onions, and cabbage had mild antibiotic properties to them. The soldiers in the field, on the other hand, were fighting a European bacterium with penicillin and canned Meal, Comfort, Individual Rations shipped in from other locales.

Experimenting with a few native vegetables, Dr. Snyrzek created a biochemical combination of penicillin and what today are known as anti-oxidants, phytochemicals, and flavonoids, natural immune system boosters, which sparked a renaissance in biomedical care.

Somewhere in his seminar notes, Ambruster knew he had seen the antidote for *nocturne's* symptoms. What did I need to heighten the antibiotics' effects? He tried to remember.

In a colleague's notebook, Ambruster found a scribbled note

in the upper left hand margin of her notes from the last day of lectures. She had written: "Indigenous plants a la Snyrzek."

Ambruster hypothesized that he needed to add natural bio-products to his patients' protocols, but from which country? The United States where the bacteria's genome originated, or from Lido Beach in Venice where the bacteria had gained strength and virility?

Picking up the hospital telephone to call down to the third floor Nutrition Department, Ambruster slowly placed it back in its charging cradle. This was something he had to solve face-to-face with Dr. Caroline Sabatini. Catching the elevator at the end of the hall, he exited on the third floor and walked over to the pediatric wing.

"Caroline," Ambruster said as he stuck his head through the open office door of an attractive brunette half his age. "May I speak with you for several hours?" His charming smile and boyish humor made it difficult for anyone to resist his requests.

"Dr. Ambruster," Caroline laughed, "yes, of course. Come in. How may I help you?"

Ambruster explained Snyrzek's seminar that he had attended and discussed the current theory that combinations of drugs, also known as "cocktails" had far better effects for HIV patients than did single dosage drugs.

Dr. Sabatini remained attentive to Ambruster's explanations, even though she had written some of the peer-reviewed articles that he was quoting.

"I can help you. We need to know if the bacteria feed on land waste or waterborne algae, amoebae, tissues, or skeletons. Then we'll match those protoglycans with vegetation and single cell proteins on the land or sea. I think since the aggressor was found in sea foam, it would be appropriate to start your patient on a diet of sea substances known to boost the immune system, such as fatty fish and red, green, and yellow seaweeds."

"Our labs in Paris are analyzing samples of the new strain sent in from multiple countries. I'll call for an analysis of its ingestion."

"Within the hour," Ambruster rose and ambled toward the door, "I should be able to start a combined antibiotic/seaweed drip for my patients. I'll report back to you after the first four-hour trial period. Thank you very much, Caroline."

Entering Julie's room a short time later, Ambruster began the antibiotic and seaweed trial on the unconscious young woman. This time, however, he approached her bedside with more confidence and less dread. This mixture of biologics had the possibility of providing the elusive cure for *nocturne*.

None too soon, he thought. I'll have to use the formula to cop a plea bargain with the prosecutor.

# Chapter 58

*The Institute of Public Policy and Safety*
*Paris, France*

**The Institute's chief scientists** and administrators gathered around the broad mahogany table in Marlin's office, all of them exchanging comments at once. As he called the meeting to order, Kate looked up to see Jake and General Schoelfield entering the room, with Lance hurriedly passing by the doorway, obviously on his way to the holding room to see Claire.

"Jake, thank God you are here," she said as she stood up. Jake quickly hugged her, and he and the General sat down at the table as Marlin called the meeting to order.

Jake slipped her a quick note that said, "Marlin filled me in on the phone as we drove here. Nice work, Kate. Wait till you hear what we found."

She just smiled. She was curious about his team's findings, but she still felt convoluted about Claire and unable to engage in meaningful conversation.

"All right," Marlin started, "as you know, Claire Martin created a hybrid of *nocturne* and released it. She is being held in the Institute's holding room until the Board of Directors can interview her. We know the genetic structure of the hybrid and her motivation for unleashing it. What we don't know is why it became such a deadly killer among people in their twenties. Every patient in their twenties is seriously ill or dying. Others who have contracted *nocturne* are ill but recovering. We need to stop this killer."

"We're the killers," Jake shouted as he rose from his seat like a heckler in a courtroom. His outburst stunned Marlin and the other scientists at the table.

"We unleashed *nocturne* five years ago, testing it on our own population. Dr. Walter Ambruster, the Institute hero who treated the patients from the first eruption of *nocturne*, and who is treating Kate's sister in Venice now, broke Institute protocol five years ago and decided to test a weaponized strain of the bacteria at the university's pier where Maria DeSanchez and Toby Hannah were infected. Toby, an Afghanistan veteran, died. Maria, one of our agents serving undercover as a graduate student, nearly died. It was Ambruster who treated them in the Emergency Room, enhancing his own reputation."

Kate grasped the edge of the table to steady herself. "Julie! We left Julie in his care!" She wanted to run from the meeting to alert the Venice police about Julie's dangerous situation.

Jake caught her eyes. "I've called the hospital guards already. Julie's safe."

Kate could breathe again. She refocused on Jake's outburst and accusations as he continued speaking.

"As Ambruster's weaponized version of *nocturne* dispersed throughout the Rehoboth Bay, it infected thousands of others, most with a lesser dose than Maria and Toby had received. At an International Youth Rally occurring that month at Rehoboth Beach, all of the teenagers fell ill, and then went back to their home countries. Today, our Base 10 labs have found that strain of *nocturne's* antibodies in the blood of all of the European victims in their twenties now. Instead of providing immunity against *nocturne,* it has made them more susceptible to the bacteria. And we're collectively responsible for Ambruster's disgraceful behavior."

Jake rarely spoke out with such passion. Under ordinary proceedings, he would have been sanctioned for his forthright accusations.

Kate's stunned expression matched that of every other scientist in the room, except for Marlin. He knew, she thought. And Ambruster started all of this? We thought him heroic in his efforts to save Maria and the others.

"He's right." Chaz Stefanich, the Institute's chief chemical engineer came to Jake's defense. "Ambruster, or any of us, are not permitted to test our lab experiments outside of the Institute without CDC approval and oversight."

"Not only that, Chaz," Kate asserted. "We play with fire every time we recombine genetic material. Ambruster's actions were criminal. Just as Claire's were. Claire's tampering exacerbated the bacteria's danger by altering an already altered genetic script. Who can predict what the ramifications of multiple modifications will be?"

"That brings us to an important point: What happened that the human body is unable to defend against this bacteria by producing sufficient, viable antibodies? How many other illnesses have those characteristics?" Chaz opened the question to the group.

Marlin, as Director, fell silent for a long time. He listened to the answers offered by the scientists. Finally, he said, "Dengue Fever. It is also one of the diseases that does not produce sufficient antibodies to ward off a second attack. The second attack is far worse than the first attack. It is conceivable that we have created a bacterium that stirs the immune systems of its hosts to produce antibodies that actually weaken the host's immune system for the bacteria's next round of attacks."

"Like preparing a food source or host for future use," Jake said.

"If that is what happened, we've set in action a bacteria that has the potential to wipe out our entire species within several generations." Marlin shook his head and turned away from the others.

Kate turned to face her colleagues. "One genetic alteration

may seem like good science to us. But we are also responsible if someone else takes our alteration to the next level. If we started the change, we need to be responsible for its behaviors down the genetic line as well.

"Claire altered our version of *nocturne* to feed off the human waste in the sewage that seeps into the coastal waterways. With such a food source, Claire hypothesized that the bacteria would be able to replicate every sixty seconds. That increased its metabolic need for a greater amount of protein food sources. It was a short jump for the bacteria to start feeding on other human proteins. The aqueous layer of the cornea seems to have been the perfect host for such a leap. With no immunity to stand in its way, the bacteria become unstoppable. We are responsible for this epidemic. It started here, five years ago."

Chaz added, "That's right, Kate. The new bacteria, encountering innumerable antibiotics flushed down toilets into the sewage system, has developed its own immunity to them, making treatment nearly impossible. What we need is a new antibiotic that has not entered our water supply, yet. The next antibiotic to be released for public use is not due out for six months."

"What about private sector antibiotics? You know which ones I mean, the ones the Army's using in Iraq?" Marlin asked.

General Schoelfield answered, "We have three we are using in combat. We like to keep those separate from the public domain to give our soldiers the best shot at having the newest drugs to prevent antibiotic failure. We have a fourth antibiotic that has never been used. Under the present circumstances, we will release whatever meds are needed in the States and in Europe to get this thing under control."

"Good," Marlin said. "Contact the pharmaceutical companies which distribute the new antibiotics to the armed forces, and ask them to send the new medications out to all coastal hospitals reporting *Bacillus nocturne* cases. Give the order Emergency Status."

"We need to tackle *nocturne's* food supply, too," Kate added. "I think we need to shut down all sewage dumping until we are certain that *nocturne* has naturally died out. Claire said sunlight and artificial UV irradiation would stop its replication, but we also want to get rid of whatever bacteria are still out there in hard to locate places."

Jake sat up straight in his chair. "Can we lace the waterways with one of the antibiotics that the army has never released for public use?"

"If one of the new antibiotics is effective against *nocturne*," the General said, "we would have to treat all the waterways simultaneously; otherwise, *nocturne's* rapid replication would allow it to develop resistance to the drug in a matter of days."

"As well as the other waterborne bacteria we will be wiping out," Chaz warned. "We'll have to monitor which other bacteria the antibiotic kills, and be ready to fight the next opportunistic bacteria which take their places."

Marlin culled their ideas. "Implement all of the ideas. We have to stop *nocturne* as soon as possible. If it mutates on its own, we will have a worse situation. Every mutation will produce a strain foreign to us, that we will have to study before we can treat."

Marlin organized his thoughts with a few jotted notes on his iPad and then began to issue orders:

"Initiate contact with the countries affected through our liaisons with the CDC and WHO. Provide the financial support they will need initially and continue to support clean up operations for both continents until our scientists say the water is safe again.

"Data-mine for hospitals that reported successful treatments for the illness and share that information with the CDC and WHO. Test those protocols in our labs. All of them.

"Implement distribution centers for drug dispensation of the Army's donated antibiotics, arrange immediate meetings with the CDC and the WHO and provide them with funding for the drug distribution, prepare press releases that a cure has been found and the steps to be used for clean-up in order to safeguard our water supply for the future. Every department here knows its job. Please begin work on this immediately.

"We need to prepare a plan, an enforceable protocol, for monitoring emerging bacteria. We will have to have teams out there monitoring for *nocturne* for years to come. We cannot take a chance of missing any resurgence in the bacteria's voracity. Everyone who survives the bacteria's current onslaught may be its victims the next time it strikes.

"And we must develop stringent policies that provide oversight for every experiment conducted at the Institute."

Every department chair recognized the pieces of the plan for which they were liable. Chairs pushed backward scraped along the floor as the staff waited impatiently to start their duties. But Jake was still not satisfied.

"When will the Institute tell the world that we were responsible?" Jake's challenge resonated around the meeting room.

Marlin appeared apprehensive as Jake spoke. As Director, he wasn't accustomed to challenges from his staff, especially his son-in-law. "I will call Ambruster in this morning. Claire is already here in the holding cell. The Board of Directors will meet with them this afternoon. I'll announce the Board's decision at a mandatory meeting by the end of the day."

# Chapter 59

*The Institute of Public Policy and Safety*
*Paris, France*

"**Dr. Walter Ambruster, on behalf of the Board** of Directors, I want to thank you for appearing before us today to help us understand your role in the epidemic that *Bacillus nocturne* is causing in Europe and the United States, and perhaps in other isolated countries around the world," said Dr. Rachel Glass, the President of the Board.

Ambruster rose from his seat to respectfully accept her greeting, then sat down heavily. He had not realized that Maria DeSanchez's mother had recently assumed the presidency. The position rotated among the Board of Directors every four years. He had been extremely busy with his research and had not given much attention to the politics of the organization, lately. Now, he wished he had.

"Dr. Ambruster, please state your present positions at the

Institute and describe your past performance as an Institute employee."

"I currently hold two positions at the Institute. I am the Chairperson of the Institute's Biomedical Department, with my office at The Institute's Rome Laboratory. I am also the Head of the Agency's Biochemical Team, meeting monthly at The Institute's Dover Laboratory. I have worked in the former position for the past four and a half years."

"Did you receive your Rome appointment shortly after the first outbreak of *Bacillus nocturne* occurred in the United States?"

"Yes, I did, Madame President. Before assuming the chairpersonships, I worked for the Institute as a professor of medicine at Atlantic University and a medical researcher at the Institute's Dover Laboratory for twelve years. I have worked for the Agency for five years."

"Dr. Ambruster, before you assumed the Chair positions at both organizations, did you express concern to the Institute about the promotion track you were on?"

Ambruster cleared his throat and lost eye contact with the Board members as he answered this question. "Yes, Madame President."

"Would you please explain, Dr. Ambruster?"

"I filed a complaint with the previous board president eight years ago, requesting a review of Marlin Stafford's evaluation of me."

"Would you please describe your complaint and whether the president decided it had merit to go before the full board?"

"Stafford refused to bring my bid for tenure before the board, citing the failure of three of my last research articles to be published in top ranking journals."

"How did this affect your career?"

"I was permitted to stay on in an untenured position, and through hard work rose through the ranks to the position of chairperson."

"And how did their decision affect your financial obligations?"

"Miserably." Anger tinged his voice and his face reddened. "I had college loans to repay, a mortgage with a balloon payment coming due, and new car payments, all of which would've been manageable if the increase in pay from a tenured position had occurred."

"How did you cover your expenses?"

"As I said, I worked long hours until I received administrative appointments, such as chairperson of committees, and then departments."

"Were those appointments as a result of your long hours working to solve the mystery surrounding the bacterial release that almost cost the life of Maria DeSanchez, and did cost the lives of others?"

Ambruster shifted in his seat and stared at the President through steepled fingers pressed against his nose.

"Yes, I believe the board wanted to reward my heroic efforts. I risked my life to be in the middle of the fray. I stayed in the emergency room for days, unconcerned for my own welfare. I stopped the spread of *Bacillus nocturne*. I cared for many patients who successfully recovered. After a few months, it had dissipated in the water, and I thought it would not return."

"Do these appointments provide an increase to your income, and if so, what is the amount of salary?"

"I don't know why you are following this line of questioning."

"Let the record show that each appointment to chairperson netted Dr. Ambruster an additional $60,000 a year."

"Dr. Ambruster, in your work for the Agency, were you called upon to weaponize *Bacillus nocturne* for possible covert use by the United States government?"

"Yes."

"Were your efforts successful?"

"Yes."

"How did you determine this?"

"The previous Chair of the Biochemical Team authorized a test in a natural setting."

"Did all of your team members concur with his authorization?"

Silence.

"Let the record show that all of the team members rejected the authorization, and the Chair withdrew the authorization after conferring with Dr. Marlin Stafford, Director of the

Agency and the Institute, who would not approve such a test."

"Dr. Ambruster, what was your reaction to this decision?"

Redness clouded his face and an icy stare replaced the congenial attitude he had tried to display. "I was outraged. Three years of research and thousands of hours of work completing a task they asked me to accomplish, and they decided not to test the weaponized bacteria. Without a test, it could never be used."

"What did you do?"

"The only thing a self-respecting scientist would do," his anger increased. "I completed the experiment."

"Where?"

"Rehoboth Bay, of course. It was the closest body of water with the most likely ability to replenish its water supply. I stayed on university property, of course. I released it at the marina."

"Let the record show that the day Maria DeSanchez and Toby Hannah were stricken by a genetically altered strain of *Bacillus nocturne*, now believed to be Ambruster's weaponized version, Mr. Hannah, then Dr. Ambruster, and then Ms. Sanchez had signed in at the university's marina, a requirement to walking out onto the pier where the kayaks are launched."

"Dr. Ambruster, would you please step out into the hall while the Board convenes privately? Thank you."

Ambruster rose slowly and started walking out of the room before he had risen to his full height. The stooped shoulders and slow gait of the man many had considered a hero five years ago spoke volumes to the people in the room.

"As President of the Board, I believe there is enough evidence to warrant an investigation by the Federal Government of Dr. Walter Ambruster's conduct and involvement in the *Bacillus nocturne* outbreak in Delaware five years ago."

"Discussion?" Senator Pete Montelli, the Institute's parliamentarian, inquired of the Board members.

No one debated the worthiness of the Board President's recommendation.

"All those in favor, please say, "Aye.""

"Those opposed, please say, "Nay.""

"In a unanimous decision, the Board has voted to turn all of the evidence of Dr. Walter Ambruster's suspected misconduct over to the Federal authorities," Senator Peter Montelli confirmed.

Dr. Glass phoned for security to accompany Dr. Ambruster to the Institute's holding cell until the Federal officials arrived.

# Chapter 60



*The Institute of Public Policy and Safety*
*Paris, France*

"**The Board of Directors from the Institute are** pleased to meet you, Dr. Claire Martin. Would you please take a seat while we ask you a few questions?"

"Yes, thank you, Dr. Glass." Claire appeared ready for discussion, leaning forward on the edge of her seat, as if she were interviewing for a position.

"This is a hearing, Dr. Martin, not a legal proceeding. However, if you would like legal counsel present, you are entitled to that representation. Would you like to consult with your lawyer?"

"I have, Dr. Glass, and she said to proceed without her." Claire fully believed the voice she had just heard in the quiet of her mind had identified herself as Claire's lawyer. The voice said Claire did not need her to be physically present, because she was always present with Claire, both representing her and protecting her.

"Dr. Martin, as a part-time employee of Dr. Kate Connors, what are your duties at the Institute?"

"I help Kate with her research."

"You assist Dr. Connors, then?"

"No, I help her. She relies on me to do the research, and then I show her how to do it herself."

"Dr. Martin, how often do you work with Dr. Connors?"

"About once a month she asks me to come to the lab because she has to travel somewhere. I am in control of the lab while she is away."

"Have you always been in control of the lab when Dr. Connors was away, or more recently?"

"Recently, definitely. I'm sorry, I can't remember if I were in control last year, too."

"That is all right. Please tell us what you remember. Do you have access to all of Dr. Connors' research when you are in her lab?"

"Yes, she trusts me completely."

"Where are you employed, Dr. Martin?"

"Why, here of course."

"And anywhere else?"

"No."

"Dr. Martin, have you ever been employed as a research professor at Peridore University in New Jersey, as your *curriculum vitae* currently states?"

"Oh, yes. Didn't I just say that? I thought I heard myself say Peridore University, also, just now." Claire seemed incredulous that Dr. Glass wasn't getting all this. Claire thought, Maybe Dr. Glass isn't as smart as me. And maybe the others on the Board aren't either.

"Dr. Martin have you worked at Peridore as a research professor for ten years?"

"Yes, I guess, if that's what you are saying my *CV* says."

"Thank you, Dr. Martin. What research have you been doing in Dr. Connors' laboratory?"

Pride crowded out the voices in her mind for a few minutes. "Why, I've re-engineered a commonly passive waterborne bacterium to replicate wildly and clean up the waste products in our bays and inland estuaries. I am a water pollution activist, you know, and I wanted to awaken the public to the harsh consequences of water pollution."

"Have you accomplished your goal, and if so, how?"

"Yes, definitely." Her enthusiasm glowed, energizing her facial muscles to produce the broadest of smiles and multiple crinkles around her eyes. "I re-engineered *Bacillus nocturne* to fight pollution. Then I conducted an experiment using multiple testing sites. I released 3 ml of the bacteria at resort beaches. I thought that if I produced a mild, waterborne illness, then everyone who became ill would start to take the notion of water pollution much more seriously. I wanted to activate the citizenry to become water pollution activists like I am." She seemed genuinely proud of her idea.

"Dr. Martin, have you been listening to the news or have you read any newspapers yesterday or today?"

"No. Much too busy getting ready for the next step: anti-pollution rallies."

"Dr. Martin, have you been reimbursed for your work at the Institute, and what do you think about the amount of money you've earned here?"

"Yes, I have. I think the money is very generous. I would work on this project for free. That's how worthwhile I believe this effort to be."

The voices offered encouragement, *You tell them, honey! Great job! Keep it coming!*

"I'm honored that the Institute gave me that huge lab, all for my own work. Isn't that incredible?"

"Dr. Martin, it may well be that you are the most incredible person we know."

Claire accepted her statement as a compliment.

"Dr. Martin, would you ever knowingly kill someone?"

"I'm shocked and offended that you would ask such a thing."

"Do your experimental releases hold any real dangers for the general public?"

"Just a brief belly-ache or two. Just enough to make them feel a little sick, but that passes quickly. I would never hurt anyone. Science is about prevention, not causal manipulation of the human populace."

The little voices in her mind became adamant. I would, I would. I would hurt somebody. I would kill somebody if they wouldn't help me.

"Can I go, now? I'm really getting sleepy."

"All right, Dr. Martin. I think we have heard enough. Thank you for coming."

"No, thank you. What an honor to be asked to speak before the Board of Directors!"

After Claire left the room, the security personnel remanded her back to her room, where she fell asleep. Awakening two hours later, Claire had lost all memory of her interrogation before the Board.

**The Board, in her absence, debated about what they** should do concerning Dr. Claire Martin.

"Madame President and Board members, discussion?" Senator Montelli saw the questions in their faces.

"Am I correct in assuming that all of you are in agreement that Dr. Claire Martin is not oriented to time and place?"

Dr. Glass looked at each board member, noting their affirmation of what they had witnessed.

"The Institute's psychiatrist has provided us with copies of her psychiatric evaluation. From the interview that you witnessed, do you believe it is a realistic evaluation?"

Again, the entire Board concurred that Dr. Claire Martin's

evaluation correctly described her present state of mind.

Senator Montelli addressed the most pressing issue. "What shall we do about Claire?  Many of us have worked with her here, and she has impressed us with her hard work and her scientific abilities. Clearly, if she can reprogram bacteria twice as fast as Ambruster did, she has a brilliant mind. Shall we waste it by having a court sentence her to a life in a psychiatric ward, or worse, prison? Or should we be responsible for her behavior because she worked among us, yet none of us recognized the early signs of her mental illness?"

Dr. Jia Zhang reminded the Board, "Her motivation was not for financial gain, as was Ambruster's. I don't believe she ever intended to kill anyone. She thought she had found a way to activate people to be responsible citizens. Her underlying goal was healthier drinking water."

"Frankly," Senator Montelli added, "had she re-engineered the original version of *nocturne*, rather than accidentally pulling up Ambruster's weaponized version, we might have thanked her for providing a weaponized version that was not fatal. She had no way of knowing she wasn't working with the original bacterium." The Senator looked toward the President of the Board for guidance.

"There are options available to us," Dr. Glass responded. "If we are turning over Ambruster to the Federal authorities, he will be tried as a disgruntled scientist out for financial gain. His greed will insulate the Institute, as an organization, from a great deal of negative public relations.

"Claire, on the other hand, poses a problem. If the reporters learn about her story, the Institute could be ruined and forced to close. Imagine the public outrage if they discovered we let a severely mentally disturbed scientist work for us who had the capabilities of genetically altering any bacteria that we study here. I'm outraged, and I have access to all the details. The public will only hear the worst of this case, without realizing how hard we try to prevent problems like this from occurring.

"There is also the issue of the Agency. It would be brought down, too. Due to national security, we cannot disclose all the good the Agency has accomplished over the years. Without those credits to our name, we could only offer a weak defense for our malfeasance."

Dr. Chen suggested, "Claire's husband is an agent. Would she qualify for admission to the Institute's Psychiatric Center in Lucerne, Switzerland? We have sent other spouses there for treatment."

"Yes, but she requires 24 hour supervision and confinement. She could be very dangerous were she to escape from the facility. She seems incapable of premeditated murder or mayhem, but she is brilliant and could start another catastrophe in the name of her next cause."

"Then let's make that a condition of her admission."

Senator Montelli called for a vote: "All in favor of remanding Dr. Claire Martin to The Institute's Lucerne Psychiatric

Center for confined, psychiatric treatment, say, 'Aye.' Those opposed, 'Nay.' The 'ayes' have it."

# Chapter 61

*Henlopen Medical Center*
*Lewes, Delaware, U.S.A.*

**"Ms. Goldenseal,"** **Dr. Howard Charleson,** President of the Henlopen Medical Center's Board of Directors, interrupted the crowd of people asking her questions, "would you please join the Director of the CDC, the hospital's Board of Directors, our physicians, and me in Conference Room C? We have some very important physicians who would like to speak with you via teleconference to discuss your cure."

"Yes," Gloria stammered, shocked by the invitation.

"Fine. We expect the conference to be ready within the hour. Gloria, thank you, sincerely, thank you for taking a risk that proved providential. You saved twelve lives with your quick thinking on the beach and untold others around the world will also benefit greatly from your use of complementary medicine. Thank you."

Gloria Goldenseal discovered that she was something of a hero at the Henlopen Medical Center. Most of the doctors and nurses in the Infectious Disease Wing of the hospital gathered around her as she stepped off the third floor elevator to check on the patients that she had brought in two nights ago from the Cape Henlopen Beach.

Forty young adults had died from exposure to the water borne bacteria on the Cape Henlopen beach the night Gloria had accompanied the EMTs; however, the twelve patients that Gloria had treated had all survived.

Gloria gave all the credit to her great-grandfather, the tribal elder who had taught her the natural healing methods that their tribe had passed on for generations. The physicians, on the other hand, knew that Gloria's combination of the old ways with modern medicine was what had really stopped the bacteria from replicating further.

Under normal circumstances, Gloria would have been censored, put on unpaid leave, lost her license, or even arrested for overstepping her boundaries in healthcare. This occasion, though, had been extremely life threatening, and she had reacted with forethought and skill. She was a hero and everyone, including the CDC, wanted to learn her treatment protocol.

I feel so humbled, Gloria thought. I didn't produce the cure. The people who came before me deserve the credit; I just took their scientific and tribal knowledge to the next step by combining their treatments.

"I recognized the symptoms," Gloria finally spoke, "from a case I had seen when I was a child, Dr. Charleson. I remembered my great-grandfather's belief in the healing powers of the mold on leather tanned and stained with vegetation from the southern Delaware area."

Gloria continued, "It made sense that his old medicine might still work today on the same bacteria in the same area of the state. Given the circumstances, direct infusion by IV seemed like the quickest way to get the antibiotic into a patient's bloodstream."

"We will all be anxious to analyze the composition of the mold that is growing on the old piece of leather that your grandfather gave to you. It may be our newest antibiotic. Thank you for agreeing to share your experiences with us and to explain why you chose to treat the victims in the manner that you did," Charleson said.

"I'll check on my patients," Gloria said, "and then share the protocol with everyone in the conference room."

Thirty minutes later, Gloria sat at a long table flanked by physicians and CDC officials anxious to hear how she had successfully treated the young adults at the beach party two nights ago.

On a large video screen opposite Gloria's table, physicians from other hospitals listened intently as she explained her protocol and her reasoning behind combining antibiotics with native plant structures.

"Miss Goldenseal," Dr. David Winters, the new Emergency Medicine Epidemiologist at Venice's Ospedale Privato, spoke, "you are to be congratulated. In a matter of minutes after seeing the patients' symptoms at the Cape Henlopen beach, you were able to diagnose and discern the correct protocol for treatment of *Bacillus nocturne*."

"What is remarkable about this brilliant woman's decision," Winters continued, "is that she came to this conclusion readily, whereas it took my research assistants and me multiple trial protocols, and excessive delving into research archives, to accomplish the same task. I am impressed, Miss Goldenseal. There is an open position waiting for you at our hospital in Venice anytime you would honor us with your presence."

Gloria smiled. "Thank you, Dr. Winters."

# Chapter 62

*The Institute of Public Policy and Safety*
*Paris, France*

**The Holding Room on the lower level** of the Institute looked like any other office space in the building, with the exception of the reinforced steel door with a heavy-duty glass window and hallway locks. The Institute had built a tiny bathroom into a privacy area about the size of a small coat closet. A small loveseat with a coffee table full of magazines sat adjacent to a large desk with a yellow lined legal size notepad and ink pen sitting on it.

When Lance looked through the door window, he saw Claire sitting behind the desk, pen in hand, face lifted toward the ceiling in forethought. She looks as if nothing is wrong, he thought. Just another day at the office. His heart sank.

Slowly turning the lock on the door, he cautiously leaned his right shoulder against the heavy door, uncertain about what would greet him on the other side.

Claire looked up, leapt from behind her desk, and smacked into him full force in her usual run to hug him whenever he came home from work.

"Lance, I'm so happy to see you, I was getting worried. It's almost suppertime. I love you," she said, drawing out the last three words for emphasis.

"I'm here now, Claire," Lance muffled his words into her soft, light brown hair. Tears welled up in his eyes as he said, "Claire, what have you done?"

"I created an agenda for the next Clear Water meeting while I waited for you, Lance. It really only took me one hour. Will you come hear me speak?"

Unsure what to say next, Lance hesitated for a few seconds while he organized his thoughts. She seems genuinely happy. Should I play along? But would that make her worse? Face it—it can't get much worse.

Finally, with a light tousle of her brown curls, Lance managed to reply, "Yes, Claire, of course. I will always be there for you, Hon. You know that, right?"

Claire searched his eyes and then softly replied, "Yes, I know that, Lance."

# Chapter 63

*The Institute of Public Policy and Safety*
*Paris, France*

**Dr. Marlin Stafford's meeting room** filled to capacity as all of the staff assembled to hear the fate of Drs. Claire Martin and Walter Ambruster. The anxiety about losing their jobs if the Institute closed, coupled with their continuing battles with *nocturne* created an unbearable atmosphere for most of them.

"Thank you, everyone for your patience. The Board of Directors convened this afternoon in closed session to question Dr. Walter Ambruster about his activities relating to the release of *Bacillus nocturne* five years ago in the Rehoboth Bay. The Board found enough evidence of criminal conduct to warrant a further investigation by the Federal Bureau of Investigation."

"They are going public with this?" Jake expressed surprise, but approval.

"Yes. The Board wants everyone to know that Ambruster's actions will reflect solely upon him, as a disgruntled employee with a vendetta in mind. The Institute administration may be reprimanded for how we handled the employee, but the Institute should remain unscathed."

"And Claire?" Kate's mixed emotions were bothering her.

"The Board decided that Dr. Claire Martin acted upon the belief that she would clean up the polluted waterways, never intending the bacteria to become lethal. They believe she had no knowledge that she had altered an already weaponized version of the bacteria. The Institute's psychiatrist examined her and confirmed that she is mentally ill and in need of treatment. Since she is the spouse of an Institute employee, they agreed to extend to her the mental health benefits that spouses are entitled to, and send her to the Institute's Psychiatric Center in Lucerne under 24 hour confinement. The Board felt this was the best solution for Claire."

For the first time all year, no one argued with the decisions of the Board. They seemed fair, if not ideal, to the scientists. As long as the Institute and their positions were secure, they could continue fighting *nocturne.*

**Kate couldn't wait until everyone left** Marlin's office. Finally, she could ask, "Against whom did Ambruster have a vendetta?" Kate's close call with the driver at the airport remained fresh in her memory.

"Me," Marlin said.

"But, why?"

"For not granting him a tenure hearing years ago. And you, Kate, for being my daughter."

"Me?"

"Last night after the fire, I reopened our files on Eduardo Manuela. You'll never guess what we found. We uncovered information that Eduardo Manuela has a mansion in Venice's old section. Same address as Ambruster's. I always wondered how Ambruster's family could afford their summer retreat in Venice. I ran a tax check and discovered Ambruster pays no taxes on the property because he does not own it. Manuela does."

"We students wondered how a professor could own a summer home that size, too. What did Ambruster teach us—Examine the patient's environment and you'll discover what caused his illness. How ironic."

"As we continued our investigation, we discovered that an injured Latin American had been staying at that address since last year, after our raid on Manuela's compound."

"He escaped? To Venice? When I called Ambruster in Venice to tell him about Julie, I thought I got the wrong number because someone speaking a Central American language answered the phone. Then Ambruster came on right away."

"What we couldn't figure out was the connection between Ambruster and Manuela. Why would Ambruster be involved with a drug lord?"

"Usually blackmail or a relative," Jake said.

"Precisely. There was talk in medical school that Ambruster disowned one of his daughters because she had married a Guatemalan drug lord," Kate added.

"Only he didn't. His connection to Manuela is solid. When the pieces started coming together, I called David Winters and had him post the guards inside Julie's room and wait with her until he was certain Ambruster had left for Paris. Julie's safe, and recovering. And we picked up Manuela on the walkway outside of her hospital."

# Chapter 64

*Psychiatric Center*
*Lake Lucerne, Switzerland*

"Will Claire always be under strict surveillance here at the Psychiatric Center?" Lance asked Dr. Bryan Wildekin, Chief of Psychiatry.

"Yes, I want a twenty-four hour watch kept on Claire the entire time she is here. She is brilliant. She could find a way to escape. Then the police would have to find her. As you know, the only way we were able to prevent Claire's arrest was to secret her out of France to this private facility. We must also be certain that her medications are working. It may take six to eight weeks for them to reach their full effect. Until then, her behavior may be erratic. Today she is compliant; she believes she's at a Swiss Spa for R and R."

"Then what will happen to Claire?"

"With your permission, we would like to enter her into one

of our newest elective cognitive therapy programs. It's experimental, but safe. If it works, it may give Claire her life back."

"I'm grateful the Institute sent Claire here, instead of prison. But now you are asking me to give permission for her to participate in an experimental program about which I know nothing."

"Essentially," Dr. Wildekin began, "we will treat Claire's mental illness using conventional methodology. When we see sufficient improvement in her psychiatric evaluations for three consecutive months, we'll want to enter her into our new cognitive therapy program. If you would like, you can wait until that time to decide whether to give your permission for her to begin the program."

"All right, that sounds better to me. Try the conventional treatments first, and then we can re-evaluate the need for the experimental program. What does the experimental program attempt to do?"

"We originally designed it to help our agents with Post Traumatic Stress Disorder. As you know, our agents face some brutal conditions when they are on duty. When they return home, their minds may repeatedly replay those traumatic events, to the extent that it interferes with their daily living. We have found a way to replace those traumatic memories with more pleasant ones. The results have been remarkable."

"Claire hasn't served on any missions. I don't know of any serious traumas that she has had, either. How would this help her?"

"We've learned that children who were physically or emotionally abused by their parents can suffer from PTSD, also. Just imagine the trauma from the young child's perspective. Their whole life is thrown out of balance. The person they most love betrays their trust and severely injures them, either physically or emotionally. Those inner scars stay with the child forever. They never forget the traumas. Unless the child, or later the adult, receives help, they may continue to vividly relive those events all their lives."

"Are you saying Claire was abused as a child?"

"Yes, severely and repeatedly. It started when she was three. She believes her relatives knew what was happening, but no one came to rescue her."

"She never told me."

"I know. For some people it is too painful to discuss. Our program is experimental, but it does help our patients."

"How does it work?"

"We help them to create new memories to replace the memories of parental child abuse. In effect, we heal their child abuse memories by supplanting them with plausible events that occur in normal families. Their overall life experiences stay intact, but they no longer recall the stark moments of their childhood. Instead, they recall some pretty happy events that occur in every child's life, like blowing out the candles on a delicious chocolate birthday cake or scrambling to pick up candy from a broken piñata. It allows the patients to reclaim their childhood."

"Will she be the same Claire I knew?" Lance asked.

"Yes, only happier," Dr. Wildekin answered.

Lance shook his head. "I don't know about this. You're asking me to approve a treatment for my wife that is experimental, and quite frankly, I'm not even sure I believe it will work. What are my other options? Does she have to be treated here? Can I arrange for our family doctor . . ."

"Lance, it will take you a while to recover from the events of the past few days involving your wife, as well. Right now, your mind is still processing what Claire has done, and it is trying to downplay the events as much as possible, as a protective coping mechanism to ease you through this difficult situation. Please understand, Lance, there are no other options. There are no other choices for treatment. The Institute's psychiatrists have all confirmed that in her present state, Claire is a threat to others and to herself. Her behavior is unpredictable. Combined with her superior intellectual ability, that makes her a very dangerous person. If she tries to leave here, the Institute will have to hand her over to the authorities for trial and incarceration."

"No choices?"

"No choices."

Lance backed his way to the door, expressionless, fallen. He paused as if considering his options but then began to realize that he had no options.

"All right. I'll sign for her treatment here using the method that you described."

"Thank you, Lance."

Dejection blanketed him, weighing his shoulders heavily forward. "What should I tell her when I leave?"

"Tell her the truth. You are going on another mission for the Institute, and you will be back in five weeks. You two have lived separate lives before because of your jobs, so this will seem like another common event to her. Each time you arrive, the Institute has agreed to set aside some vacation time for you to spend with Claire. It will be like your regular Rest and Relaxation after a mission, but the R and R will be for both of you, and we'll be here to support you two as she adjusts to her treatments."

"How long will the treatments take? How long will Claire be confined?"

"Lance, she has major and multiple problems. It may be a long time. I think we can help her be more comfortable with herself and others. That alone will be a big, first step. Our goal is rational thinking and behavior. In the meantime, she will be safe here."

"How long? Tell me how long you think she will be confined."

"In years?"

"Years?" Fear creased his heart.

"For someone with as serious an offense as Claire has committed, the treatment protocol will cover a span of at least five years, but we never let anyone leave until we are certain they can function well in society and are no longer a threat to themselves or others. We will observe Claire in progressively responsible living conditions during a second five year period before we will release her."

# Chapter 65

*Base 3*
*Dover, Delaware, U.S.A.*

**"Kate, Jake, this is Lance calling you** for a video conference. Can you click on?"

Kate and Jake had just finished breakfast at the hospital with Julie and Luke when the video on Kate's computer began chiming. Hearing Lance's voice, Jake hurried over to turn the video camera on.

"Hey, Lance." Jake called out. "Julie has totally recovered, and we are taking her home today. How are you? And Claire?"

Lance hesitated, uncertain how to begin. "I'm so happy Julie is well again." Another long pause and then slowly, Lance organized his convoluted thoughts. His mind finally had pieced together all of the anguishing events of the last three days.

"I wanted to talk to you today to let you know how very sorry I am that Claire was responsible for Julie's illness and the devastation that *nocturne* caused. I feel responsible, too. Somehow, I missed, totally missed, the signs that Claire was in trouble. I really let her down, and you guys, and thousands of other people who had to suffer because of my negligence. I'm really sorry, and I don't know how to repay the time and sorrow this has caused you and everyone else."

"Lance, it's not your fault. This has been a terrible time for all of us. The Institute and the Agency kept us so busy the last several years that none of us were spending enough time with our families and friends. How could you know? Anything that seemed suspicious in retrospect is just that—retrospect. It's always easier to see the problems after the issues are resolved."

"Jake's right, Lance," Kate said. "Whenever Claire said or did something unusual, we just brushed it off and said, 'Oh, that's just Claire.' But, it wasn't Claire. It wasn't her normal behavior. We were so busy getting our work done that we failed to see how she had changed. I'm as culpable as anyone. I failed to renew her Psychological Review. Her reality unraveled right in front of me, and I didn't see it happening. I'm so sorry that I didn't help her."

"Lance, how is Claire reacting to her confinement at the Institute's Lucerne Psychiatric Center?" Jake asked.

"The Institute arranged for her stay there, for which I am grateful. I saw her last night. She's . . . comfortable, and seems to be herself again, at times, except she's unaware that she did anything wrong. She thinks she's vacationing at a spa. I'm not certain how long that will last. The doctor said they expect her behavior to be erratic for a while."

"I'm sorry, Lance," Jake said.

"Me, too. Out of all our missions, this is the hardest thing I've ever had to deal with. I feel riddled with guilt. And I should, despite your assertion otherwise. If only I had paid more attention to Claire. I just want our old life back, but that is never going to happen, now."

"If we could make that happen, Lance, we would. Jake and I are here for you. We'll help you and Claire however we can."

"Thank you. I really needed to hear that from you. I'm going to need some help reconstructing our life. I can tell that already. I don't know where to begin, but I think your forgiveness is my first step down the long road to redemption."

# Chapter 66

*Three months later*
*Lido Beach, Venice, Italy*

**Crystal tossed a handful of sparkling sea foam** high into the air and giggled as it dispersed into thousands of iridescent bubbles. Her memory of Julie's ordeal at the beach was fading away, leaving her with a sense of caution rather than fear. She raced around the beach beneath the flecks of sea foam, playing with her parents, but deftly turning her cheeks away whenever the foam drifted too close to her eyes.

After an hour of splashing in the surf with Crystal, Kate and Jake sunk into their lounge chairs at the water's edge. Since *nocturne's* last outbreak, they kept Crystal close to themselves whenever they were near the water. Immediate treatment would be their first line of defense if *nocturne* ever struck again.

"I'm glad that the Agency gave us a reprise of our interrupted vacation," Kate said.

"Yes, but they could've chosen the Alps instead," Jake said.

"Just as dangerous there if *nocturne* infiltrates the water supply. At least here we know the way to the closest emergency room."

"True, but it would've been nice to spend some time with Lance and Claire. I wonder how she's doing. It's hard to think about her parents abusing her when she was three years old, like Crystal."

"How different Claire's life would have been if her parents had given her the unconditional love she deserved or if someone had stepped up and reported the child abuse."

"I've thought about that, too," Jake said.

"We should be able to travel to Lucerne to see Claire and Lance in a few weeks. European health officials reported a few cases of *nocturne* this week, but they acted quickly to contain them."

"That's good. When do you think the new health and research regulations will be approved?"

"With the world focused on protecting the balance of nature and the scientific community weighing the dangers of multiple recombinant DNA, we're likely see new regulations before summer's end."

"We need to restore the balance of nature, but how do we restore the balance in our lives? We've gone through a horrible three months, and we're overstressed, overworked, and exhausted."

"One of my first professors in graduate school recommended a way to handle stress: 'Equal pleasures for equal stressors.' She meant we could recover from any number of stressors as long as we had an equal number of pleasures to counterbalance them."

"Wisdom," Jake said as a grin crossed his face. "I'm for tipping the scale in favor of pleasures."

"Well, yes, that would build up our resilience," she laughed. "We'll need to pool every resource we have and keep building up our reserves while we prepare for the next heavy assignment the Agency has planned for us."

"Us?"

"I saw my file on Dad's desk. I opened it when he left the room."

"You didn't!"

"I did. I think he knew I'd look."

"And . . ."

"We can take Crystal with us. Our assignment is at Julie's medical school, my alma mater! Two semesters. Investigative work only."

"Right on! More time on the beach!"

"It's a new Agency policy. Some lighter assignments in the mix to offset the more difficult ones."

Kate's memories of missions past flooded her mind, but within a few seconds they receded. She recognized them as counterpoints to the joy she felt today—listening to the rhythm of the lapping waves, the melodic calls of sandpipers, and

Crystal's arpeggio laughter. Life is a nocturne, she thought—a balance of melody and melancholy, harmony and hostility, diverging into dissonance yet returning to resolution. Our lives together, caring for Crystal and giving her all the love she needs, will be our opus, our creative work, far more important than any other work we will ever do.

CPSIA information can be obtained
at www.ICGtesting.com
Printed in the USA
LVHW041412020920
664858LV00018B/1377